# SIGNAL FIRES

BY THE SAME AUTHOR

NOVELS

*Black & White*

*Family History*

*Picturing the Wreck*

*Fugitive Blue*

*Playing with Fire*

NON-FICTION

*Inheritance*

*Hourglass*

*Still Writing*

*Devotion*

*Slow Motion*

# Signal Fires

## DANI SHAPIRO

Chatto & Windus
LONDON

1 3 5 7 9 10 8 6 4 2

Chatto & Windus, an imprint of Vintage, is part of the Penguin Random House group of
companies whose addresses can be found at global.penguinrandomhouse.com

Penguin
Random House
UK

First published in the United Kingdom by Chatto & Windus in 2022
First published in the United States by Alfred A. Knopf in 2022

penguin.co.uk/vintage

A CIP catalogue record for this book is available from the British Library

HB ISBN 9781784744960
TPB ISBN 9781784744977

Typeset in 12/16pt Sabon LT Std by Jouve (UK), Milton Keynes
Printed and bound in Great Britain by Clays Ltd, Elcograf S.p.A.

The authorised representative in the EEA is Penguin Random House Ireland,
Morrison Chambers, 32 Nassau Street, Dublin D02 YH68

Penguin Random House is committed to a sustainable future
for our business, our readers and our planet. This book is made
from Forest Stewardship Council® certified paper.

MIX
Paper from
responsible sources
FSC
www.fsc.org    FSC® C018179

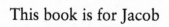

This book is for Jacob

For if the earth is a camp and the sea
an ossuary of souls, light your signal fires
wherever you find yourselves.
Come the morning, launch your boats.

CAROLYN FORCHÉ
FROM "MOURNING"

# August 27, 1985

# Sarah and Theo

A  ND IT'S NOTHING, really, or might be nothing, or ought to be nothing, as he leans his head forward to press the tip of his cigarette to the car's lighter. It sizzles on contact, a sound particular to its brief moment in history, in which cars have lighters and otherwise sensible fifteen-year-olds choke down Marlboro Reds and drive their mothers' Buicks without so much as a learner's permit. There's a girl he wants to impress. Her name is Misty Zimmerman, and if she lives through this night, she will grow up to be a magazine editor, or a high school teacher, or a defense lawyer. She will be a mother of three or remain childless. She will die young of ovarian cancer or live to know her great-grandchildren.

But these are only a few possible arcs to a life, a handful of shooting stars in the night sky. Change one thing and everything changes. A tremor here sets off an earthquake there. A fault line deepens. A wire gets tripped. His foot on the gas. He doesn't really know what he's doing, but that won't stop him. He's all jacked up just like a fifteen-year-old boy. He has something to prove. To himself. To Misty. To his sister. It's as if he's following a script written in Braille, his fingers running across code he doesn't understand.

"Theo, slow down." That's his sister, Sarah, from the backseat.

Misty's riding shotgun.

It was Sarah who tossed him the keys to their mom's car. Sarah, age seventeen. After this night, she will become unknowable to him. The summer sky is a veil thrown over the moon and stars. The streets are quiet, the good people of Avalon long since tucked in for the night. Their own parents are asleep in their queen-size bed under the plaid afghan knitted by one of their father's patients. His mom is a deep sleeper, but his dad has been trained by a lifetime as a doctor to bolt awake at the slightest provocation. He is always ready.

The teenagers aren't looking for trouble. They're good kids—everyone would say so. But they're bored; it's the end of summer; school will resume next week. Sarah's going into her senior year, after which she'll be gone. She's a superstar, his sister. Varsity this, honors that. Bristling with potential. Theo has three years left, and he's barely made a mark. He's a chubby kid whose default is silence and shame. He blushes easily. He can feel his cheeks redden as he holds the lighter and inhales, hears the sizzle, draws smoke deep into his lungs. His father—a pulmonary surgeon—would kill him. Maybe that's why Sarah threw him the keys. Maybe she's trying to help—to get him to *act*, goddamnit. To take a risk. Better to be bad than to be nothing.

Misty Zimmerman is just a girl along for the ride. It was Sarah who asked her to come. Sarah, doing for Theo what Theo cannot do for himself. Change one thing and everything changes. The Buick speeds down Poplar Street. Misty stretches and yawns in the passenger seat. Theo turns left, then right. He's getting the hang of this. He flicks the directional, then heads onto the parkway. As they pass the mall, he looks to see if Burger King is still open.

"Watch it!" Sarah yells.

He swerves back into his lane, heart racing. He almost hit the guardrail. He gets off the parkway at the next exit and eases up on the gas. This was maybe a bad idea. He wants to go home. He also wants another cigarette.

"Pull over," Sarah says. "I'll drive."

Theo looks for a good spot to stop. He has no idea how to park. Sarah's right—this is stupid.

"Actually no, forget it. I shouldn't," she says.

They're almost home. It's like a song in his head: *Almost home, almost home, almost home.* Just a few blocks to go. They pass the Hellers' house, the Chertoffs'.

As he leans forward, the lighter slips through Theo's fingers and drops into his open shirt collar. He lets out a yelp and tries to grab it, which only makes matters worse. He arches his back to shake the burning metal thing loose, but it's wedged between his shorts and his belly. The smell of singed flesh. A perfect shiny half-moon will remain. Years from now, when a lover traces the scar on his stomach and asks how he got it, he will roll away. But now—now their futures shoot like gamma rays from the moving car. Three high school students. What if Sarah had gone out with her friends instead, that night? What if Misty had begged off? What if Theo had succumbed to his usual way of being, and fixed himself a salami sandwich with lots of mustard and taken it with him to bed?

The wheel spins. The screams of teenagers in the night.

*Theo no stop jesus fuck help god* and there is no screech of brakes—nothing to blunt the impact. A concussion of metal and an ancient oak: the sound of two worlds colliding.

The fender and right side of the Buick crumple like it's a toy and this is all make-believe. Upstairs, on the second floor of Benjamin and Mimi Wilf's home, a light blinks on. A window opens. Ben Wilf stares down at the scene below for a fraction of a second. By the time he's made it to the front door, his daughter, Sarah, is standing before him—*thank god thank god thank god*—her tee shirt and her face splattered with blood. Theo is on all fours on the ground. He seems to be in one piece. *Thank god thank god thank god.* But then—

"There's a girl in the car, Dad—"

Misty Zimmerman is unconscious. She isn't wearing a seat belt—who wears seat belts?—and there's a gash in her forehead from which blood is gushing. There's no time to call an ambulance. If they wait for EMTs to get here, the girl will be gone. So Ben does what's necessary. He leans into the driver's door, hooks two hands beneath the girl's armpits, and drags her out.

"Your shirt, Theo!" he barks.

Theo's belly roils. He's about to be sick. He pulls his shirt off and throws it to his father. Ben lifts Misty's head, then wraps the shirt tightly around her skull in a tourniquet. His mind has gone slow and quiet. He's a very good doctor. He feels for the girl's pulse.

Mimi is on the front steps now, her nightgown billowing in the wind that seems to have kicked up out of nowhere.

"What happened?" Mimi screams. "Sarah? Theo?"

"It was me, Mom," Sarah says. "I was driving."

Theo stares at his sister.

"That doesn't matter now," Ben says softly.

6

Up and down Division Street, their neighbors have awakened. The crash, the voices, the electricity in the air. Someone must have called it in. In the distance, the wail of a siren. Ben knows before he knows, in that deep instinctual way. He couldn't see in the dark when he dragged the girl out of the car. He registered only the head wound, the uncontrollable bleeding. He now knows: her neck is broken. And he has done the worst thing imaginable. He has moved her. In the days to come, he will tell the story to the authorities, to the life-support team, to Misty's parents. The story—that Sarah was driving, with Misty riding shotgun and Theo in the backseat—will not be questioned. Not this night, not ever. It will become the deepest kind of family secret, one so dangerous that it will never be spoken.

# December 21, 2010

---

# *Benjamin*

THE BOY IS at his window again. It is 10:45 at night, surely a time boys his age—he is nearing his eleventh birthday—should be asleep in their beds, dreaming their twitchy, colt-like dreams. But instead, like clockwork, here he is: dark hair glimmering in the light cast by the full moon, small hands grasping the windowsill, his thin neck craned upward through the open window, searching the sky. The boy's breath makes vaporous clouds in the cold. Now he picks up that gadget, pointing it this way and that like a compass, its eerie, milky-blue glow illuminating his pale face. What the hell is he doing? It's all Ben can do not to open his own window and yell across Division Street to the kid: *Be careful!* The words are in his throat.

*Where are your parents?*

But he can see the parents too, the entire house, except for the boy's room, lit up in the night like a love letter to Con Ed. The mother sits at the kitchen table, bent over a magazine, a wineglass near her elbow. The shape of the father can be made out in the gym they built over the garage. The man is rowing like a maniac, as if propelling himself toward a drowning person.

The house across the street used to belong to the Platts, and before that, to the McCarthys. Back when he and Mimi had first moved into the neighborhood, when Division Street actually divided (though it was considered rude to talk about it) the more desirable part of town from the houses closer to the train station, there were no home gym additions, no pool houses like the one that seemed to spring up overnight behind the Berkelhammers' old house, no outdoor fireplaces and elaborate sound systems built into mossy stone walls.

A lone car slowly makes its way down Division and turns on Poplar. In the distance, the yowling of a cat. The stiff leaves from the holly bush scrape against the kitchen window downstairs. Ben had meant to ask the gardener to dig it up last fall before it rotted any more of the house's old clapboards, but with everything else going on, it had slipped his mind. Now, it's about to be somebody else's problem. The new owners, a couple he hasn't met, are relocating from Cleveland. Along with two small children. And one of those sad-eyed basset hounds.

So this is how he's going to spend this last night, then? Wrapped in his flannel robe, gazing out his bedroom window, absorbing every sight and sound of this place where he has lived more years than any other? He is committing it all to memory.

Forty years.

He and Mimi used to make fun of people who'd say treacly, asinine things like *it all goes by so fast*. But now, here he is. Forty years since he and Mimi moved into this house. Mimi was pregnant with Theo, and Sarah was in diapers.

They were probably not so very different from the Cleveland couple, imagining just how life would be. Downstairs, all the rooms are filled with boxes. These are stacked floor to ceiling and labeled according to destination:

*S. W.* for the china, Mimi's silver, most of the good linens. All to be shipped to Sarah in Santa Monica, though why she could possibly want more stuff than she already has is beyond him. His daughter has never been the sentimental type, but maybe now, in middle age, she is softening.

*T. W.* for the thousands of records—actual vinyl—for which Theo has purchased and restored a turntable in his Brooklyn loft. Also being shipped to Theo are boxes labeled *B. W. Files,* representing Ben's medical practice dating back to his residency. What else can he do with the files? Burn them? No. He will leave them in the care of his son.

The boy has spotted him. As he has for the last several nights, he raises his hand and waves—a child's wave, fluttering his fingers. Ben unlatches his window and slides it upward. The cold air hits him in the chest.

"Hey, kid!"

He knows the boy's name well. Waldo, a hard name to forget—but it feels too familiar to use it. Even though the family has lived across the street for a decade now, they've tended to keep to themselves. When they first moved in, Mimi never had a chance to walk over with her usual plate of cookies and a note welcoming them to the neighborhood. She used to keep copies of a list of helpful hints: the A&P on Grandview gets its fish fresh from Fulton Street; the second-grade teacher is a weak link, but Mrs. Hill, who teaches third, is a gem. Ben can see Mimi still, as she was during those years of what they now call parenting, as if describing an activity like jogging or hiking. Her wavy dark hair piled into a messy knot. Her long legs tucked into ski boots. Her easy laugh.

These folks leave first thing in the morning, the father in a brand-new Lexus hybrid, the mother in a Prius—cars that don't make a sound—and as dusk falls they return, gliding silently into the garage, the automatic doors closing behind them. The boy doesn't play on the street the way Sarah and Theo used to. None of the neighborhood kids are ever out in their yards. They're carted around by their parents or nannies, lugging violins or cellos in their cases, dragging backpacks that weigh more than they do. They wear soccer uniforms or spanking white getups, their tiny waists wrapped in colorful karate or jujitsu belts.

"Hey, kid!" Ben calls again. "What are you doing?"

Young Waldo is holding the contraption—it looks to be a black book slightly larger than a paperback, but for the glow—up to the sky, as if suggesting that maybe God read him a bedtime story. Ben fumbles in his bathrobe pocket for his distance glasses. Now he can see the lettering on the boy's sweatshirt. A Red Sox fan. A surprise, here in Yankees territory. It can't be easy for him at school, then. Especially this year, when the *Red Sox suck!* chant has turned out to be all too true. The boy's long bangs fall over his eyes.

"Too bad about Pedroia," Ben calls out.

"*And* Youkilis. *And* Ellsbury." The kid sounds personally aggrieved. His voice is unexpectedly high and musical, like a flute. Still, he keeps the black book trained on the sky.

"What is that thing?" Ben asks.

"Star Walk," the kid answers.

"Is that some kind of game?"

The kid flashes Ben a look—part disappointment, part incredulity—that he can read all the way across Division Street.

"No," he says. "It's not a game."

"Okay, then."

"Do you wanna see?"

"Well, I—"

Ben hesitates. Though he has kept an eye out for the boy over the years, he doesn't know him, after all.

"Come on, I'll show you."

Through the kitchen window, the mother is silhouetted against the flickering lights of a television screen. The dad is still rowing.

"Isn't it past your bedtime?"

"I'm not tired."

Waldo reminds Ben a bit of Theo at that age. Theo had been bigger, heftier, and when he couldn't sleep he would pad down to the kitchen, slap some salami and dijon on a piece of bread, pour himself a glass of milk, as if only the weight of a full meal would settle him down for the night. Mimi would scold Theo, then, about not brushing his teeth, and would privately fret that maybe he was getting too heavy. Oh, how Ben wishes they had known then a fraction of what he knows now! That all those little worries (cavities! a few extra pounds of baby fat!) were nothing, in the scheme of things.

"I'll meet you at the magic tree," the boy calls. "In two minutes!" He ducks his head back inside and pulls down his window, disappearing into his darkened room.

Ben closes his eyes briefly. *The magic tree.* He knows that's what this generation of neighborhood kids calls it. And why not? A majestic oak at the corner of Division and Birch (all the streets west of Division are named for trees), its trunk is now close to five feet in diameter. It is encircled—depending on the season—by dozens of varieties of wildflowers, tall, fragrant grasses. Every other bit of greenery in the neighborhood is regularly manicured and trimmed by landscapers, but the oak presides over its own small patch of jungle, a primeval piece of real estate. People who don't know the story—newcomers to the neighborhood—surmise that the family who lives at 18 Division, Ben's house, must be responsible for the tree. They couldn't be more off the mark. But Ben won't set them straight.

He walks downstairs through the narrow passage left open by the floor-to-ceiling boxes lining either side of the front hall. Pulls his old down parka from the coatrack near the door and throws it over his bathrobe. What a sight he must be! An old man, stepping onto his front porch, wearing what appears to be a floor-length skirt, fuzzy moccasins, and a ratty ski jacket that has seen better days.

The boy is already waiting by the tree. Now, he too has the vantage point to see his mother pouring herself another glass of Chardonnay in their house across the street, his father rowing. But he is not watching the secret lives of his parents unfolding as if on a television screen. No, he's more interested in that thing, what was it called . . . that star thing. He is holding it open to the sky.

"Hi." Ben offers his hand. "We haven't formally met. I'm Dr. Wilf."

"I know," says the boy. Of course, he knows. Otherwise he wouldn't have left the safety of his house in the middle of the night to meet a perfect stranger. Would he? Ben feels a surge of protectiveness toward the kid. He wants to march across the street and knock on the front door. *It's eleven o'clock at night. Do you know where your son is?* The boy's face, up close, is beautiful in the way of all boys his age, his skin smooth and luminous. The fringes of his eyelashes are so long they cast shadows over his cheeks. His thin neck and narrow shoulders. Ten going on eleven. A boy on the verge of enormous change. A boy (here he thinks of Theo with a pang) who is about to wade into a sea of unknowability from which it will take him years to return.

"I'm Waldo."

"Hello, Waldo."

Ben glances at the contraption. The screen seems to be mirroring the clear, moonlit sky. Stars shine against a purplish-black background. Strains of music emanate from the device—strange, otherworldly. Ben now sees that it's one of those new, immensely desirable pieces of equipment, though he can't remember what it's called. He's seen stories on the news of people lined up outside stores, standing all night just for the privilege of buying it before anybody else. He wonders if the kid's father stood in line. From the intensity of his rowing, he strikes Ben, perhaps unfairly, as a man who might need to be first.

As Waldo tilts the screen, lines form, shapes emerge as if the heavens were opening up to them. A bull. A snake. A crab. A child holding a harp.

"Look at this." Waldo slides his index finger down one side of the screen. The screen-stars wheel through the screen-sky, while above them, high above Division Street, a jet glides through the night. The lights on its wings blink steadily. It's heading, most likely, to JFK. The actual stars seem curiously immobile, less compelling than the jet or the simulation of stars on Waldo's screen.

"When's your birthday?" Waldo asks abruptly.

"The sixteenth of January."

"What year?"

"Are you asking how old I am?"

"No—that's not the point!" The kid always seems on the

verge of extreme, near-explosive frustration, as if the world around him cannot—will not—conform to his expectations.

"Nineteen thirty-six," Ben says. "January 16, 1936."

"Around what time?"

Ben has to think about this. Does he even know? The last person who probably cared enough to remember the time of his birth was his own, long-gone mother. But then it comes to him.

"Close to nine at night."

"And where?"

"New York City. Brooklyn, actually."

The kid sets something in motion then, sets the galaxy spinning, and the date on the screen scrolls back, back, back at a dizzying pace. Although the ground is cold and damp, not quite yet frozen, and despite knowing that he will pay for it in his bones tomorrow, Ben sits down right between two of the oak tree's tremendous roots. His scrawny, old-man legs peek out from his bathrobe, and he covers them with the soft plaid flannel. The boy kneels next to him in his Red Sox pajamas and ski jacket. The dates on the screen continue to spin, the shapes in the sky morphing, one into the next. He can hardly keep track. A bear. A lion. A sailboat.

Ben looks up Division Street at the few lights still on in houses whose occupants he no longer knows. He used to be able to tell you just about everything about the families who lived in these homes. For better or worse—for better *and* worse—he knew about Jimmy Platt's little drug habit, Karen Russo's affair with Ken the golf pro, the gambling problem that eventually forced the Gelfmans into foreclosure. He knew that Julie Heller regularly smoked a joint when she took her standard poodle for his late night walk, that Eric

Warner had gone to rehab, though no one had ever gotten to the bottom of why.

Theirs was a neighborhood like any other, with the secrets and heartaches and lies, the triumphs and moments of grace that weave their way through all communities. He had often felt stifled by it—and God knows, it had driven Mimi crazy—but still, he had taken some comfort from the fact that this was *his* neighborhood. *His* people. In making the decision to settle in a particular house on a particular street, they had all thrown their lot in with one another. Their kids had run in and out of one another's houses. Had smoked their first cigarettes together, been best friends, then sworn enemies, then friends again. The parents were like witnesses, bystanders, learning to get along (*for the kids' sake*, Mimi used to say) and sometimes even liking one another enough to go on joint vacations.

Now, the neighborhood has battened down its hatches for the night. Alarm systems on. Lipitor ingested, or Prozac, or Klonopin. Maybe, for a lucky few, Viagra. Couples, mostly men and women in their thirties and forties—nearly half his age—lie in bed together or apart, reading or drifting off while watching some nighttime medical drama. Babies, toddlers, schoolchildren, teenagers—all letting go of the day, surrendering to tomorrow.

All except Waldo.

"You're seventy-four," Waldo says.

"You did the math in your head."

"Look." Waldo hands Ben the device, which is heavier than it looks. "There it is."

It takes Ben a few seconds to realize what he's looking at: the sky of his birth. "Canis Major," Waldo says. "A very cool constellation. Canis Major contains Sirius—the Dog Star. The brightest star in the night sky."

Ben touches the screen, tracing the dog with his index finger: a large-pawed animal, seated, his head alert, as if awaiting further instructions. Waldo leans over and taps a circle in the upper-left corner of the screen.

"Canis Major is a constellation, included in the second-century astronomer P ... Ptol ... Ptolemy's forty-eight constellations," Waldo reads out loud, "and still included among the eighty-eight modern constellations. Its name is Latin for 'greater dog,' and it is commonly rep ... rep ..."

"Represented," Ben prods the boy.

"I know!"

"Sorry."

"... *represented* as one of the dogs following Orion, the hunter. See also Canis Minor, the 'lesser dog.'"

"I'd certainly rather be born under a greater dog than a lesser dog," Ben says.

Waldo glares at him.

"You're making fun of me."

"No."

"You're joking, then."

"Well, yes."

"This isn't a joke."

In the glow cast by the contraption, Ben sees that Waldo's eyes are brimming with tears.

"Okay, buddy." Ben pats his hand awkwardly. "I'm sorry. I didn't mean—"

"Everybody thinks this is stupid, or something."

The boy is trying hard not to cry, but his sharp little chin is quivering.

"Who's 'everybody'?" Ben asks.

"I dunno."

"C'mon."

A long pause, during which Ben notices that the skin around the boy's nails is raw and puckered, picked and bitten to the quick.

"My dad," Waldo finally says. For the first time, he looks across the street at the windows above the garage, which have gone dark.

"Now, I'm sure that's not true," Ben says, even though he knows no such thing.

A small, involuntary shrug from Waldo, who refocuses on the screen and touches another constellation.

"Pyxis," he says, his voice cracking.

The shape of a compass appears in the sky below the great dog Canis. "Pyxis," Waldo reads, "Latin for 'box,' is a small and faint constellation in the southern sky. Its name is also Latin for a 'mariner's compass.' It should not be confused with Circinus, which rep . . ."

Ben lets Waldo struggle with the word, his brow furrowed in concentration. His heart breaks for the boy; still so small, trying to hold the whole world up on his narrow shoulders.

". . . *represents* a draftsman's compass," Waldo completes the sentence. He is crying now.

Ben wants to hug the boy, but instead he slings one arm over Waldo's shoulders. Waldo leans his head against Ben, a gesture so simple and sweet he very nearly loses it himself. The poor kid's whole body is shaking.

*It's okay, buddy,* Ben whispers. *It's gonna be okay.*

Without thinking, he sways back and forth, the way he used to with Theo, with Sarah, not only when they were babies but right up until this age, this precipice. He would hug them fiercely, then find himself swaying, rocking, as if on a dance floor after the music had stopped.

"My dad doesn't want me to talk about this stuff," Waldo says. Looking straight ahead at his house across the street. "He told me"—here, a great, heaving breath—"he told me that if I keep talking about it, he's going to take Star Walk away from me, and my telescope too."

"Why do you think he doesn't want you to talk about it?" Ben asks.

"He says I'm wasting my time with things that don't matter. He says I'm living in a dream world."

Waldo tips the device from side to side, and the whole star-filled sky, the myriad constellations along with the outlines of their shapes and forms, expands in both directions.

"And why do you think it's so important to you?" Ben asks. Had he ever been this patient with his own son? In the years before Theo became inaccessible, in those precious years when he would still have allowed himself to be seen, to be known—had Ben taken the time? The answer isn't a simple yes or no—but even so, the lost opportunities are too painful to contemplate. He cannot have that time back. He doesn't get a do-over.

"I guess it makes me feel better," Waldo says.

"How come?"

"When I'm freaked out . . . when I think bad thoughts . . . the whole idea that out there . . ." He trails off as if the sheer expenditure of so many words has exhausted him.

"What kind of bad thoughts?" Ben asks.

"Oh, you know."

"No, I don't know. Tell me."

"Like, about dying and stuff."

Ben nods. Dying and stuff. Of course.

"Anyway, out there"—Waldo gestures not to the sky above them but to the screen, which Ben realizes with a start is more real to him than the stars above—"is so massively huge, and here, we're just . . ."

"What?" Ben asks. The kid is a curious combination of expressive and restrained, as if his very spirit were doing battle with everything he's been told he's supposed to be.

Waldo jumps to his feet.

"Andromeda, Antlia, Apus, Aquarius, Aquila," he recites. "Ara, Aries, Auriga, and that's just the *As*. There's only one *B:* Bootes. Lots of *Cs*, though. Caelum, Camelopardalis, Cancer—"

"You've memorized the constellations."

"I'm working on the stars now."

A shiver goes through Ben, and he slowly pushes himself off the ground, steadying himself against the trunk of the magic tree. How long have they been out here in the freezing cold? He can barely feel the tips of his fingers. He clenches his hands, then releases them. Across the street, the mother turns off the lights in the kitchen.

"Waldo? I think we'd better both go to bed, kid."

"One more thing," Waldo says. "Let me just show you one more thing, please?"

Ben's not sure he can handle one more thing, but what choice does he have? Waldo presses the bottom-right corner of the screen, and now they are flying over the curvature of the earth, skating above the surface of oceans and continents until the entire planet recedes and two neon green lines bisect to show their exact location on the globe. A small neon figure stands in the center of a circle perched on the easternmost edge of the United States, the state of New York, the town of Avalon, the street . . . their street. Division Street.

"Here we are," Waldo says, pointing to the neon figure. "That's us."

Ben touches the screen. He moves his finger fractionally to the right. Names of towns, cities, states whiz by: Danville, Ohio; Roseville, Michigan; Erie, Pennsylvania; Concord, North Carolina. Continents collapse. Lyon, Istanbul, Phuket, Taipei, Cairo, Tel Aviv. From this distance, everything is connected. The East Coast to the Midwest to the South. America to Europe to Asia. The sky of 1936 to the sky of 2010. From this distance, it seems possible that it's all happening at once: this life, that life—an immeasurable number of lives all playing themselves out in parallel motion. He is at once a newborn at the Brooklyn Jewish Hospital, a kid playing stickball on Classon Avenue, a bar mitzvah boy all squirmy in his new suit, stumbling through the words of his Torah portion. He is a college student, a sleepless medical intern, a young husband. He is watching his daughter's birth. He is moving with his young family to Division Street. He is hearing his son's first lusty wail. He looks down at the screen and sees Mimi's face as if she herself were a constellation. *My darling. I am coming.*

# Shenkman

H E PUSHES BACK with his legs, smooth and hard. Thinks of his old coach's word: *fluid*. Hinges his upper body, then slides forward, arms extended. The briefest pause of recovery, as the flywheel spins. Drive, recovery. Drive, recovery. He counts. *One, two*. Full lungs at the catch, empty at the finish. He gives the RowPro a quick glance. *Fuck*. He's 6K into this race and two sculls are ahead of him. Best not to focus on that. On the wall in front of him, the flat-screen TV displays the surface of a lake. In his mind, he is there, not here. Gliding along Lake Winnipesaukee. He's tried music—turns out he doesn't like listening to music. He's tried checking out the shows everybody talks about at work. But he can't watch a show set in a 1960s ad agency while rowing. It's crazy-making. *Meshugenah*. It's taken him a while to real-ize that this—the deep twilight blue of the lake, the ripples he imagines are cast by his blades—this is what he's been looking for. Here, in this gym above his garage, paid for with plastic, here is where he forgets about the rest of his life.

Alice is on the other side of the house, and Shenkman knows she's lonely and slightly pissed off—that these hours of the day are when she expects to be with him and talk about ... well, whatever. Office politics. His mother. Their plans over spring break. Waldo. This, above all, is the subject he wants to avoid.

*One, two.* His trapezius muscles burn.

It's been almost an hour since he tucked Waldo in for the night, but he's pretty sure his son isn't sleeping. He knows that Waldo gets up and opens his window—Shenkman can see every open door and window in the house on the burglar alarm monitor. He's been trying to let it go. Hoping Waldo grows out of it. It borders on obsessive, and if he and Alice start talking about it, they're both going to have sleepless nights. No—this is better. Better to cut through the frigid waters of Winnipesaukee until his arms give out.

At least once a day, Shenkman has a long talk with himself. He promises himself that he'll be easier on Waldo. He hears the tone of his own voice, criticizing his son. What he really wants to say, what he means, is *I love you and want the world for you.* Instead, what comes out is more like *Jesus will you stop picking at your fingers* or *Put the napkin in your goddamn lap.* There's something he finds utterly impossible, unreadable, unreachable about his son. He tries not to think too much about it, but it creeps into everything, into every waking minute of the day. He's stopped trying to get Waldo to do the kind of father-son things Shenkman thinks they should be doing. They don't throw a ball around, for instance. And the episode in which Shenkman, against Alice's better judgment, forced Waldo to join the Avalon Astros is best left in the annals of their family history, never to be mentioned again. He can still see Waldo standing in the middle of the soccer field, his arms dangling by his sides—his boy genius—completely lost and confused while his teammates zigzagged around him.

Shenkman has two hundred meters left to go. On his Row-Pro screen, he's now only four meters behind the leader. Lindgren, of course. Lindgren is just edging him out, and eight others are trailing. Shenkman trained hard yesterday, sprinting and resting for a solid forty minutes. He overdid it, maybe. *One, two.* On the screen, it's always a perfect day, the sky a preternatural blue. A stand of trees shines like emeralds. His heart rate is a bit higher than he'd like, but he steps it up a notch. Pulls a hair's breadth in front of Lindgren. *Fuck you, Lindgren.* Fifty-eight meters left. Shenkman goes back to Winnipesaukee. *One, two.* Behind him, he pictures the buoys of the finish line, neon in the distance. He hears the slap of his blades as they flatten against the water's surface, then go vertical and slice silently down. He tells himself not to look at the monitor, to think only of the finish line.

He crosses it, panting. Sweat pours down his back. His heart hammers. Only then does he look at the final results on the RowPro. The last remaining scull—that guy from New Zealand—slides to the finish line, and now all the sculls are lined up like perfect little soldiers. He rubs his stinging eyes with a towel, then squints at the bottom of the screen to see the winner. Lindgren. By an eighth of a second.

Shenkman strips, leaves his drenched clothes in the gym hamper. He pulls on a pair of clean sweatpants and wishes, not for the first time, that he had sprung for a bathroom when they built the addition. Sauna, steam, the works. But it was enough of a luxury—a home gym that only he would use—and there was no way he could justify it to Alice. In the beginning, he had tried to get her interested in working out, mostly to alleviate his own guilt—but Alice wanted nothing to do with it. *Your man cave,* she called it. And installed the hamper, so that he could deal with his own stinky workout clothes. Alice never sets foot in the gym. She doesn't know about RowPro, much less about Lindgren.

Downstairs, the front door opens and closes. Shenkman crosses the enclosed breezeway just in time to see the dark blue of a Red Sox sweatshirt disappearing up the stairs.

"Waldo!"

Waldo freezes.

"What the hell are you doing?"

"Nothing, Dad."

"Were you just outside?"

"No."

"Don't lie to me."

"I'm not!"

Shenkman tries to hold on to the promise he made himself, but it's like grasping a handful of air. He can feel himself going from zero to a hundred miles an hour, temper-wise. He takes a deep breath. Still sweating. He tells himself not to be too hard on Waldo. It only makes things worse. He's about to let it go—his jaw clenches from the effort—but then he sees the iPad tucked under Waldo's arm.

"Were you just—"

"Dad! Dad, I'm sorry!"

"That's it." Shenkman takes the stairs two at a time. He grabs the iPad from under Waldo's arm. It's all he can do not to throw it down the stairs and smash it to bits. "You're done."

"Please don't take it away. *Please.*"

"You can't say I didn't warn you."

Waldo looks even smaller and paler than usual, his face a

greenish white. How long had he been outside? And how could he have slipped out of the house without either Shenkman or Alice noticing? He was not even eleven years old, for God's sake! What eleven-year-old leaves his house in the middle of the night? Alice emerges from their bedroom at the top of the stairs. Her reading glasses are perched on the bridge of her nose, and she's holding a sheaf of legal briefs.

"What's going on? Waldo?"

He runs to her and flings himself on her, burying his head in her chest.

"My God, you're freezing!"

She glares at Shenkman as if this might be his fault.

"Mom, tell him not to take Star Walk away," Waldo cries into the thick chenille of Alice's robe.

"Honey, we'll talk about it later," she says, stroking his hair. "After we've all calmed down." She's always soothing Waldo, trying to make things better in the short term, but Shenkman has a different take on things. He's convinced that Waldo is being spoiled—not just in that way that all kids these days are spoiled but actually being rotted away, bit by internal bit, his character eroded by his parents' lack of conviction. Shenkman holds the iPad tightly in his hand, reminds himself that the thing cost almost five hundred bucks.

"He was outside, Alice."

"That's impossible."

"Ask him."

Alice takes Waldo by the shoulders and disengages him from her bosom, holds him at arm's length and scrutinizes his face as if a map of the truth might be found there.

"Waldo?"

He blinks away his tears.

"Is this true? Did you leave the house?"

A tiny nod.

Shenkman can see that Alice has now hit the long skid into the dangerous territory where he spends most of his time. Anger—she is slower to anger than Shenkman, but fear sets her off—overtakes her. A bright red spot appears on each cheek.

"What were you doing out there?"

"I was just looking at the—"

"What were you thinking?" She gives his shoulders a quick, almost violent shake. "Don't you know that it's dangerous to—"

"I'm sorry!"

"Stop apologizing!" Shenkman explodes. The eruption of his own voice surprises him. He was going to let Alice run with this for a while and avoid being the bad guy for once. But no. His love for his son is a vast and forceful thing; whatsoever threatens Waldo must be destroyed. But given that it's Waldo who appears to be hurting himself, what can Shenkman do? What can he do?

"You're grounded!" Shenkman yells. He hears his own father's voice echoing in his head. Words, phrases he never thought he'd say are a part of his everyday vocabulary: *because I said so* and *now you listen to me young man* and *as long as I'm paying the bills.*

God, he hates himself.

Waldo detaches himself from his mother and runs to his room. He slams the door behind him so hard that the crystal chandelier in the dining room tinkles—a bizarrely merry sound, given the circumstances. His sobs are audible from behind his door. His fists pound the headboard. Shenkman knows that Waldo would kill him right now if he could. And who can blame him? Shenkman is about to turn away, defeated, and head back into his man cave, but Alice is looking at him, shaking her head. Her hair has loosened from its scrunchie and falls softly over her face, the way Shenkman likes it. Is it so wrong, to have the thought that his wife is pretty? Waldo has inherited her delicate features, her pale, porcelain skin.

"That was unnecessary," Alice says quietly.

"Do you think?" It comes out angrier than he intended. Everything seems to be coming out angry, as if he has only one setting.

"You could have defused it. Instead of . . ."

"Alice, I didn't know how. I saw him coming in from outside with that stupid fucking thing, and I just—"

"Lost it." Alice completes the sentence for him.

"Yeah."

"And now you've told him he's grounded."

"Uh-huh."

"How are we supposed to do that? Skip his piano lesson, and jujitsu? Just have him come home after school tomorrow so he can sit in an empty house, staring at the walls? What exactly is that supposed to accomplish?"

Shenkman registers that Alice is more pissed at him than usual.

"I wasn't thinking." But then he shifts gears. "You got mad too, you know."

"I didn't yell." Her eyes, those same dark fringed eyes she gave to Waldo, flash at him. "I didn't threaten. I wasn't . . . violent."

"I wasn't violent!" Shenkman yells.

Alice's shoulders slump. She looks like she's sprung a leak, her whole body deflating.

"Let's just drop it. We'll revisit this in the morning."

Shenkman would almost prefer it if she'd keep fighting with him. Always the lawyer, she is cutting her losses.

"Alice, I . . ."

But she's already walking back upstairs, heading to Waldo's room. No doubt she'll snuggle up to him, wipe away his tears, strike some sort of bargain. She'll tell Waldo that his father loves him—that he didn't really mean what he said. Of course Waldo can have Star Walk back. Of course he's not grounded.

Shenkman turns back to the gym. Not that he's going to work out again, though the thought does cross his mind. He eases himself onto a mat, stretches out his legs, and tries to touch his toes. His muscles are frozen solid. His lower back aches, and a sharp pain shoots down the outside of his right hip. He hopes like hell it isn't sciatica. Forty-two years old, and rowing like he's still eighteen. Who the hell does he think he is? Middle-aged, is who he is. His body is letting him know, just in case he's forgotten.

The iPad dings from the top of the hamper. He's still not used to it—the only way he could justify the expense was to share it with Waldo, but that's over now. He reaches for it, then scrolls down. A dozen messages, all from the office. Nikkei opened low. Spam from wine merchants, golf resorts. Credit card offers. A news alert about the death of a ninety-eight-year-old senator whose name doesn't ring a bell. And then—there it is—Lindgren. The subject line reads *Yo, dude!*

Jesus, really? Shenkman knows nothing of what's happened to Lindgren over the last twenty years, other than that the guy has stayed in good enough shape to beat him by an eighth of a second. Lindgren might never even have crossed his mind if it wasn't for RowPro. From the very first time Shenkman logged on to race, there was Lindgren's name on the board, as surely as if they were both back on Winnipesau-kee, rowing the Meredith Bay course.

Lindgren seated in front of Shenkman, their movements as precise and aligned as a corps de ballet. Lindgren, his wheat-colored hair whipping in the breeze.

*Wassup?* the body of the email reads. Nothing else. Just one word. *Wassup.* Wassup with you, Lindgren? It sure isn't an alumni class note, along the lines of *Jack Lindgren and his lovely wife Melinda recently welcomed their third child, a son called Chip. The Lindgrens divide their time between Manhattan and Newport, where they have rewarding careers as fill-in-the-fucking-blank.*

Shenkman's thumb hovers over the delete icon. Does he really want to go back there? To engage Lindgren? In college, it seemed they would know each other forever, but the truth is that they had nothing in common, even then. Nothing except a very particular athletic ability that landed them in the second and third positions on varsity crew. If he reconnects with Lindgren, he'll have to tell him about his life. He'll have to account for the past twenty years. *Wassup.* Graduate school, check. Career in an unremarkable state of ascendancy, check. The distinct feeling that perhaps somewhere along the way he made a wrong turn, check. Lovely wife who has recently started taking antidepressants, check. Suburban house slightly beyond his reach, check. But more than this, more than this: one beautiful, complicated, delicate, infuriating, brilliant, dreamy, terror-inducing boy, check.

He powers down the thing, and Lindgren goes dark.

# *Sarah*

S HE IS PLAYING a game on her phone. It's like Scrabble
on speed. L-I-E becomes L-I-E-S. She spots an N and it
becomes L-I-N-E-S. Anything not to think. If she were
someone who carried a flask (could she possibly become
someone who carries a flask?), she would take a swig now, or
two. The airplane wine has worn off, leaving her unpleasantly
buzzless. The driver is wearing a cap; his hands are precisely
at ten and two o'clock on the steering wheel. He hasn't
engaged her in conversation. Her assistant booked the car
service and probably had her flagged as a VIP.

S-E-E-M. S-E-E-R. S-E-E-I-N-G. Her phone rings. An image
of Peter replaces the word game on the screen. An early morning shot taken at the beach. He's wearing a wet suit, leaning
against his surfboard. Early mornings in Malibu, the waves
are a great equalizer. Oscar-winning directors, powerhouse
agents, out-of-work screenwriters—the surf doesn't care. The
surf would just as soon pull any of them under.

"Hey," she answers.

"Everything going smoothly?" Peter has her on speaker-phone in his car.

"More or less."

"Where are you?"

"Just passing Irvington."

"You're almost there."

A pause. Is Peter distracted by traffic? He had a pitch meeting earlier in the afternoon. She debates asking him how it went. It's been a long time since she's heard a note of optimism in his voice, and she just isn't up for the dejection, the bitterness, the *story*. The last time she asked, he suggested that maybe the only reason he was brought in to pitch is that he's her husband.

"I should be with you," he says.

She closes her eyes.

"I know."

"Sarah, I feel so bad about this. If you had given me even one day's notice, I could have shuffled things around."

"I know," she repeats. Her voice sounds wooden to her own ears. Why is she punishing Peter? What he's saying is perfectly reasonable. It was only late last night that she bought the ticket—full fare, business class. Completely nuts, really. But that's what happens when you wait until the last minute. You spend too much money, further alienate your children, and make your husband feel guilty and useless. She's the one who should feel guilty. Who does feel guilty.

She takes a deep breath, tries to impersonate someone rational. "I know it was impulsive, Pete."

*Impulsive.* Ha. Dr. Baum would consider this an interesting choice of word. It's been coming up a lot, lately. As in, *We need to get to the root of this impulsive behavior.* As in, *These impulses are going to get you into trouble.*

"I honestly didn't think I needed to be here," she rushes

36

on. "But then I pictured my dad—doing this all alone, and Theo is just incapable of showing up—"

Wait. On Yom Kippur she vowed not to bad-mouth her brother. *Lashon hara*, one of the two most serious sins according to Jewish law. The other being murder. It's a kind of murder, to speak ill of someone, isn't it? She couldn't stand such scrutiny herself.

The driver turns left on Poplar, right on Division. She isn't ready for this. Not for the angle of the streetlight against the dark blue mailbox on the corner; not for the crunch—an East Coast sound—of the car's tires against the last of autumn's leaves raked into piles along the edges of the street; not for the twinkly white lights of the wreath hanging on the front door of the Hellers' house, which will always be the Hellers' house to her, no matter who now lives there. And there's that fucking tree. She gives it a quick, sideways glance, as if it might blind her. What had she thought? That anything would have changed? Or perhaps that she would have changed?

Peter is saying something.

"Sarah? I think I'm—" The connection is breaking up. He must have hit that dead spot on Mulholland.

The driver slows to a stop. "Here we are, ma'am."

"Just give me a moment."

She fishes through her purse for a compact, looks at herself in the two-inch mirror. Her skin is blotchy in the car's overhead light, her eyes glassy. And she's getting a zit between her eyebrows. Wrinkles *and* breakouts: on the list of things she hadn't known about entering her forties. Really, there should be a guidebook, along the lines of *What to Expect: The Toddler Years. Should be able to* cook a decent coq au vin, balance a checkbook, manage a household. *Might be able to* sleep at night without the wonders of Ambien. *Might even be able to* enjoy sexual relations, though not necessarily with one's own husband.

She sits still, the engine idling, and looks through the closed window at the house of her childhood. The porch light is on, as if her father is expecting company, even though he has no idea that she has pulled up in a car outside. The wicker love seat and two chairs cast long, hulking shadows across the wide front steps. If her mother were here, the furniture would have been covered, protected by custom-made tarps for the winter. The house looks a bit beaten up, badly in need of a paint job. The black iron numeral 1 in the 18 above the door is askew. One of the front shutters is missing, and the window boxes are filled with the brown husks of dead geraniums. The strong wind blowing east off the Hudson River a few blocks away has done its work. The dampness. She can feel it even before she opens the car door.

Her phone rings again. She's expecting Peter, but instead the screen reads *No Caller ID*.

"I can't talk to you now."

"Where are you? I waited for an hour."

"I'm in New York."

A long silence.

"Aren't you going to say anything?"

"Like what?"

"Like maybe, you're sorry? Like maybe, you should have let me know so that I wasn't just sitting at the bar like some fucking moron?"

"I'm sorry," she says.

"You know, you don't sound very sorry. But let me tell you, if you think you can—"

She ends the call and turns the ringer to silent.

She steps onto the sidewalk and peers up at the second

floor. The light in her parents' bedroom is on. Her teeth chatter. She pulls the collar of her thin cashmere coat around her neck. She should have let her father know she was coming, but she just couldn't do it. She kept thinking maybe she'd change her mind. Back at LAX, looking for her flight on the departures board, she had been nearly overcome by the desire to close her eyes and point at a destination. Madrid. Acapulco. Tucson. She could have done it. She had a credit card and a passport. So now what? Ring the doorbell? Knock? Peel back the doormat and feel around for the spare key?

The driver, she realizes, is waiting for her to go inside.

"It's okay, really," she says. "I'm going to take a little walk."

He looks at her, unsure. Can he leave the slightly wobbly, shivering VIP customer standing on a suburban curb?

She steels herself. Looks him in the eye. "Really," she repeats. "It's okay."

The car pulls away, its taillights slowly receding. She looks across the street. Johnny Platt's old house. She has no idea who lives there now. One light burns in Johnny's old room. She'll just circle the block, she promises herself. That's all. Besides, it's too cold to stay outside any longer than that. In her impractical heels, she navigates the uneven sidewalk. It's been well over thirty years (an impossible fact she quickly files away) since she was a kid playing hopscotch on this very concrete. Susan Stern broke her ankle flying off her bike right here, in front of the Gelfmans' house. Noah Kantrowitz puked into the azalea bush the month after his bar mitzvah. How many thousands of times in her life has she passed the privet hedge lining the Mintzes' property? (*Imagine*, her mother had sniffed. *A privet hedge in Avalon.*) Once Sarah was finally old enough to cross at the light on North Elm on her own, she took this route to school each day, Theo trailing behind her.

*Wait for me!*
*Walk faster!*
*I can't—my books are too heavy.*
*Not my problem.*

God, she had been a lousy sister. She's still a lousy sister.

A single leaf skitters across the street and gets caught in a drain. No cars, this time of night. She rounds the corner. Ready or not. Tries to take a deep breath. It's even colder than she thought. Her heels click sharply up the front walk, an unnatural sound amid the rustle of tree branches, the dead suburban quiet. The light in Johnny Platt's old room has gone out. Now, the only night owl left is—

"Waldo?"

A voice—her father's voice—seems to come out of nowhere, startling her. She takes a step back, very nearly tripping on a loose stone. She wheels around.

"Waldo!" Her father's voice again. "Is that you?"

The sound is coming from above, Sarah realizes.

"Who's there?" Her father sounds frightened. "Waldo, no joke, you'd better tell me if—"

The second-floor window of her parents' bedroom is open. She squints up, blinded by a spotlight flooding the front lawn.

A long, stunned silence. All she can really make out is the outline of her father's head, his gray hair fanned out.

*Mimi?* It comes out in no more than a whisper. Still, he may as well have shouted. Oh, no. He doesn't think—please not.

"Dad, it's me," she says quickly. "It's Sarah. I just flew in from—"

The window comes sliding down, and less than a minute later, the front door swings open and there he is, Benjamin Wilf, in his big old flannel bathrobe and ancient fur moccasins, a scarf she crocheted for him when she was in middle school wrapped around his neck.

"My sweet Sarah."

He holds out his arms to her. Three big steps and she practically collapses into him, his robe soft against her cheek. Although it must be a decade since he's smoked a pipe, she catches a faint whiff of black cavendish tobacco. It's all she can do not to weep. Her father's hand strokes the back of her head as if no time had passed, none at all. She isn't a forty-two-year-old woman in the midst of a stupid, stupid affair. She isn't fighting off an incipient hangover. As she stands in the doorway of her childhood home, hugging her elderly father, the air turns briefly golden and bright. She is once again a girl, and he—he is a man in his prime. So handsome, so capable, you would trust him with your life. A very good doctor (that's what everyone always said about Benjamin Wilf, until they stopped, until all that followed mention of his name was a prolonged and awkward silence). Now, they sway together like an old couple, dancing. With her eyes closed, the scent of black cavendish, she can almost imagine that they are still that same beautiful young family with their whole lives ahead of them, waiting to be lived.

"Sarah." He breaks her reverie. "What in the world are you doing here?" He ushers her inside. The front hall is filled with boxes.

In the yellow light of the chandelier, she looks at him. It's been only a few months—since Labor Day, when they all went to Santa Barbara for the long weekend—but Benjamin seems to have aged ten years. The bags under his eyes are wrinkled and heavy. His mouth has settled into its downward creases, making even a smile look like an effort.

"I came to help," she says.

His eyes flicker away from hers for a moment. Of course.

41

He's too kind, too gentle a person to say it out loud: these dozens of boxes, taped up, labeled neatly, stacked to the ceiling, have been packed alone. She pushes away the image of her father going through the house, room by room. What to keep? What to store? What to throw into the enormous Hefty bags she sees piled in the living room? Now, there's nothing left to do. Nothing but the actual act of leaving. He may not have needed any help with that. In fact, it only now occurs to her, he may not have wanted company at all.

She waves a hand in front of her. "I'm sorry," she says. "Theo and I should have—"

"It's not your job to take care of me," he says. "And anyway, it's not like I'm going very far."

He glances at Sarah to see if she's going to challenge him on this. No, not far, not if you're measuring distance. Four blocks—just to the other side of North Elm. But where he's going is light-years away, and they both know it. She says nothing. What can she say? *At least you and Mom will be together again, living under the same roof?*

"Come, sweetheart. Let me see if I can still find us some tea."

Tea is the last thing she wants. She is well beyond the comforts of chamomile and honey. She follows Ben down the hall, narrow to begin with but now almost impassable, into the kitchen. Her phone is vibrating in her front jeans pocket. Again and again it thrums against her hip bone. Can she ask her father for a real drink? It's a familiar calculation: shame versus craving. She never knows which one will win. Actually, that's a crock. Craving wins. Craving trumps shame every time.

She modulates her voice into something super-casual.

"Have you packed up the liquor cabinet, Dad? I wouldn't mind a nightcap."

"You're in luck," he says without missing a beat. He turns

from an open box of pantry goods and crosses the kitchen to another box by the back door. "I was planning to leave all the booze for the gardener." He slices open the tape with a knife, then pulls out a dusty bottle of brandy that probably hasn't been touched in a decade.

Ben moves a pile of dishcloths from a chair and motions her to sit. He takes a lone juice glass from the dish rack, pours her a healthy shot. Then he drags a large wooden crate next to the chair and lowers himself down. He pats her knee as she takes what she hopes appears to be a reasonable sip of brandy.

"I'm afraid there are no sheets on your old bed," he says.

"I'll sleep in my clothes."

"You should have told me you were coming."

"It was last minute."

He nods.

"Your brother called earlier."

*Good of him. At least he remembered.*

"He says he'll stop by later in the week. I think this was just too hard," Ben says.

Now it's her turn to nod. And take another sip. *Too hard.* What does that mean, too hard? The fucking phone again. She has seven missed calls. It figures. Of all the men she could have had sex with—not that she flatters herself, but there were, to be honest, quite a few—she had to go pick someone ... what was Dr. Baum's word ... *unbalanced*? It seems inevitable now that Peter will find out about it. That her girls will disdain her; they'll side with their father in the messy divorce that is sure to follow.

Her gaze falls on the empty kitchen wall, the spot where their family schedule used to be. Mimi organized their lives in columns on a Pottery Barn chalkboard. Ben's column had notes about the meeting of the zoning board, the hospital dinner dance (*make sure tux is clean!*). Theo's was all about tutors. If they had known he was going to end up opening one of the hippest restaurants in Brooklyn (she's read all the reviews online), they might have eased up a bit on the homework help. And Sarah's was all social stuff. *Sleepover at Amy's Saturday. Lauren's sweet sixteen.* Each Sunday afternoon, Mimi would take the eraser and make small, efficient circles around the chalkboard. There was something satisfying about watching their weeks evaporate into dust, the future yet to be filled in.

Ben is yawning, his mouth wide open, gold fillings visible. He must be exhausted. It's nearly midnight here, though for her it's still early. She wonders if she might be able to pour another nip of the brandy once he goes to bed.

"I don't mean to be rude," he says.

"Not at all, Dad."

"The movers will be here at seven sharp," he says. "Do you think you can fend for yourself? There are still some crackers and cheese in the fridge, I think. And the TV hasn't been disconnected."

"Dad?"

She hadn't meant to speak. She inhales deeply—oxygen to the brain—trying to clear her thoughts. She is on the verge of saying more than she wants to. Words she'll regret tomorrow. She wants to tell him about her life, but that would be the height of selfishness, wouldn't it? The older she gets, the more alone she feels. The mess she's made of her life is none of her father's business. Especially not now.

"Are you okay, Sarah?" Ben has become suddenly focused. She remembers this look. Doctor Ben. At once kind, sensitive, and laser-sharp.

"I'm fine, Dad."

"You don't seem fine at all."

The phone again, against her hip.

"Jesus!"

"What? What is it? God, Sarah, are you in some kind of—"

She tries to pull herself together. She didn't fly across the country to upset her father. She's here to help. To be a good daughter. To do one right thing.

"No, no—it's nothing."

"Obviously it's not nothing."

"Perimenopause—it's making me emotional." She smiles her careful, hotshot-producer, red-carpet smile. "Please, don't worry about me. I'm good."

For a brief moment a world of sorrow crosses Ben's face like a passing shadow, before his features rearrange themselves into something safe and bland. Like father, like daughter. They will march on through.

"Okay, then. You're sure?"

She doesn't trust herself to speak.

"I'm here if you ever want to talk," he says.

Her eyes sting. How many times in her life has she heard him say exactly that?

And it was true. He had always been available. Ready to listen without judgment. At times it had made her a bit lonely, her father's steadiness.

He stands and stretches, his thick white chest hair visible where his robe falls open.

"Good night, sweets. Sorry to be such a party pooper."

"I'll walk you upstairs," she says.

They walk single file through the narrow, box-lined hall. Ben turns off the outside light, as he has every night for forty years. Does he think, as they climb upstairs arm in arm, of the years he carried her on his back, her small legs kicking with glee? Of the light that used to seep beneath Theo's closed door, Led Zeppelin playing? Does he think about the family photos that lined the now-empty walls? Mimi had framed every class picture of Sarah and Theo from kindergarten all the way through high school, so that walking up the stairs was like watching time-lapse photography. They got older with each step: missing teeth, adolescent awkwardness, graduation gowns.

At the top of the staircase he pauses, as if unsure which way to turn. The bedrooms are stripped bare, floors littered with empty hangers, rolls of packing tape, collapsed cardboard. Her breath catches at the sight of the stained mattress and box spring in the center of the master bedroom; they seem obscene, almost grotesque, like old naked bodies. It feels as if the house she was raised in were nothing more than an elaborate stage set. Now the play is over. The reviews are in. And the whole apparatus is being struck.

They're striking the set. A violent word.

Her father sighs, tousles her hair like she's a kid. "See you in the morning," he says.

She stands and watches as he shuffles over to the stained mattress. She'll head downstairs in a minute, pour herself some more brandy and sit for a while among the boxed-up remnants of her family's life. She doesn't believe in ghosts, but ghosts are all around them. The people who owned the house before them, and the owners before them, and the ones who built 18 Division at the turn of the century. She has to believe that they're all here. That they've made an indelible mark. That all their joys and sorrows, their triumphs and mistakes and hopes and despair are still as alive as they ever were. That no one ever truly, completely leaves.

# *Theo*

THE NEW SOUS chef somehow managed to fuck up the roux. Or rather, he should say the ex–new sous chef, because anyone who can fuck up the roux cannot possibly be trusted. Still, he shouldn't have lost his temper like that. Sent him packing. It must be some kind of record: three hours from start to finish, and now he has his kitchen to himself, which, if he's honest, is the way he prefers it.

Eleven o'clock, and the second seating is finishing up the intermezzo, a simple blood orange and mint-infused sorbet. He plates the last course—a trio of baby lamb chops served with caramelized carrots—as Carlos piles the sorbet dishes in the sink behind him. Two desserts, and then Theo will emerge from behind the heavy burgundy curtain that separates the dining room of Twelve Tables from the tiny kitchen. When the restaurant first opened, there was no curtain, but after the *Times* review it became impossible. Everybody wanted to be friends with him. They hovered while he chopped and sautéed. He never moved from a single spot in the center of the kitchen; the copper pots gleaming overhead, the sink, the double oven, the butcher block of German knives all within easy reach.

*Theo, you must try the wine.*

And then the producing of a decanter.

*It's a 1989 Domaine Leflaive Chevalier-Montrachet from our cellar.*

The slow, breathless extraction of the crumbling cork. The drama of it, as if they were soldiers in hazmat suits dismantling a bomb. Then the swishing and sniffing. The wine, rich and golden as a sunset in the Côte de Beaune. All the while he was at risk of burning the butter; of forgetting the thick-crusted French bread heating on the lowest rack.

*Theo, when will you be getting morels?*

*Are you open for New Year's?*

*Can we book a table for our friends? They're dying to get in.*

So finally, he hung the curtain and hired Carlos. Propped a SORRY, WE'RE CLOSED sign in the window overlooking Vanderbilt Avenue. The people with reservations at Twelve Tables know to ignore the sign, and the rest are kept from knocking or just walking in. They peer through the window, their breath fogging up the glass. What is this place? Theo has kept the bright yellow corrugated metal awning of the bodega. SWEET—GROCERY—TROPICAL PRODUCTS.

The *Times* review has brought Wall Street brokers and hedge fund guys from across the river. Folks who used to drop a few grand for dinner at Per Se are now on the austerity plan. They show up in town cars, without reservations. They circle the block, confused. Where is the restaurant? They consult their Zagat guide or OpenTable. They resort to maps.

"I'm sorry," Carlos goes out and tells them. "We have only twelve tables, and we're fully committed for both seatings."

"Can we book a table for tomorrow night? For next week?"

"I'm sorry." Carlos is unfailingly polite. This is his first sobriety job. He's been with Theo since the day he got out of rehab and answered the ad on Craigslist. "We are fully committed."

They can't believe it, these people who are used to being able to make things happen. It drives them crazy. And so they try and they try. Their personal assistants call. They send chocolates from Vosges, black market caviar, artisanal salumi. They drop names. They will be coming with a very important person: Fran Lebowitz, Derek Jeter, Nancy Pelosi.

The first of tonight's two desserts is a dense gateau au chocolat, served with a small glass of a house-made black walnut digestif, to be followed by a bite-size donut hole drizzled with caramel sauce. With a wooden spoon, he stirs the caramel. Tastes it, then adds a pinch of sea salt. These are some of his favorite moments. The low buzz of the evening winding down on the other side of the curtain. The perfection of the meal. The loneliness that he will feel in an hour, when the last of the diners has departed, when Carlos has washed the final dish, when there is nothing to do but go home—that loneliness is still far off.

"Hey, Big T." Carlos brings in the last of the lamb trio. "They're stuffed. Their word, not mine."

By this point in the evening, some diners—mostly the ladies—are pushing food around on their plates. To be fair, they're on the eighth course of a ten-course meal. The foie gras ravioli on a braised cabbage leaf. The slice of pancetta on a bed of wilted spinach topped with a poached egg. He tries to keep portions small. The consommé with lobster tail had been served in a ramekin that could fit into the palm of his hand.

Extreme dining, some critics have called it. Pathological

dining. The reviewer from *New York* magazine accused Theo of being a control freak. Backlash, but still, it stung. What's wrong with comfort food? That's how he likes to think of it. Comforting food for discomfiting times. He is providing far more than dinner. Each night, he peeks through the curtain and sees little miracles. In the jeweled light cast by Turkish lanterns dangling from the ceiling, across the scattering of mismatched tables—some covered with checkered cloths, others bare and scarred—what he sees in the flickering glow are faces transformed, over the span of hours, from agitation to contentment. From heartache to something like joy.

The young couple at table two—friends of his fishmonger—weren't speaking when they arrived tonight. By the time Carlos set the frisée salad in front of them, they were holding hands. The stage actress Anouk Levy is at her regular table by the window, dining alone. She has been widowed for six months. At first, she would read a book between courses, or obsessively check her iPhone. She would leave food on her plate, her fingers nervous in her lap. Now, she sips her demi-bottle of cabernet, soaks up the poached egg with the crust of her bread. When she leaves, tall and regal and very un–Prospect Heights in a black sheared mink, she will offer Theo a half smile and a nod. *Merci.*

His patrons—his regulars—are his family. The truth is that he loves them. He may not see them outside the restaurant (he hardly has a life outside the restaurant), but here at Twelve Tables they are everything. He dreams of them. Frieda and Joe Glasser, who drive over from their brownstone near Brooklyn College. Marty Adelson, his longtime accountant, who dines every Friday with his elderly father. Celia Gabriel, a food editor turned blogger. Dozens of people whose weeks are shaped by their dinner reservations.

And what do they surmise about Theo Wilf?

He plates the gateau au chocolat. Pours the nocino into delicate, small digestif glasses he scored on eBay. Pops the donut holes into the oven to warm.

That he is a large man, with a big, round belly. A man of appetites.

No wedding ring. They might wonder: Does he live alone? Is he straight or gay?

He hands two plates to Carlos. He'd better not leave the kitchen—not until the donut holes have been served, espresso orders taken.

She has been in the restaurant since the beginning of the second seating. *She.* He knows her name—Harper Loomis— but tries not to say it, or even think it. Ever since he was a kid, he's avoided the names of girls he likes, as if the very syllables are too much to bear. *She.*

He has questions for her—each lined up patiently behind the next—questions he will never ask.

*Were your parents* To Kill a Mockingbird *fans?*

*What's the last thing you think about before you fall asleep?*

*If I could cook you one perfect meal—tell me, what would it be?*

Instead, he steals glimpses of her through the burgundy curtain. Each week she comes in with a different date. Sometimes she is with men, sometimes women. Tonight it is a woman. They have been consumed with each other the whole evening, their heads bent close, thighs (he is sure) touching as they sit side by side on the restaurant's only banquette. They form a beautiful picture, the two of them. She, with her spill of shiny black hair, flash of white teeth; her companion, small and fair, her eyes lined in dark, smoky kohl.

He samples the nocino. Imagines himself sitting next to her. He would feed her forkfuls of the gateau. Raise the glass of nocino to her mouth. Watch the black walnut stain her lips. Then he'd lean over and—

Oh, fuck's sake. Who is he kidding.

The donut holes are warmed in the oven. He pulls out the tray, transfers them to a small bone china plate, drizzles each one with the thinnest layer of caramel.

"Big T?" Carlos again.

Theo wishes Carlos would stop with the nickname. He knows that somewhere along the way he's crossed the line between portly and fat. He also knows—as his father is fond of telling him—that he's no spring chicken. Men have heart attacks at forty. Major myocardial infarctions from which they don't recover. Especially men who cook ten-course dinners every night, tasting each ingredient—the foie gras, the pork belly—along the way.

"Big T, some lady's on the phone. Says it's important."

The ringers are supposed to be turned off in the restaurant. And he doesn't carry a cell phone.

And the number is unlisted. All this for a reason. So what the hell?

He glares at Carlos. First the sous chef, now this. People disappoint you. The more you rely on them, the greater the letdown.

Carlos wags the receiver at him. "Sorry, man."

It's probably that woman from *Bon Appétit*. She keeps calling. The more he fends her off, the harder she tries. She wants to do a profile on him. A human-interest story. He has tried to convince her that nothing about him is of human interest.

"Take a message."

"Lady sounds upset, man."

He takes the phone, wedges it between his shoulder and ear as he turns on the espresso machine. Watches the blinking green light as it warms up.

"Theo Wilf," he says.

"Theo, it's Sarah."

For a disorienting moment, it doesn't compute. The din of the restaurant—the dull clink of spoons against dishes, forks against crystal, the rumbling chorus of voices—it all recedes into a cottony silence. And at the center of that silence, piercing him so deftly it is as if a sliver of glass had entered his bloodstream, is a nameless foreboding.

Sarah calling him here means—what? He didn't even know she had the number. She sounds agitated, her words slurred. He tries to breathe all the way into his stomach. Fill his whole body with air like a helium balloon.

He tries to speak, but nothing comes out.

"Mom's disappeared, Theo."

The words do not compute. Here in the innermost part of his inner sanctum, his kitchen, the heart of his restaurant, he feels a wave of dizziness. He holds on to the edge of the counter.

*Momsshdishapeeredzzztheo.*

"Slow down." He clears his throat. "Sarah, slow down. I can't understand you." The green light on the espresso machine has stopped blinking. Moving slowly, methodically, he tamps down a few scoops of dark Italian roast—fully loaded—then twists the handle, locking it into place. *Disappeared.* Places a demitasse cup beneath the nozzle. Pulls the lever. As if continuing what he had been doing before the phone rang might throw these last minutes into reverse. He had planned to bring Harper Loomis her espresso himself.

*Disappeared.*

"Someone just called from ... the place. Avalon Hills. They can't find her."

He looks at the clock on the oven. It's nearly midnight. Everything is cushiony and weird. He feels pinned to the spot by his sister's words, and by the childish desire to reject them. What did they say to each other when they were kids? *Take it back!* As if actions, words, the passage of one moment to the next could be undone.

"I'm here in Avalon. I flew in tonight."

"Oh, shit, I'm sorry. I know I should have—"

"Theo, stop and listen to me." He presses the receiver hard against his ear. She's still slurring her words. Is she drunk? "No one has seen Mom since bingo. That's what they said. Since bingo."

"This doesn't make any sense," he says, mostly to himself.

Carlos is hovering nearby, pretending not to listen. Theo turns his back, hunches over the dirty dishes in the sink.

"They've looked everywhere. She's gone."

Carlos taps him on the shoulder.

*Boss?* he whispers.

"Not now!"

But then Carlos points in the direction of the espresso machine. The demitasse cup has overflowed, spilling all over the counter, dripping onto the floorboards.

"Shit!"

"Theo!"

"No, not you," he says. "Something else."

He dumps the first demitasse cup and starts over.

"Let me take care of this, T," Carlos says quietly.

As Carlos efficiently fills the orders—espresso, cappuccino, doppio, macchiato—Theo tries to take in what is happening.

His mother. The last time he visited was well over a month ago, on a raw November day. The wind whipped against his face as he rode his motorcycle up the Saw Mill River Parkway. She was standing just inside the sliding doors of the lobby. She wore an old pair of jeans and a sweater of his father's. On her left hand, her wedding ring. Her hair—now completely silver—hung in one long braid down her back.

She looked so much like herself that he forgot. For a split second he forgot, and engulfed her in a hug. They had always been a family of huggers. Even during his teenage years when they barely talked, he would wrap his arms around his mother and it was as if the two of them understood that no matter what, they were bound by a powerful and immutable love.

But just then, she felt like a bird in his arms. A trapped, panicked bird, wings beating. She pulled away from him, quivering.

*Mom, it's me—Theo.*

She stared at him hard, as if from the other side of a vast, dangerous landscape. Then vaguely, politely, as if she knew she had met him once but couldn't quite place him, she offered him her hand.

*Of course. Hello, Theo. So nice to see you again.*

"Theo?" His sister's voice. "Did you hang up?"

His cheeks are damp.

"Theo! Are you there?"

His mother doesn't recognize her husband, her children, her own name. She doesn't know what day it is, or who is president. And she's somewhere out in the world alone. Hasn't been seen since fucking *bingo*, for crying out loud. For all he knows, Mimi is shuffling along the streets of Avalon in her pajamas. The forecast calls for snow.

"I'm here."

He unties his apron and grabs his leather jacket from the hook by the emergency exit. On the other side of the curtain, in a parallel universe, an eruption of laughter. He tosses the restaurant keys to Carlos. His motorcycle is parked outside. From Brooklyn, he can be there in forty minutes, tops.

"You okay, T?"

"You're gonna have to lock up, bro."

"No problem."

The phone is still pressed to his ear. On the other end, he can hear his sister breathing. It is a sound at once familiar and elusive, like a forgotten strain of a childhood lullaby.

"I can't do this alone," Sarah says. "I haven't woken Dad up yet to tell him, and—oh, Jesus, Theo, can you imagine? Please, can you just—"

He's not good at this. Words aren't his thing. He's never been able to say what he feels. But people shouldn't make the mistake of leaping to the conclusion that he doesn't feel. He feels plenty.

"I'm on my way," he says. *I love you,* he wants to say, but can't. *I'm sorry.* But the words won't come. He wants to reassure her. *Everything's going to be all right.* But that would be a lie. His sister is drunk. His mother is missing. His family has unraveled bit by invisible bit. There was nothing that could have been done—Theo tells himself this—nothing at all that could have prevented it. Now, they are separate. Each in a private, tattered universe. He shakes a few remaining donut holes into a wax paper bag, then folds it into his backpack.

# *Waldo*

THE FRONT DOOR closes behind him with a soft click. Not that they're listening, anyway. He spent the last half hour crouched in the hallway, his ear pressed to their door, straining to make out the two voices he knows best in the world. His mother's harsh whisper. The low, persistent rumble of his father's voice. Then, once in a while, a word or two would let loose—*psychiatrist, medication, not normal*—like the first pebbles of an avalanche trickling down a mountain. Avalanches have to begin that way, right? With just a single stone? He's thought a lot about this. How would you know? How would you know the difference between normal and scary?

They're up late, his parents. And it's his fault. It's always his fault. His father will be grouchy in the morning. He will straighten his tie into a knot, his mouth tight as he shrugs on his suit jacket. His mother will look wan, exhausted in her skirt and high heels as she goes through the motions of packing his sandwich. *Not normal.*

They will call his name. *Waldo! Time for school!*

After a minute or two, they will call again. This time sounding irritated.

*Waldo, get down here, slowpoke!*

Another few minutes, and his father will march up the stairs, taking them two at a time. *Don't make me come in there, young man!*

His father is right. He isn't like the other boys in Avalon. He doesn't care about playing baseball—though he can recite the batting average and on-base percentage for every player in the Red Sox lineup if anyone cares to ask. He hates football, and the kids who play it. Ditto lacrosse. And don't get him started about Harry Potter. Basilisks, Grindylows, Nifflers—who cares? When there's so much that's real in the universe, why make things up?

Outside, on Division Street, the clear, moonlit sky has given way to clouds. The moon is a smudge. The air smells like snow. Across the street, Dr. Wilf's bedroom light is off. Waldo stops to consider: Does he have everything he needs? Mittens, hat, scarf, coat. Long underwear under his pajamas. Wool socks. Sneakers. He's even brought a bag of chips in case he gets hungry. And he has ten dollars—his past two weeks' allowance—stuffed into his pocket along with a half-eaten roll of Life Savers. He hasn't thought much beyond that. His mind is at once wild and quiet, like the way it sometimes is if he's played too many video games. Soon, his parents' whispers will give way to silence, punctuated only by his father's snores.

*Waldo, goddamnit, if I've told you once, I've told you a thousand—*

In the morning, his father will throw open Waldo's bedroom door. And what will he see? A perfectly made bed, hospital corners and all. Pillows fluffed, his two stuffed bears sitting propped up just the way the housekeeper leaves them each day.

*Alice! Alice, Waldo's gone!*

That'll show him. Waldo moves quickly down the front walk and—where is he going?—heads in the direction of North Elm. He pulls his hood over his woolen hat. Hunches down and makes himself smaller. His heart is beating fast. He doesn't want to think about his mother. If he thinks about her, he'll turn around and run home. She is all around him, inside and outside, like a smell. Like skin. Like the vapor his breath is making in the freezing-cold air.

The iPad is tucked inside his zipped-up jacket, close to his chest. He knew he would find it in the gym. It was right there next to that dumb rowing machine—his father loves that machine so much he should have *married* it—and when he turned it back on, it was still almost fully charged. He wonders how long it will take—how many hours—before the battery gives out. He stops on the corner of Birch and Poplar and pulls it out, aiming the screen at the cloudy sky. Star Walk can see through the clouds. The constellations are there, unchanged since he showed them to Dr. Wilf what seems like a thousand million hours ago. Chamaeleon, the lizard. Hydrus, of course. The keyhole shape of Mensa.

*Why do you care?* He closes his eyes. His father's voice is never far away. *What the hell difference does it make?* He's never been able to explain. How can he tell his father that his head is filled with noise, and that this is what makes it all go quiet? The hush of the night sky. The wheeling stars. The ancient shapes. They make him feel cozy and safe, as if he were under a vast blanket. As if his mom were tucking him in, sitting on the edge of his bed, rubbing small circles against his back. As if she would sit there all night, watching over him.

A car speeds past, music thumping through closed windows. He stops and waits behind a tree. What will happen if someone sees him? What if they call the police? He's small, even for eleven. His wrists are thin, his legs are like sticks. His neck so narrow it makes his head look big. Sometimes people ask him what grade he's in and when he says sixth, they can't hide their surprise. Even though he skipped a year, he looks like maybe a fourth grader. And sixth graders who look like fourth graders shouldn't be walking around Avalon in the minutes after midnight.

Maybe he should just go home. His parents would never know he had been gone. The spare key is in the backyard, under a loose piece of flagstone on the patio. He knows the alarm code. His bed would feel warm right about now. His bears he still sleeps with. Their button eyes and matted fur. A pang rips through him, deep and jagged like something sawing at his insides. He doesn't feel safe out here—but he doesn't feel safe in there either. He can't stop seeing his father, vein bulging in his forehead, grabbing Star Walk out of his hands. Gripping the iPad like he might just smash it.

No. He pokes his head out from behind the tree. The car is gone. He keeps walking, each step taking him farther away from home. A destination is forming in his mind, somewhere just beyond his reach—but as with the constellations above the cloud cover, he tries to trust it. One foot in front of the other. He hums a tune. The theme song from *SpongeBob SquarePants*.

He reaches North Elm, which he isn't allowed to cross by himself. But he isn't supposed to run away from home, either. The rules he has lived by, *eat all your green beans, say please and thank you, look grown ups in the eye,* all these and more have vanished, vaporized like each breath, here one moment, visible, tangible, then gone.

His nose is running. His eyes tear. He should have brought his ski mask, goggles. And he doesn't have the lip balm his mother always makes him use, the one that smells like mangoes. His lips are already chapped from licking them in the cold.

What now? He looks both ways on North Elm. Not a car in sight. The traffic light turns from red to green. Back to red. Back to green. He stands there, frozen. What is he afraid of? Kids in school are always making fun of him, calling him a scaredy-cat. His teacher, Mrs. Hardy, tells him not to pay attention. That he'll have the last laugh someday, but someday seems a really long way off. On Facebook, they're mean to him. They call themselves his friends, but they're not friends. They write all sorts of things. *Answer a question about Waldo Shenkman. What's one word you would use to describe Waldo Shenkman? Dumb. Dreamer. Nose picker.* He's stopped looking.

He holds his breath and runs across North Elm as if diving into a lake. Lets out his breath only when he gets to the other side. Now he's in a foreign land, away from the houses and corners and trees of his neighborhood. He's not far from the center of Avalon, though he wouldn't know exactly how to walk there. The train station is nearby. And he's pretty sure that not too, too far from here is the parkway and the mall.

A light snow has begun to fall. He sticks out his tongue. The snow tastes like metal. How can something that falls straight from the sky taste like something already on the earth? These are the kinds of questions that get him into trouble at school. The questions that puzzle his teachers and make his classmates hate him. But it isn't his fault if he thinks about these things! *Not normal.* He stuffs his hands deep into his pockets and keeps going. Now he's leaving tracks.

In the distance, an unfamiliar *whoosh.* He hears it through the thick wool of his hat covering his ears. *Whoosh ... whoosh ...* Way down the road, in front of him, he sees a green sign. The entrance to the main route—he doesn't know the name of it—that leads to the parkway that leads, eventually, to New York City.

He doesn't want to go to New York City. No, no, no. That's too far away, and he doesn't know anybody there. He's visited a few times with his parents and all he can remember is the wind, whipping through the immense gray canyons, the people on the streets, all moving too fast. The smell of pretzels, chestnuts. The blurry destination in his mind becomes a little bit clearer, as if a dial inside of him were being adjusted. Left foot, right foot. The snow is covering the ground now. He should have worn boots. He trudges along, his toes cold. He doesn't have a watch on. How long has he been out here?

He pulls out the iPad. It says 12:53. He's been gone for less than an hour, and he's already worried. Maybe the kids at school are right. *Crybaby. Scaredy-cat.* He makes his way along the edge of the ramp that leads to the main route. *Whoosh.* He has to be very careful. In his dark blue down jacket, hood pulled up, tartan plaid pajama bottoms, he is practically invisible. *Watch out for cars!* He can hear his mother's voice. *Your head is in the clouds!* He hugs the side of the road, moves quickly to the other side of the dented metal divider. If he's right—and please let him be right—he has only a short way to go. He's driven this route with his mother a thousand times. He wishes he'd paid more attention.

His stomach is flip-floppy. There aren't many cars on the road, but they're driving really fast, as if everybody wants to get home so late at night. He sees a flash of movement in the sparse woods: a family of deer, their necks turning toward him, eyes gleaming. What does his father call them? *Rodents. Vermin.* They eat the expensive rosebushes. He keeps moving. Counting his steps. Trying not to think about anything bad. About how far from home he is. Too far to go back. He can't change his mind.

There, now he can see it. Eureka! The entrance to the mall, all lit up like a welcoming planet. The signs—WHOLE FOODS, POTTERY BARN, WILLIAMS SONOMA, NEIMAN MARCUS— are familiar. The parking lot stretches for what seems like miles. When he was a little kid, his parents brought him here to pick out a jungle gym for the backyard: a custom-made maze of cedarwood, with slides and doors and a sandbox. He never really played on it that much. But there's the store. He sees it all the way on the edge of the mall near some of the smaller stores that sell Hallmark cards and candy and pajamas. Play Heaven, it's called. When he thinks of the last time he saw his dad truly happy, it might have been that day. *Choose anything you want,* his father said. *The biggest slide. How about a climbing wall? That's my boy.*

The wind slices through him as he crosses the parking lot. Christmas lights are everywhere. Santa and his reindeer prance across the Pottery Barn windows, and the Neiman Marcus mannequins are wearing glittery gowns. The music that's usually piped outdoors has been turned off for the night. No "Joy to the World." No "Jingle Bell Rock." He wishes the music were playing. He wishes the lights were on throughout the mall, and that the parking lot were full of cars. He wishes—he's mad at himself for it—but God, he wishes his parents were here. Both of them. His father and his angry eyes. His mother and the way she folds him into a hug. He has gone too far, and the distance is unbearable. He feels like he might just float away. Like he might lift off the ground and disappear, up, up, up, until he's part of the great blanket above him. He'll break apart into thousands of pieces and become Constellation Waldo.

On the sidewalk outside Play Heaven, a cedar play structure smaller than the one his parents got him is all set up and on display, complete with slide and sandbox. On the wooden door, a handmade sign says WELCOME! Maybe he can just rest for a few minutes. Figure out what to do. It has to be warmer in there than it is in the parking lot. He's started to cry, and his tears are sticking to his eyelashes, freezing in place on his cheeks.

He bends over—he's too big for this, really—and pushes the door open. Inside the play structure, it's dark. Dark the way it is in the middle of the night when he has to get out of bed to pee. The way that shapes, so ordinary in the light of day—the staircase, the chest of drawers in the hall, the bathroom scale, the toilet—become hulking and foreign. The way he fights off his aloneness by reminding himself that his parents are just down the hall.

Except that his parents aren't just down the hall. *Whoosh . . . whoosh . . .* He is inside a play structure on the edge of a mall off a route he cannot name, miles away from home. He sits on the cold concrete and pulls the iPad from inside his jacket once again. It's 1:18. The battery is still nearly full. The music slows down the rhythm of his heart. He takes a ragged breath.

Wipes his eyes. The stars above are unchanged. No matter what happens down here, Chamaeleon is still up there. And

64

Hydrus. And Mensa. Nothing bad will happen. Not if he keeps remembering.

He rummages through his backpack for the bag of chips and rips it open. He consumes them two, three at a time. When does it become light out? He checks Star Walk. The sun will rise at 7:08. He counts on his fingers. Can he last that long? Things will look different in the morning. That's what his mom always says. He wedges himself into a corner and wraps his jacket around him as tight as he can, like a sleeping bag. And like a child counting sheep, he closes his eyes and starts at the beginning: *Andromeda, Antlia, Apus, Aquarius, Aquila, Ara, Aries . . .*

# *Mimi*

W HERE IS HER family? It's been hours since she last saw them. They had been on the beach near the hotel. The kids were building a sandcastle complete with a seashell roof.

Their tanned, curved backs, spines like two perfectly matched strands of pearls. Dark, wet hair plastered to their small heads like baby seals. *Theo, wait . . . let me!* Sarah's voice rose above the waves. But hold on. Wait a minute. That's not right. Her bedroom slippers slap against the snow. Theo and Sarah aren't old enough to be on their own—at least not for so many hours.

Sarah's just turned thirteen, and Theo's eleven. They shouldn't be on the shore of an unfamiliar island by themselves. What island is it, anyway? Bermuda? Barbuda? She got so absorbed in her crossword puzzle, and then she took a nap—*26, 5, 17, bingo!*—and now she can't find them.

She follows the white line. Surely the white line will lead her to her babies. Ben must be looking for them too. He had gone inside the hotel before her nap. Something about a patient, an emergency with a patient. *Paging Dr. Wilf.* But he'd promised her a vacation. A real vacation, away from the hospital, from the beeper, from the phone ringing at all hours. A bolt of anger flashes through her. He had promised! And now they've misplaced the children.

Her fingers are stiff, her hands turning blue from the cold. Who knew how cold it could be in Bermuda/Barbuda? She needs to get rid of the hideous bracelet weighing her down. Leather, rubber—what is it? Ben must have bought it for her on the beach from one of those vendors. A fancy thing but ugly, with that bulbous, watch-like face. She tears it off her wrist with a sudden, startling violence and drops it to the ground as she follows the white line.

A truck rumbles toward her, headlights blinding. The long, loud bleat of a horn. She jumps back as the driver zooms past, lowering his window, shouting something at her that she can't understand. She feels herself shaking. Where is she? She has lost the thread. Images, memories pour through her like sand through an hourglass. Her children are newborns, they are teenagers. She can't keep track. They seem to be everywhere, all at once. What's this? Theo at age five, holding up a lilac for her to smell. Cupping her cheek with his pudgy hand, mimicking her. His soft lips pressed against hers. Her little lover boy. And Sarah, her wet hair in two braids. Sitting at the kitchen table, bent over her homework. A cold glass of milk by her elbow. She's in sixth grade, seventh, eighth. She is growing, growing, now she's—

*Stop,* something tells her. *Stop there.* But the images churn. Inside her is nothing but an ocean. Waves cresting, receding, cresting again. Sarah, panting on the front porch, her eyes wild. *What happened?* Her daughter looks at her wordlessly.

Blood smeared on her white tee shirt. Dirt on her chin. The Buick, its front crumpled into the oak tree like a piece of aluminum foil. Smoke rising from its hood. The wail of a siren.

Mimi stumbles toward her baby girl. *Sarah! My God, Sarah—what on earth?* The moment is as alive as it has ever been, as if she herself were a tree, sliced open, revealing story after story.

But wait. Where is she?

Right. She is looking for her children. She has misplaced them on the beach.

They are lost, and she's following the white line.

Up ahead, there are bright lights. Letters, words, signs. She can almost make them out in the distance. It looks like a carnival, a country fair. A roller coaster, a Ferris wheel. She catches a whiff of cotton candy. She feels relief trickle through her like something slow and warm. That must be it. *Thank god thank god thank god.* Theo and Sarah must have gone to the carnival. Just wait until she has a word with them. They know better than to wander off like that, especially in a foreign place.

The white line curves into the country fair. Blinking lights, red and green. They mean something, but she doesn't know what. No one is in the vast, empty field! It stretches out before her. Black, endless. They all must be over there, near the blinking lights. Ben probably has them. Right now he's probably bought them enormous cones of cotton candy.

The field is full of thousands of white lines, glowing in the dark. She stands in the center, unsure of which way to go. She trains her eyes on the red and green lights and moves toward them. Toward Ben and the kids. Her breath is short. The hem of her nightgown stiff and wet against her calves. She clutches the top of her terry-cloth robe and closes it around her neck like an overcoat.

Where is her car? She must have misplaced that too. So many lost things. If she had her car, she could pick up Theo and Sarah at school. They must be waiting outside for her. She hates to be late. Usually they walk home together, but not when it's snowing. Sarah is probably waiting at the curb in her bright orange down jacket and the angora hat Mimi knitted for her. Jumping up and down to keep warm. Theo, his jacket unzipped, head bare. Legs poking out of gym shorts straight from basketball practice. *You'll catch your death of cold!* No. Wait. They're on vacation. Her car is parked in the garage of their house in Avalon. *Slap, slap, slap* go her bedroom slippers against the snow-covered asphalt.

The wind feels like something solid. Like a wall she has to break down with each step. *Slap, slap.* Again, Sarah on the front porch. Her lips are moving. One word lobbed after the next—impossible to grasp or understand. Mimi's watching a movie, a horror flick, with the volume turned off. Her daughter has blood on her white tee shirt. The Buick is wrapped around the oak tree. The radio still playing. Cyndi Lauper singing. *If you're lost, you can look, and you will find me.* The windshield shattered. Glass glinting all over the sidewalk, the summer lawn. *Time after time.* A police cruiser—no, two police cruisers—come screeching around the corner. Ben is on the ground, bent over a girl. A bullhorn blares. *Sir! Move away from her!* Ignoring the cops, Ben yells back. *It's okay—I'm a doctor.*

Now Mimi's very nearly across the vast, dark fairgrounds. She looks around at the red and green blinking lights. Where did the Ferris wheel go? The roller coaster? They were here a minute ago. How could they have just disappeared? Her throat is tight with fear. Her fingers and toes so numb she can hardly move. But then she spots it. There! They must be in that sweet little house. Oh, they're playing tricks on her. A game of hide-and-go-seek. Those kids. They've always loved to play tricks on her. To see if they can fool her, make her jump.

She picks up her pace, nearly tripping. *Come and get me!* Now she's almost there. She had been so silly to worry. They're all crowded inside that little house with the crooked sign on the front. She's sure of it. WELCOME. The word comes to her, even though it's been a while since letters have arranged themselves in a way that makes sense. WELCOME. She hunches down and pushes the door open. The wind bangs it shut behind her.

In the dim gray shadows, she can barely see anything at all. The walls creak and quake in the wind. She's on a boat. She's crossing a lake in—where are they again? New Hampshire? Maine? It doesn't matter. Somewhere in New England. She is on her way to collect her children, but the boat won't move fast enough, no matter how hard she paddles. The shoreline shifts. It keeps changing.

"Who are you?"

A child's voice. Hoarse, almost a whisper. Huddled in the corner—*thank god thank god thank god*—there he is. His dark hair falls over his face. His knees are pulled up to his chest. Her boy, her beautiful boy.

"Theo!"

She lunges toward him. He's only two steps away from her. He presses himself even farther into the corner, his lips trembling. He covers his face with his hands, looks at her through his fingers.

"Theo!" She looms over him, nearly losing her balance. "Where's Sarah? Why did you run off like that? Oh my God, Theo, I've been so worried. I've looked for you everywhere—"

"My name isn't Theo!" The boy starts to cry. "Go away! Get out of here!"

"We were on the beach—you were building a sandcastle and then—"

He jumps up and—still pressed against the wall—begins to inch himself toward the door. He never takes his eyes off her. He appears to be . . . what is it? She has no frame of reference for the look on her little boy's face. What is it? In all her years as a mother she has never seen anything like it, and she feels it in her heart. A cracking. A devastation. Her son is scared to death. The thought comes to her from far away. He's terrified of her.

"Go on! Get out of here! My parents . . . my parents are coming . . . they're right over there. I'm telling you."

"What are you saying? I'm your—"

"Leave me alone, lady!"

Her legs give way and she pitches forward. The side of her head hits the cold ground, but it doesn't hurt. Not at all. She is weeping, and it's coming from that same faraway place. Tears puddle into a small crevice in the concrete. What could she possibly have done to hurt Theo?

She looks up at him. Gathers what few words she has, pulling them from the depths.

"I'm sorry," she says. "Whatever I've done, I'm sorry."

He stops moving.

"Please."

In the thin slats of light piercing the shadowy darkness, she can see that he is shaking from head to toe.

"I would never hurt you. I promise."

His eyes dart around the little house, as if looking for any other possible mode of egress. Then, slowly, he extends a mittened hand and pulls her to her feet. She can't stop crying now. The sounds coming out of her are hardly human. What's wrong with her? It had been such a beautiful day on the beach, and now she's gone and ruined everything.

"Lady?" Theo has her by the shoulders. Why is he calling her that? "Lady, you're bleeding."

She touches the side of her face, and her hand comes away streaked with blood.

She wants to reassure him. A surface scratch. Ben will fix it later. He'll apply peroxide, antibiotic ointment. But the words won't come. Her mouth moves, but she can't talk anymore.

"You're not okay." He unwraps a scarf from around his neck. "Here, take this."

She stares at him. Her boy. She lets him wrap the scarf around her.

"And here." He digs into the pocket of his jacket and comes up with a knitted hat.

He holds it out to her. "Put this on."

She can't move.

"Lady, put on the hat. You're gonna die from the cold."

*Theo, where's your sister? Where's your father? Where has everybody gone?*

He wipes his nose with the back of his mitten. *Haven't I told you, always use a tissue?* He reaches out and gently fits the cap over her long gray hair, pulls it over her ears.

"Listen, lady, I can't give you my jacket because then I'll die from the cold too."

Her teeth are chattering.

He takes some kind of machine thing from inside his jacket, then pushes a button and the screen lights up like a television. His face is pale, aglow.

"Listen, it's four more hours until sunrise," he says. "When the sun comes up, everything will look different."

She tries to nod.

"That's what my mom says, anyway." He lets out a ragged sigh.

*But I'm your mom!*

"You'd better sit close to me," he says. "I learned in nature camp that with our body heat, we can keep each other warm."

He helps her into the corner where he had been sitting. She scoots over on the cold, hard ground until she is right next to him. One of her slippers falls off, her foot bare and blue.

"Wait," he says. He digs through his backpack and emerges with a pair of rolled-up socks. "Use these."

She stares at him. Mute, immobile. He stares back.

"Okay." He separates the socks. "Okay," he says again, "put them on." She bends forward, tugs on the right sock. Then the left. Her skin is a little wet, which makes it difficult, but still she does it. She stuffs her feet back in her slippers.

"That's better, isn't it?"

He sits back down next to her, their arms and legs touching. Their breath clouds mingle in the air.

She begins to cry again. *Where is Sarah? Where is Ben?* She swipes at her cheek, angry with herself.

"Do you like the stars?"

He speaks slowly, quietly, as if he himself were not a child.

"Yes," she manages. Anything to keep him close.

"I have something cool to show you."

He lights up that screen again, and she looks down in the darkness and sees the whole night sky. A bull. A snake. A crab. A child holding a harp.

"That's Taurus," he says, pointing. "And that star there is Alpha Persei, the brightest star in the constellation of Perseus."

He runs a finger along the screen and they are moving

back, back, back, away from the earth, away from this place, everything spinning.

"See? It can show us exactly where we are."

They are up in space, looking down at Earth. Strange music surrounds them. She sees oceans, continents. From here it all seems so simple. The spinning stops. She sees a tiny figure encircled in the center of a grid.

"That's us," he says. "That's where we are in the world. See? Don't you feel better?"

She looks at her boy. His soft, downy cheek, pale blue in the glow of the machine. To think she almost lost him. Her breathing slows down. The music becomes a wordless lullaby.

She has never been so happy.

# December 31, 1999

# *Shenkman*

NEW YEAR'S EVE, his least favorite of all holidays. Amateurs' night out. People getting hammered, all that sloppy hugging and kissing. And for what? As a kid, when all the other neighborhood kids tried to stay up past midnight to watch Dick Clark's countdown and the ball descend over Times Square, Shenkman would try like hell to fall asleep. That moment when the clock struck midnight— the ending of one year becoming, in an instant, the beginning of a new one—that moment was intolerable. Who wanted to be awake for a whole lot of nothing? Tick, tock.

This year, though. This year the drumroll has been loud and ceaseless. Y2K compliance and readiness—or, at least, the perception of compliance and readiness—has been the firm's focus. It's a public relations problem, that's what it is. Clients are panicked. Attorneys are mobilized, ready to take on class-action suits in the event that, at the stroke of midnight, the rollover causes havoc. Which it won't. The event horizon has been dealt with. The IT guys have been on it for years. Data expansion, windowing, date repartitioning—the rollover problem has effectively been put off until the end of 2900, which maybe he should care about, but he doesn't. Still, newscasters won't shut up. They fill the airwaves with endless chatter. Every Silicon Valley bigwig has become a talking head. It amazes Shenkman, the inanities that pass for insight. Morons have lined up to buy gold, canned goods, firearms. They're stocking up on batteries, radios, water, just in case time gets turned back to 1900, the electrical grid fails, the markets crash, and rioters take to the streets.

And for another thing—here he realizes his priorities are perhaps in the wrong order—Alice is having a baby. He means, *they're* having a baby. *He's* having a baby. A boy. He's seen evidence of this on the endless stream of sonograms they have endured since the day the pregnancy test showed two parallel bright red lines—like railroad tracks into the unknown—but still, he doesn't quite believe it. The three hundred bones that make up a baby, the head, the toes, the penis and scrotum (hence, a boy), the ripples along Alice's belly like ocean swells. He carries the most recent printout in the billfold of his wallet, and more than once he has pulled out the flimsy gray-white paper and examined it as if for clues. Who is baby boy Shenkman? And what does he, Shenkman, know about being a father? He knows nothing. Precisely zero. All he knows is what not to be, how not to behave.

*Everything's okay,* he reminds himself. *You can do this.* Mentally he pulls back on his oars. He glides through the depths, a team player. *You can do this.* He tells the other voice in his head—the one that sounds suspiciously like his own father telling him he's a piece of shit—to shut up.

"Honey?"

Alice is calling him. But he takes another minute, standing at the kitchen window of their new house, gazing across Division Street. Thirty-one years old, and for sure he had no business buying this house. Well, that's not entirely true. Sure, they're mortgaged up the wazoo, he and Alice. But they've pored over spreadsheets, assessed the risks. There's every reason in the world to bank on a steady climb—their combined salaries and bonuses, the health of the real estate market—into a promising future. Still, he can't help it. That voice is in his head again. *Who the hell do you think you are? You're nobody. That's who.*

"Honey?"

Five more weeks. That's all the time they have left to be just the two of them. Before the arrival of baby boy Shenkman. They haven't settled on a name yet. The biblical ones are still on the table. Isaac, Aaron, Moses. *Moses Shenkman.* His son will be a boxer. The first great Jewish boxer of the twenty-first century. *Isaac Shenkman.* His son will be a Harvard-educated neuroscientist. *Aaron Shenkman.* His son will be an actor, one of those handsome-in-a-Semitic-way funny guys, like Adam Sandler or Ben Stiller.

Dusk is falling over Division Street. Across the way, the older couple who live in the pretty clapboard house pull into their driveway. They emerge from their car, each carrying a Stew Leonard's shopping bag. They're both wearing navy-blue down jackets. The husband holds the wife's elbow, guiding her over an icy patch on their front walk. They don't look too worried about Y2K. They're an attractive couple, spry and distinguished-looking. Like Shenkman and Alice in thirty-odd years, if they're lucky. He wonders if they're entertaining tonight. They must have grown kids. Maybe grandkids, even.

He checks the fridge to be sure the champagne is chilling properly. He's beaten back his Grinch-like holiday phobia just this once and has sprung for the good stuff: Cristal and a small tin of beluga. He's not sure if Alice is allowed to eat caviar or if it's on the verboten list, along with sushi, cured meats, unpasteurized cheese. But he figures a celebration is in order. They will raise a glass to each other, to the new millennium, to the unborn Isaac/Aaron/Moses, to the beginning of their family life in this family home, in this suburb that they chose because of its good school system and easy commute to the city.

They have been careful.

They have done their homework. All will be well.

"I've been calling you." Alice appears in the doorway. She's gripping the frame, and her face is paper white. "My—"

She doubles over her huge belly.

"My water broke," she manages to say.

Only then does he see the dark stain soaking through her pregnancy leggings, dripping onto the floor. His mind races with what to do. What to do? He knows how to analyse the risks in a vertical merger, identify suitable targets, restructure equity, but his pregnant wife—Alice!—is crouching down now, squatting, a vein bulging in her forehead, she is screaming something, at least it sounds like screaming, though it seems to be coming from a great distance, and he is glued to the spot. Holding a tin of beluga in his hand. *Do something!*

His feet move, his hands move, his fingers dial the three emergency digits, he fumbles for the obstetrician's service number, conveniently located in the kitchen drawer, but his hands are shaking and he comes up with a menu for Empire Szechuan and a slip from the dry cleaner instead.

Alice is still squatting, doing the patterned breathing exercises they learned in Lamaze.

"Hee, hee, hoo!"

Two quick exhalations, and then she blows the breath through her mouth.

"Hee, hee, hoo!"

But she's not supposed to do that kind of breathing until she's in full-on labor.

What's she doing? He sits down on the floor. The ambulance is on the way. She stumbles forward, and he catches her by the shoulders.

"Look at me, Alice!"

Her eyes are wild. She's off somewhere and he can't reach her. Her face contorts with pain.

"The baby's coming," she says between breaths.

"That's impossible," he says, trying to soothe her. But what does he know? Her water has broken. They've lived in this house for two weeks. He doesn't know the neighborhood. Where the hell is the hospital? He should know how to get to the hospital. They've been there only once, for a tour of the new maternity wing.

"Fuck you!" she screams. "Fuck you, Shenkman—I hate your fucking guts!"

He's heard this sort of thing happens. Women go crazy. They call their husbands names that they don't mean. He tries to stroke her head, her hair plastered down with sweat. She jerks away from him. *Do something.*

He races into the front hall, then flings the door open and runs down to the sidewalk, scanning the street in both directions. Where's the ambulance? He's never in his life called 911. How long should it take?

Inside the house, Alice lets out another scream.

He turns to rush back in, but stops when he hears something. A voice is calling from across the street.

"Excuse me?"

It's the older man in the blue down jacket. He's standing on his front porch, shading his eyes in the encroaching dusk as if trying to make out something on the horizon.

"Is everything all right?"

"My wife—" Shenkman stammers.

The man waits for him to finish. His graying hair shines in the light cast by the sconces on either side of the front door. Just the other day, Shenkman and Alice had admired those sconces and considered knocking on the door to ask the couple where they had bought them.

"My wife is in labor," Shenkman says. "Her water broke, five weeks early, and—"

He hasn't even finished the sentence before the man has come bounding down his front walk faster than Shenkman would have thought possible, and is now next to him. Leading him back into his own house.

"I'm a doctor," he says. "Let's go. Where is she?"

"In the kitchen—make a left over—"

"I know the way."

Alice is now on all fours, her belly swaying low. "Hee, hee, hoo!"

The man bends over her. She looks questioningly at Shenkman over her shoulder.

"Alice, this is our neighbor—he's a doctor," Shenkman says. As if he can possibly take credit for conjuring a doctor out of thin air.

"Ben Wilf," the man says tersely. "When did your water break?"

"Half an hour ago," Alice pants.

"How many weeks are you?"

"Thirty-four and a half. I want my doctor!" Her face is red, her dark bangs stuck to her forehead. "Where's my doctor?"

"How far apart are your contractions, Alice?"

"I don't know. Three minutes—maybe less?"

"What number baby is this?"

"First. First baby."

"Towels." Wilf turns to Shenkman. "Lots of them."

*Jesus. Jesus Christ.*

Shenkman barrels upstairs, opens two doors before he finds the linen closet.

Grabs an armload of towels. He and Alice just picked them out together at Waterworks last week. A plush, mossy green that now seems to mock him. Fancy towels, a Poggenpohl kitchen, the brass bed they had shipped from an antiques store in North Carolina—who did they think they were, that they would get to live such a life?

*Please,* he finds himself praying into thin air. *Please, please, please.*

Alice has removed her pregnancy leggings and panties. She's back in a squatting position.

"Cover as much of the floor as possible," Wilf directs.

Shenkman gets on his hands and knees, spreads the towels in two thick layers beneath his wife like a mossy green island in the middle of the kitchen floor.

Alice moans, a low, deep animal sound. Wilf checks his watch.

"But we can't have the baby here," Shenkman says. He realizes how ridiculous this sounds, but there's a part of him—a not insignificant part—that believes saying it will make it so. This isn't the way it's supposed to be. In his mental picture of this auspicious moment, they are in the hospital's state-of-the-art birthing suite. Alice is soaking in the jacuzzi. The lights are low. A CD is playing the sound of steady, rhythmic ocean waves, the call of birds. The doula has been called. The mohel has been notified. Everything has been checked off the list.

"I'm sure we'll get to the hospital before—"

This inspires another *fuck you* from Alice. God, he wishes she would stop saying that.

"Do you have gloves?" Wilf asks. Shenkman shakes his head. Never has he felt so useless. He's the go-to guy. The contingency man. The one who has always—ever since he was a kid—been prepared for any situation.

"Go across the street and ask my wife for my medical bag," Wilf says.

Shenkman just stands there like the fucking idiot he's always known, deep down, he really is.

"Go on!"

Alice moans again.

Wilf checks his watch again. "Two minutes apart," he says.

He stands and strides over to the sink. Runs the water until it's steaming hot and washes his hands with antibacterial soap. Wilf commands the kitchen as if it were an operating room, pulling a white china bowl from the cupboard and filling it with hot water.

He brings the bowl and the soap over to Alice.

"We're going to sterilize the area," he says. His voice soothing and calm. He turns to Shenkman and gives him a look. *What are you waiting for?* Shenkman snaps out of his stupor. Bolts out of the house, looking again for the ambulance, which is nowhere in sight. Not even a siren in the distance. *One, two. One, two.* The slap of his blades against the lake. The deep, powerful slice down into the depths. He knows what it is to push himself as hard as he can. *You can do this.*

He sprints across the street and up the front walk of 18 Division, then knocks on the door.

"Coming!" He hears a woman's musical voice from inside. The latch clicks open, and the elegant, rangy older woman he had watched getting out of the Volvo wagon is framed by the doorway, wearing a chef's apron. She's beautiful, with startling green eyes and a generous mouth. Her hair is long and wavy, threaded through with silver like her husband's. Shenkman guesses she's in her early sixties.

"My wife is in labor," he says. Breathless. He wants to be very clear. The woman's eyes are so kind he feels like he might cry. "An emergency. Dr. Wilf—"

A hand flies up to her mouth. "Oh!"

"He asked me to get his doctor's bag."

"You mean she's—but did you call—"

"It's happening fast."

Something crosses her face, an expression so fleeting that Shenkman hardly notices it. Only later will he consider what it might have meant: concern, pride, a fierce protectiveness.

"Come in." She ushers him into the front hall. "Please wait here—I'll be right back."

She rushes upstairs. Shenkman hears floorboards creaking above his head. His palms are damp. His eyes feel pinned open, as if he's forgotten how to blink. The house is so quiet, except for the footsteps of Mrs. Wilf, that he can hear the *tick, tick, tick* of the antique hall clock—probably an heirloom passed down from grandparents, maybe even great-grandparents.

He watches the second hand as it makes its jerky,

mechanical progress. In the warm glow of the Wilfs' foyer, he sees a series of family photos lining the staircase. A boy and a girl, both with the dark wavy hair of their mother. Will he and Alice ever have pictures like this? Or is he standing in the center of the exact moment when it all turns to shit? He shakes away the thought, as if the thought itself might have the power to bring them harm.

Mrs. Wilf comes quickly down the stairs, carrying a sturdy black bag.

"Here it is," she says. She seems to hesitate for a moment before handing it over, and Shenkman wonders if there's something else he's supposed to say or do. But then she thrusts it at him. "You'd better hurry."

As he runs back across Division Street, he hears a siren. It sounds too far away. It might not even be for them.

In the kitchen, Dr. Wilf is crouched down over Alice. She steadies herself on the towels with one hand flat against the wall.

"Okay, Alice." Wilf still has that calm, measured tone. "Push on the count of three. One, two . . ."

Alice grimaces, bearing down. Her face is a color Shenkman hadn't known was possible.

"Good. Now some quick breaths."

Tears roll down her cheeks.

"This is . . . too hard . . ."

Shenkman goes to hold her hand, and again she swats him away. It is as if he were on the other side of a plexiglass partition, an audience of one, watching a performance unfold. His wife and the doctor are in their own world. A world in which there is no room for him.

"Breathe. Don't push again until the next contraction."

She is staring into Wilf's eyes as if he were her savior.

He checks his watch again.

Another contraction overtakes her, and she lets out a wail.

"Now? Okay, *go*. Give it all you've got, Alice."

She's lying on her back now, knees apart. Shenkman folds more towels so she'll have extra padding against the cold kitchen floor. She grips the necklace Shenkman gave her for Hanukkah—a gold chain with a blank charm, waiting to be engraved with their baby's name. Wilf reaches down. His jacket is tossed to the side; his shirtsleeves are rolled up to his elbows. Who the hell is this Wilf, anyway? Fate has put them in his hands. After the research, the diligent parsing of *New York* magazine's best doctors issue, the pulling of strings to get on ridiculous wait lists, they have ended up with their next-door neighbor. All he knows about the man is that he wears an L.L.Bean down jacket and shops at Stew Leonard's.

"Great job," Wilf says. As unruffled as an airline pilot during turbulence.

*We're experiencing some light chop, folks.*

"Blow out through your mouth."

Shenkman watches his wife trying to breathe. *Please be okay.* He understands with vicious clarity why people strike bargains with God. If Alice and the baby pull through this, he will . . . what. He will work harder, do better, be kinder. He'll be the best damned father in the whole world. He thinks he hears a siren growing closer, but he doesn't trust his own ears.

"I love you, Al," he says. Hoping she won't start cursing at him again.

"The baby's crowning," Wilf says calmly. "Push again, Alice. You've got this."

His expression shifts.

"Keep pushing," he says. Suddenly very still and watchful.

"What's wrong?"

"Nothing," Wilf says, but it doesn't look like nothing. "Okay, Alice—I need you to give a half push, let's get the head out—"

Footsteps pound up the front steps. The squawk of a two-way radio.

"Steady—" Wilf mutters.

Alice screams.

The front door—Shenkman had left it wide open—slams and three EMTs burst into the kitchen, but Wilf doesn't even seem to register them.

"That's it—"

"Make room, sir."

Wilf's hands are blocked from view by Alice's thighs.

"Come on, Alice—keep pushing."

Shenkman moves so that he can see. He hovers over Alice, looking down. She's so small and fine-boned, and her belly is enormous. The whole thing seems completely impossible.

There's his baby's head. The head!

Wilf cups the back of the skull, which fits into the palm of his hand. A pulsing, dark red thing—oh, God, the umbilical cord—is wrapped around its neck. Wilf slips two fingers between the cord and the neck. The baby's neck.

"Sir, please make room!"

Shenkman holds out a hand, palm flat. *Stop.*

"He's a doctor," he says quietly.

The squawk of the radio again.

Alice has gone white.

In one fluid motion, Wilf lifts the cord up and around the head, which then turns to the side as if escaping a noose. Another push and out comes the infant—the shoulders, the surprisingly robust chest, the skinny little legs—in a flood of reddish water.

Only then does Ben Wilf let out a long, slow breath. His eyes meet Shenkman's. "There," he says. "The little guy just needed an assist."

The EMTs have fallen silent. Three men in rubber boots standing in a row.

Alice—Alice is weeping.

Wilf places the infant right on Alice's chest.

"Here's your baby boy, Alice."

Everything has gone blurry, and it takes a second for Shenkman to realize that he has begun to cry. He sits on the floor next to Alice, wipes the sweat off her brow. Then he reaches out—he's afraid to touch—and strokes the tiny hand. He counts five fingers. Then five on the other hand. And ten toes. And tiny blond eyebrows. A penis that—he notices with pride—is pretty big, proportionally speaking. It's all there—his son—all three hundred bones having grown and somehow attached to each other in the right places.

Ben Wilf stands up, allowing the EMTs to finish up the job. As they tie the umbilical cord, he goes to the sink and scrubs his hands, which are covered in blood. He watches, drying himself with a dish towel. Then he unrolls his sleeves and picks his down jacket up off the floor.

"I don't know what we would have done without you," Shenkman says.

Wilf shifts from leg to leg. Uncomfortable with the potential for a display of emotion, Shenkman recognizes—since he is much the same way himself. *Don't worry,* he wants to say. *I'm not going to hug you.*

"It was the neighborly thing to do," Wilf responds.

"Seriously, I—"

"Happy New Year," Wilf says. He pauses. "Have you decided on a name?"

Shenkman and Alice look at each other. Suddenly Isaac/Aaron/Moses doesn't look like an Isaac/Aaron/Moses. The circumstances of his birth have made him unusual. An unusual boy who needs an unusual name. A boy—he swallows hard, remembering the bargain he made, a bargain he intends to make good on—a boy who deserves the best of him, from this day forward.

"Waldo," Shenkman blurts out of nowhere.

Alice smiles at him, delighted. The baby is already at her breast. "That's it," she says. "Waldo Shenkman."

# Sarah

S HE STILL ISN'T used to LA, three years in. After majoring in film and English at Wesleyan, she had debated about graduate school but instead got a job working as an assistant for a film production company in New York. She stayed within a ninety-minute radius of Avalon—close enough to go home for the occasional weekend, though she almost never did. Each evening during those happy-ish early years, she lugged a tote bag full of scripts back to her apartment. She lived in a three-bedroom walk-up near Columbia with two roommates, and the production company's offices were on lower Broadway, so often she started her evening's reading on the 1 train. Sarah thinks about that time often. Her early twenties. It all now seems so long ago. She hadn't met Peter yet. Hadn't had the girls. Hadn't begun her quick ascent to a job she hadn't even known she wanted.

Now, it's the strangest New Year's Eve ever, and she and Peter are throwing a party. When they first moved to the craftsman bungalow in West Hollywood, one of her new friends told her that everything social in LA happens in back-yards. She didn't understand what this meant, but she came to realize that—unlike in New York, where friendships and relationships played out in public, in restaurants, bars, cafés, and on sidewalks—in Los Angeles people invited friends over. Even modest homes like theirs had backyards kitted out for entertaining. A pergola, heat lamps for chilly nights, a grill and pizza oven built into a stone wall encircling their terrace. They don't have a pool. Another thing a friend told her when they were contemplating their move west. *Don't buy the big house.* In other words: this is a fickle business; your fortunes may change.

She first met Peter on the page. His was one of the scripts she lugged uptown in her tote bag. His agent had submitted it as a sample. Rabbit Rabbit (that was the name of the company) was looking for a screenwriter to adapt a debut novel by a young Australian writer, and Sarah had been culling through dozens of scripts in search of a spark. This was something she had learned as she climbed into bed each night with stacks of pages and a glass of wine. At first, she read every word, aware of her responsibility. But it became clear that it was possible to skim simply in search of a spark. Sparks were rare. Peter's script was smart, irreverent, fresh. He had a unique voice—something they can't teach you in film school. She brought his script to her boss, who asked her to set a meeting.

Now, Sarah places a vase of lilacs on the long teak dining table beneath the pergola. They will be twelve for this Y2K dinner party, not including all the children. No one wants to leave their kids home—not this year, when rumors of wide-spread computer failure and mass hysteria have had people hoarding bottled water and canned goods and emptying their bank accounts, just in case. Every recent conversation has carried a whiff of macabre world-is-ending humor. In the weeks leading up to New Year's Eve, very little business has gotten done. It seems the whole world is in a state of suspended animation, waiting to see what happens when the clock strikes midnight on a new century.

She's hired a few local teenage girls to watch the kids so the adults can party like it's 1999, as their invitation suggests they do. As she lays out the pale blue cloth napkins, the dove-gray stoneware plates, she hears Peter through the open patio doors, shopping bags rustling. One of the teenagers is in the sunroom with Syd and Livvie, newspapers spread across the wood floors, making Play-Doh out of flour, salt, cream of tartar, vegetable oil, and food coloring. It's a cozy domestic scene, the pretty table, the husband back from the market, the twins, their fingers stained pink and blue—she observes it from a few angles: a wide shot, a slow pan. It is she herself, Sarah Wilf, who is missing. She's *here,* sure. But some essential part of her is not fully present. This has been true of her for so long that she hardly even notices, anymore. And certainly no one else would notice. She looks the part, she knows that. She has always looked the part. She is tiny, delicate, very pretty; she thinks this with zero vanity, it's just a fact. She inherited her mother's striking coloring: eyes that change with the light, sometimes green, sometimes amber; a long tangle of dark curls. A heart-shaped face. An innate composure. It all adds up—the degree from the right school, the string of jobs each more excellent than the last. No one would know that she is only, ever, a few steps away from the abyss.

Peter joins her on the terrace, arms full of chopped wood for the chiminea.

"You should have seen the lines at Trader Joe's," he says. "It's like erev Armageddon."

Sarah watches her husband as he builds a small pyramid of logs in the chiminea. He's taken to life in LA, even though she's had the greater success since their move. He's grown his hair longer and wears baggy khaki shorts, faded tee shirts, Birkenstocks—the latter without irony. Most mornings, after he drops the girls at preschool, he drives to a café where he sits for hours, hunched over his laptop like every other customer. Sarah remembers a screenwriter they know—a guy who'd gotten credit on one big hit he hadn't even written— telling them that he often sits on his deck in Malibu, watching the flights arriving and departing LAX. *Screenwriter coming in,* he'll think as a plane lands. *Screenwriter going out* as a jet takes off, making a wide half circle over the ocean, then heads east.

Peter has also adopted the laid-back manner of an Angeleno. Sarah's pretty sure it's bullshit, the whole nonchalant affect. LA is a town fueled by ambition, and at the center of that ambition is the industry; that's how it's known, the industry. Everyone else—real estate brokers, hairdressers, dentists, accountants, dermatologists, personal trainers, restaurant owners, house cleaners, gardeners, even cops and firefighters—circles around the industry like satellites orbiting the earth.

"What time are they coming?"

"Eight. I didn't want to get started too early or we'll be drunk and asleep before midnight," she says. She's gathered a pile of sleeping bags and blankets in the sunroom for the kids. Her parents used to do that on New Year's Eve. They'd had a long-standing dinner party for neighbors and nearby friends, and all the kids would come in their long johns. Sarah and Theo used to love that night, the children outnumbering the grown-ups, the sense that their house was where everybody wanted to be. When did they stop the tradition? Never mind. She knows exactly when they stopped the tradition.

She doesn't really like the chiminea—it looks like a fancy terracotta crematorium—but it came with the house and tonight it will be festive, or so she hopes. The families coming are all new friends, the kind you make when your kids are little. Syd and Livvie go to preschool with a few of them, and then there's the synagogue. She wonders how long they'll stay in this house, in this neighborhood. Unlike her parents, who moved into 18 Division when they started their family and have no intention of ever leaving, it seems most people Sarah knows move every few years, acquiring bigger houses, better zip codes.

"I'm going to work for a couple of hours," Peter says. "That cool?"

She bites her tongue. Of course it's cool. It has to be cool. She'd rather mix them cocktails—margaritas, maybe?—and relax with him before their guests come, but she doesn't want to get in the way of his work. She is exquisitely sensitive to her husband's ego. It wasn't supposed to be this way. Peter was supposed to be the brilliant and brilliantly successful screenwriter. Hadn't she discovered him? And Sarah would have the solid but less glamorous career, behind the scenes, as a D-girl—they still called the young women in film development D-girls—writing script coverage, eventually working her way up the ladder to something like associate producer.

Instead, a film she produced two years ago—one that began as a script she had found in the slush pile and became a passion project her bosses let her run with—was nominated for that rarest of honors, Best Picture. It was made for under $5 million and cleaned up at the box office. Which made her, Sarah Wilf, a hot commodity herself. Studios came courting, and fancier production companies offered her a shingle. She splurged on a strapless black Dior gown for the Oscars, and Peter bought his first tux. His adaptation of an Ishiguro short story was in development, and it seemed to them both that they'd be back at the Dorothy Chandler Pavilion again soon. Many times. For each of them. *Don't buy the big house.*

Peter's adaptation went into turnaround, like everything else Peter has written, including that fantastic first script that was the start of their lives together. An unproduced screenplay is like a tree falling in a forest. No one sees it, no one reads it, except for the producers who occasionally continue to raise his hopes, then crush him. Peter is nearing forty. He looks younger. His daily surfing habit keeps him tanned and fit, his light brown hair now bleached a sandy blond by the sun. But Sarah worries. Hollywood is a quietly punishing culture. Lately, Peter's manager hasn't been returning his calls. *I don't have him,* says his chirpy assistant, who is invariably named Jennifer. Meetings have been pushed off indefinitely. And when he does have a meeting, afterward he hears nothing. The industry's version of a pass is simply silence.

For the time being, Sarah is making more than enough to support them all. They can send the girls to the best preschool that feeds into the best elementary school. They can join the gym and Wilshire Boulevard Temple. They drive two nice-enough cars, employ a host of babysitters. Just last month, they endured a weekend at Disney with Syd and Liv. But she is worried about Peter, in the long term. He's more gifted than many produced screenwriters—but he just can't seem to catch a break. There's luck involved. Luck, and also, she has to admit, a certain kind of temperament. The writers who make it tend to be a type: kinetic, fast-talking bundles of energy who keep their ears to the ground and know all the players. Networkers. How she despises that word.

She fixes herself a margarita and puts her bare feet up on the wall. She's breaking one of her rules—never drink alone—but tonight, she needs to take the edge off her loneliness before the guests arrive. Maybe she'll even break another of her rules: only one cocktail, then stick to wine. She has a lot of rules, mostly revolving around drugs and alcohol. She never drinks on Sundays. She sticks with white wine and stops at three glasses, max. She doesn't do coke, though some of their friends do. Peter smokes pot, but she's not into it. She doles out her drinks like they're medicine, which in a way is what they are. She numbs her feelings, because they are bigger than she is. And not just the painful feelings—the joyful ones too. She is filled with love for her daughters, with gratitude for her work, for the life she and Peter have built. All of it swells like a wave, threatening to overtake her: happiness, pride, terror, insecurity, and the terrible, terrible loneliness that goes away, however briefly, only after a couple of drinks.

But she doesn't want to be thinking about this. She wants to enjoy the slight, pleasant buzz and think about the evening ahead. She hears the doorbell ring and for a second panics that she told people the wrong time? But no. It's probably a delivery. Peter will get it. She takes a long sip.

One of the babysitters peeks her head out. "Hey, Sarah? Someone's here to see you. I wasn't sure if I should open the door."

Pushing aside her quick, sharp annoyance with Peter (did he not hear the doorbell?), she looks through the glass panes that frame the front door and sees the back of a man's head. Thick, dark, unruly hair. She looks more closely. A gray tee shirt hanging from beneath an army jacket, dirty jeans. She has one hand close to the alarm system's panic button as she turns the knob and opens the door just a crack. You never know.

"Can I help you?"

He turns around. Tanned, thirty pounds thinner, eyes behind mirrored shades. Her life—her history, the whole of her childhood—standing there, shifting from foot to foot. At once alien and utterly familiar. Smiling, uncertainly. As if he may have rung the wrong doorbell.

"Hey, Sis."

"Theo."

She says his name softly. Like maybe she'll need to take it back. It has been five years since she's laid eyes on her brother. While she was living uptown and writing coverage on slush-pile scripts for an annual salary that barely covered rent and ramen—often having to call her parents to ask for a hundred bucks here or there to tide her over—Theo had dropped out of Bard and was living back home. Twenty-two years old and spending his days hiding in his childhood bedroom, the door affixed with a plastic sign from grade school: Theo's Room.

Her parents tried not to burden her with their worries, but she could hear it in their voices. Whenever they spoke by phone, her mother was chipper and full of news and neighborhood gossip, as if her grown son were not regressed, increasingly hermetic, and upstairs playing video games. It was Ben who was more straightforward with Sarah. *This may be serious,* he finally said one evening. There was something hesitant in his cadence, something unsaid between them, but still, what he did say was frightening. Sarah had looked up Theo's symptoms—Google was brand-new, but she was learning how much information was now at her fingertips—and as best she could tell, Theo was either suffering from incipient schizophrenia (he was the right age for it) or just going through a rough patch. She'd also read up on neuroplasticity. Theo had always lagged behind, in terms of his emotional agility, from the time he was a little kid trailing her on the way home. And also, he was a guy. Guys were slower to mature, generally speaking. So none of this was definitive or very helpful.

It wasn't until she persuaded Theo to meet her in the city for dinner that she saw for herself just what kind of shape he was in. His handsome face was distorted by bloat. His forehead shone with sweat. Was he wearing pajamas? Maybe not, but they might as well have been. Wide, loose flannel pants stuffed into snow boots, and a gray hoodie on top. She took him to a cheap Italian restaurant near her apartment where they sat across from each other in the candlelit dark, two people who had started with the same parents, in the same place, the same home, the same town, but now were living vastly different lives.

Sarah ordered one glass of wine, then two, then three. Theo ate his linguini and then polished off her barely touched chicken parmesan. The ghost of Misty Zimmerman was at the table with them, as surely as if she had pulled up a chair. Misty would have stood near Theo at their high school graduation—their surnames both at the end of the alphabet. Misty would have gone to one of those good small New England schools: Bowdoin, Amherst, Middlebury. She was gifted at languages. She had been in AP Spanish as a sophomore. Who would she have become? Expressionless, she turned her lovely head back and forth, watching the two people responsible for her death.

Sarah and Theo had never talked about it, not once since

that August night less than a decade earlier. Now, Sarah sometimes wonders whether talking would have been better. Silence didn't make it go away but instead drove the events of that night more deeply into each of them. Neither of them had ever been able to unsee what they saw, unhear what they heard. The scream of a girl about to die enters the world's playbook on repeat. There is no running from it.

"Theo?" Sarah took another sip of wine. "What are you going to do?"

"I don't know."

"You can't just keep going like this."

"Why not?"

Her brother looked everywhere but directly at her. Searching for modes of escape.

"For one, you're killing yourself. You're killing Mom and Dad."

He flinched a bit at that.

"For another, it's just such a fucking waste."

"A waste of what, Sarah?"

She faltered here. She wanted to say *potential,* but was this even true anymore?

"Look, Theo—if you're hurting because—"

Now he looked straight at her.

"What?"

He didn't seem capable of speaking in complete sentences. Just a few bleated words strung together. She couldn't. She just couldn't go there. If she started talking about that long-ago night, the torrent of words might set loose everything she had so meticulously packed away.

"Nothing," she said softly.

And then later that week, when Mimi called her weeping—*Theo's gone*—Sarah once again had the sense that she had utterly failed her brother. *What do you mean, gone?* Her heart thudded. *He left a note.* Sarah felt a pain in her stomach so sharp she nearly fainted. *Not exactly a note,* her mother went on. *A clue. A copy of Bruce Chatwin's* In Patagonia.

Now, Sarah becomes aware of Syd and Liv, clinging to her legs, peering around her as if she were a tree trunk they were hiding behind.

"Girls, this is your uncle." Something catches in her throat. "Mommy's brother. Your uncle Theo. Theo, these—"

Her voice catches seeing Theo with Syd and Liv. She moves forward as if to hug him but instead punches him in the shoulder as if they were five and seven years old again. She has been here, building her life, such as it is. She's been busy having her babies, making a home, trying to figure out how to be a grown-up. But a piece of her has been missing. Now, she is standing in the house of Theo. The city of Theo. The country of Theo.

"This is Syd and Liv," she finishes.

He slips off his backpack, resting it against the front steps. Then he crouches down so he's on eye level with the girls.

"Hey," he says. "You guys are twins, aren't you!"

Syd nods. Liv is sucking her thumb, a habit she had given up.

He laughs—a rich, deep peal of a laugh that she would know anywhere. He looks so good. So . . . changed, as if he's shed that lost-boy carapace and emerged whole. Complete. He's become a man, Sarah realizes. Five years. Five years interrupted only by the occasional cryptic postcard from Patagonia and, later, from Buenos Aires. *I saw the remains of the giant sloth.* Or, *Working in a tearoom.* Each time one arrived, she would study his childish scrawl. Was he telling her something? Sending her a code to crack? She'd call her parents and let them know that Theo had been in touch. Over the phone, she would hear the quick intake of her mother's breath. Her father's careful silence.

Theo picks up his backpack and follows her inside. Syd and Liv have rarely been so quiet. She hears Peter rustling around upstairs. It seems impossible that her husband and brother don't know each other. Theo vanished and then, within months, she met Peter—two of the most important men in her life passing each other as if through a revolving door, coming and going in a strange, cosmic symmetry.

Early in her relationship with Peter, Sarah had considered whether to tell him the whole story. She had never spoken of it with her parents, never told a friend or her therapist. Sometimes, one of her teenage babysitters would remind her of Misty Zimmerman—a flash of long hair, sleepy eyes, tanned legs, a braided rope bracelet—and she would feel pressure behind her eyes, as if Misty were always alive inside her head, clamoring to get out. But if she told Peter, what good would it do? It would become a thing. Something real. She'd have to contend with his questions. With his *knowledge*.

Peter rumbles in his bare feet down the stairs.

"Pete?"

Sarah, Theo, and the girls are still standing near the front door.

"Peter, this is my brother, Theo."

Peter's eyebrows shoot up. "Whoa, man. Wow! Hey!"

Theo sticks out a hand. He has a tattoo, Sarah sees, on the inside of his wrist. It looks like it might be a word. She tries not to stare.

"I hope it's okay if I crash here," Theo says. "I mean, if it isn't too much—"

"Of course!" Sarah and Peter say in unison.

"I can't believe I'm finally meeting you," Peter says. "The mysterious, elusive Theo."

"Not so mysterious," Theo responds. His eyes dart to the door. She remembers that look. He could leave again. He could leave and never come back.

Sarah shoots her husband a glare that he doesn't register. She wants to tell Peter that this isn't a drama, this isn't a plot point. It's her fucking *life*.

"We're having a party tonight." She rushes to fill in the awkwardness. God, now she wishes they weren't having a party.

"Am I invited?"

She tries to imagine Theo in conversation with any of their new friends. What in the world will they talk about? *Buenos Aires, how interesting! Sarah, did you visit?* Her head throbs. She needs another margarita.

"Come on." She grabs Theo's backpack and heads up the stairs. It reeks of all sorts of organic matter she doesn't want to think about too much. He'll need a shower. And clothes. He's a little bigger than Peter, but she can rustle something up for him. A linen shirt. A pair of khakis. Her mind turns to the practical. She's a producer. She'll produce this. If she sticks with the details, everything will be manageable.

She turns to him, five years' worth of questions swirling, still unformed. *Why did you go away? Why have you come back? Whatever you learned, can it possibly be worth the pain you caused?* She thinks of her mother and father, and the way Theo's disappearance has been a burden they've carried, lightly at first (surely he'd come home soon!), then weighing them down more and more with each passing year. Their most self-protective qualities—her father's silence, her mother's proud soldiering on—have loomed larger, a shadow cast over their younger, better selves: humor, irony, playfulness, delight have faded away.

She feels a familiar flash of anger—that kindled rage always ready to burst into flames—but just as quickly, it's doused. Theo, in her home. Improbable, all but impossible, as if a baby elephant had escaped from the Santa Barbara Zoo, trotted down PCH, made its way all the way up Sunset, and were now calmly grazing in her backyard.

Theo reaches out and touches her lightly on the arm. "You okay?" he asks.

"What do you mean?" Defensive. *What-do-you-mean-am-I-okay-of-course-I'm-okay-I'm-always-okay.*

He looks at her as if searching for something. Then his eyes slide away. "Never mind."

"No, what?"

He's wearing the dustiest, dirtiest pair of sandals she's ever seen, which causes a momentary distraction. This, she knows how to deal with. She makes a mental note to include toenail clippers in the pile of clean clothes. And shaving cream. A razor.

He touches her arm again, as if making sure she's real.

"What?" She persists. Some small, stubborn piece of her wants to hear what he thinks, even if it hurts. He gazes at her steadily, for the first time reminding her of their father. The corners of his mouth struggle into a small smile.

"Looks like a beautiful life, Sarah," he says.

# *Theo*

FIVE MINUTES BEFORE midnight. The turn of the year, the turn of the millennium. He's lying on a deck chair near the chiminea. The dinner guests have risen from the table, flushed, sated. Sarah outsourced most of the meal from a Turkish restaurant on Ventura, and it was pretty good overall. Her friends were nice enough, though they all spent way too much time talking about their kids. But what does he know? He doesn't have kids. He probably will never have kids.

He's feeling a little disoriented and tells himself this is normal. He's been back in the States for just three days. What did he think? That he'd be able to reinsert himself seamlessly into life as he once knew it? When he landed at LAX, he'd taken a taxi straight to Sarah's house. When it pulled up to the front, he told the driver to keep the meter running. Theo got out of the car and peered up at the craftsman bungalow nestled behind massive old trees. On the front porch, there were wicker chairs, a love seat with striped cushions, plants in huge ceramic pots. Two tricycles. He examined the scrap of paper to be sure he had the right place. Sarah lived here? The driver tapped his horn, and Theo climbed back into the taxi. He gave the driver another address, in East LA: a motel owned by a cousin of the chef at La Cabrera.

Life as he once knew it is gone. Poof. What was it his mother used to say? *Time stands still for no one.* Each morning for three mornings, he returned to West Hollywood and loitered outside Sarah's home. He can't imagine his sister's life. She has kids, for Christ's sake! His nieces followed him around tonight chanting *Uncle Theo! Uncle Theo!* until they finally fell asleep with the other children piled into the sunroom. Can he be Uncle Theo? He wonders if he has been gone so long that there's no coming back. When he thinks of his parents, his throat tightens. They too must be different. Older, for starters. He's queasy from the two whiskeys he drank in quick succession early in the evening. His system, he realizes, is in shock.

"Chocolate-covered strawberry?" One of the babysitters is passing a tray around, now that the kids are asleep. He takes a strawberry he has no intention of eating. Inspects it. Sniffs, and catches the slight but unmistakable scent of fertilizer just beneath the more overpowering dark chocolate. No one else would detect it. Among the chefs in Patagonia, he had earned the nickname La Nariz because of his unusual sensitivity to smell. Just from a whiff, he could tell the difference between lamb meat from Chubut Province and Tierra del Fuego. La Nariz. His nose preceded him. He must tell Sarah about the berries in Argentina—gooseberries, delicate white and red currants that grow in the wild during the winter months.

He has been surprising himself for days now. Surprised by

his own actions, the way one might be if watching a close friend do something totally out of character. He is at a slight remove from his own life, as if narrating it rather than living it. Here is Theo Wilf, announcing an extended leave—perhaps a permanent one—from La Cabrera. Here is Theo, in his one-room flat in Palermo Soho, packing up his shorts, a favorite apron, his notebook of recipes. Here he is, leaving an envelope of pesos for the landlord. Watch Theo as he goes to Ministro Pistarini to catch his flight, carrying little more than the backpack that he first arrived with five years earlier. When he bought his ticket, he debated: New York or Los Angeles? His parents or Sarah? The possibility of neither did not occur to him. It was the end of the twentieth century. He had been gone a long time. Long enough to become a different person— if it was ever possible to become a different person. Now he was ready to see his family.

Or at least, so he thought. Maybe he should have stayed a few more days in East LA, where the smells and sights and language were familiar. The chalupas roasting on street corners. The music blaring out of car windows. The staccato rhythm of rapid-fire Spanish. Now, Sarah is standing next to Peter on the far side of the pergola, beneath a hanging lantern that bathes them both in a luminous glow. Peter is clinking his glass with a spoon, a god-awful sound that fills Theo with shame. Sarah is wearing a loose black dress, and she has gone barefoot all night, gliding like a small, graceful queen among women encased in shiny fabric like well-wrapped gifts. She is lovelier than ever, but it is her sadness that lights her from within.

She is incandescent in her misery. He sees that—and he knows he is the only one who does.

*Clink, clink, clink.*

So this is Peter. He seems like a nice-enough guy.

*Clink, clink, clink.*

A hush falls over the party. The guests turn to Peter, ready to be entertained.

"We just want to say—"

He has his arm around Sarah, protectively. Or perhaps possessively. Theo's not sure which.

"—it's less than two minutes until we're officially in the year 2000, and assuming that we don't lose electricity and phone service and rioters don't take to the streets—"

A chuckle ripples through the crowd.

"—Sarah and I are grateful to share this auspicious moment with each and every one of you."

*Hear, hear!* A smattering of applause.

"To friends and family!" someone calls out.

Peter tips his glass in the direction of the impromptu toaster, and then at Theo. "Nothing's more important," he says.

Small clusters of people continue their conversations, but the atmosphere is alive with change. With the ticking of the clock. They are the generation that has been born in one millennium, and will die in another.

*One minute!*

Theo leans back in his deck chair and closes his eyes. He is walking the road along the Chubut River in the direction of the cordillera. The mountain peaks in the distance are covered with ice caps. He walks many hours each day, as many as his legs will allow. A stray dog circles, then runs off. A farmer stops his truck, offers a ride. If he keeps moving, keeps putting one foot in front of the other, he will be all right. Now—he cannot control the path his mind takes—he is in the kitchen of La Cabrera. Walking, cooking. It's all motion. A whirl of activity so that he can avoid . . . he doesn't know quite what he's avoiding. Thought. If he doesn't think, he can't get into trouble. He turns four steaks on the grill in quick succession. Crushes a clove of garlic into softened butter. Adds a dash of sea salt. Finely chopped basil.

"You doing all right?"

Theo startles. His eyes blink open. Sarah is sitting on the edge of the deck chair. A breeze blows a few strands of dark wavy hair across her cheek. The plains of Patagonia are more real to him than his own sister.

*Nineteen, eighteen, seventeen . . .*

"I don't get the point," he says.

"Of the countdown, you mean?"

"Yeah."

"Me either."

They sit quietly, the two of them, watching the guests.

"Champagne?"

A babysitter hands them each a flute. He touches his glass to Sarah's.

"It's depressing," she says. "At least I find it depressing."

*Twelve, eleven . . .*

Theo knows she wants to ask him why he's come back. The better question is, why did he leave in the first place? But they won't talk about it—not tonight. She tilts back her glass and downs it. Wipes her mouth with the back of her hand. Their eyes meet only fleetingly. In the space between them, there is a whole lost world: street names, phone numbers, summer barbecues, broken bones, family dinners, shadows on walls, stolen turns, dappled light playing against floorboards. French toast sizzling in an iron skillet. Pages of homework strewn across the dining room table. Beethoven quartets on Saturday afternoons. The smell of black cavendish tobacco.

*Seven, six, five . . .*

In his sister—her bare toes pointing toward each other, pigeon-like, her bitten nails, her small ears—he remembers everything he's tried to forget. He's not walking the road along the Chubut River now. He's not in a blur of motion in the center of a kitchen, preparing fourteen dishes at once. He sits still. What choice does he have? His father's tortoiseshell reading glasses resting on top of a half-finished paperback. The creak on the third stair. Icicles, in winter, that would hang like spears from the eaves above his bedroom window. The way his mother would answer the phone, the three musical notes of her hello.

"Will you stay for a while?" Sarah is asking him.

He doesn't know the answer, and he doesn't want to lie.

"I mean," she says, "I'd really like you to stay for a while."

She has softened, all the prickly edges he saw in her when he arrived have melted away, and what is left is a beautiful, vulnerable girl. In their backyard in Avalon, a hammock strung between two strong poplars. The two of them, deep in the ropes, limb over limb, inseparable.

*Two, one . . .*

*Happy New Year!*

A few renegade noisemakers screech. Time seems, for an instant, suspended.

Kisses, slaps on backs. The further popping of corks. He leans forward and gives his sister a hug. He fights past the lump in his throat, the sting in his eyes.

"I'd like that too," he says. But what he really means is that he'd like to take this suspended moment—the new millennium already careening inexorably forward—and roll it back instead. Back, back through layers of time to a split

112

second when things could have gone differently, if only they had known. There must be that second, bobbing and darting in the aliveness of their shared history, unmistakable, glowing like a firefly in the darkness. If only they could pinpoint it and stop it there, right there, at the small but indelible spot that somehow they missed the first time around, if only, then perhaps their whole family could begin again.

Oh, who is he kidding.

They both lean back on the deck chair, side by side, and gaze at the clear night sky.

"We'll see," he says.


In the morning, he rises before all the others. The house is quiet, spotless. He had heard them hours after the last guests left, cleaning the kitchen. You'd never know a party took place the night before. He opens the fridge. Last night's leftovers look sad and exposed in the bright light of the refrigerator. They'll sit here for a few days, untouched, and after the kitchen starts to smell vaguely of garlic and lamb, they will get tossed into the trash.

He pulls out the platters and lays them on the butcher-block countertop. Grabs a deep china mixing bowl from the cupboard. Well-used copper pans dangle from an iron rack. He reaches up for a large skillet and sets it on the stove. Theo lifts a full carton of eggs from the fridge's side door. He sniffs them. Fresh enough, and definitely organic. He whisks the eggs with one hand as he begins to dismantle the platters with the other. Decides against repurposing the kofta—he doesn't imagine his nieces have acquired the taste. There is smoked salmon, though, which he will sauté in a bit of butter. He examines last night's cheese platter. The blue is strong.

His nose tells him it's from back east—Vermont, maybe Maine. He takes a nice small piece of manchego and dices it into the whisked eggs. Ideally the cheese would be at room temperature, but once it slowly melts in the pan it will make little difference.

It seems they have only 2 percent milk, but it will do with a bit of cream mixed in. He's making it up as he goes along—his favorite way to cook. It has been years since he's followed a recipe, with the notable exception of desserts. Red and yellow peppers—good, local ones. An onion. A head of garlic. Sarah's knives need sharpening. Now, he searches the kitchen for ramekins. Individual quiches, he's decided. Not traditional quiche with that waste of a crust but a flourless quiche, light and elegant as a soufflé. The little girls will like it, he's sure. His nieces! Today he will learn how to be Uncle Theo. He'll get down on the floor and play with them. He'll make them necklaces out of pasta shells.

Music runs through his head as he sous-chefs for himself. In the kitchen at La Cabrera they played Los Fabulosos Cadillacs on the radio. The samba beat. The bluesy slide guitar. There was always a din emanating from the cavernous, brick-walled dining room. *Theo! La señora de la mesa numero diez quiere su carne a término medio!* Outside, people sipped champagne and waited on the sidewalk. The occasional impromptu tango.

The onion, peppers, garlic are in neat, camera-ready piles on the chopping block. Chives—he needs chives. And dill for the salmon. He noticed a small herb garden last night. He slices a pat of butter into the skillet and turns the flame on low. What time do they wake up in this house? It's just about seven thirty.

Outside, even through the thick walls of the bungalow, he

hears the caw of a crow. He wipes his hands on a dish towel. Then heads to the patio doors, the heavy, cool knob in his palm, and twists it open.

The sound—the metallic blast of a siren—is so jarringly loud that he jumps back, stunned. His teeth rattle. *Eee-ooo-eee-ooo.* Only a half second later does he realize that he has let out a scream. The siren just keeps blasting and blasting. *Eee-ooo-eee-ooo.* A voice, a man's voice: *The system has been breached.* Theo looks around wildly and only then sees the keypad by the patio doors. Of course. What an idiot. Of course, there's an alarm system, he now realizes as he vainly jabs his finger at every possible button, trying to stop the horrible noise.

"What happened?"

Peter and Sarah appear in their sweats. Sarah is rubbing her eyes.

*The system has been breached. The system has been breached.*

"I'm so sorry, I—"

"Shit," Peter says.

*The system has been—*

Peter strides across the kitchen, then presses a code into the keypad, silencing the siren.

"Now they're going to show up," he says.

"But—"

"No, when the alarm goes off, they don't call. They come. Either security or the cops. That's the way it works."

"Oh, man. I'm really sorry."

Syd and Livvie toddle in, looking shell-shocked. Livvie—or is it Syd?—is sucking her thumb.

"It's okay. Not the biggest deal in the world. What were you doing, anyway?" Sarah asks.

She walks over to the coffee maker, taking in last night's disassembled platters, the Saran Wrap balled up on the island, the chopped vegetables, the bowl of eggs. The grated cheese spilled on the counter.

"I was making breakfast," he says. He can't remember the last time he felt so useless. He shouldn't have come here. Shouldn't have gotten his hopes up. He despises his own childish optimism.

The doorbell rings within minutes.

"Everything's all right," Peter says to the security guy. "False alarm."

"We'll need your password, sir."

"Sarah? Sarah, do you remember the password?"

"Hold on, what's that smell?" Sarah asks.

It's then that Theo remembers the skillet. He rushes over to the stove and removes it from the flame, but it's too late. The butter is burned.

# Mimi

BEN IS SPENDING a long time in the shower. It's been at least forty minutes since he closed himself off in the bathroom, the water running. Forty minutes since he came home from across the street, pale, sweating, his shirt stained with rust-colored blood. His hands—those beautiful doctor's hands, strongly veined, with long, elegant fingers—trembling. She's gone upstairs once already, listened at the bathroom door to be sure he's okay. She waited to hear him moving around and, satisfied, she headed back downstairs to the kitchen.

It's a boy. Ben told her that much. A healthy boy, slightly premature, around six pounds by his estimation. The lungs seem fine, though he'll need to be checked out at the hospital. They're calling him Waldo. Yes, Waldo.

"So why are you shaking?" she asked him. "It's all okay then, isn't it?"

He hesitated.

"It almost wasn't."

A shiver ran through her.

"What do you mean? Is everything—"

"Yes," he cut her off. Unusually sharp. "I don't want to talk about it."

Home birth. She shudders. She knows that it's all the rage. Young women these days actually choose to deliver their babies at home with midwives. They fill their bathtubs with aromatic oils. Their music of choice plays on the stereo. They have birth plans. As if giving birth were something that can be planned. Thank God her Sarah didn't consider going that route, especially with twins. A doctor's daughter through and through, she availed herself of everything Cedars-Sinai had to offer when Syd and Liv were born.

She thinks of the young couple across the street. She hasn't met the wife, though she had seen her lumbering in and out of the house, her huge pregnant belly preceding her. The husband looked so panicked when he came to ask for Ben's medical bag—of course, he was panicked! But there was something more. A vulnerability, a softness in his face that made Mimi want to embrace him, to take his head onto her shoulder and pat down his hair. *There, there.* He must be around Theo's age. Thirtyish. But unlike Theo, he's married, a new father, and living in the house across the street. *Please, please, please.* The word fills her so often that she doesn't even notice it anymore. She sends it out the door, down Division Street, like a paper airplane, up the river, over the ocean, across the equator. If she puts her whole self into that single word, that concentrated thought, she has some notion—she knows it's magical thinking—that it will reach her son. That wherever he is, he will have the thought: *It's time to come home.*

The water upstairs stops. She hears the shower curtain

sliding open. The fan in the bathroom being turned off. It's dark out now—that deep, unremitting black of an early winter evening. She drifts around the downstairs, turning on lights. The outside porch light. The table lamps in the living room. The wrought-iron chandelier in the dining room with its sixteen candle-shaped bulbs—wasteful, but somehow festive. My goodness, it's hard to believe that the twentieth century is coming to an end. She feels it as a pang of loss. The years she had her babies, years in which she was a young mother, nursing, singing lullabies, walking them up and down the uneven sidewalks, holding hands, lifting them high on her shoulders. The years of preschool, grade school, middle school, high school. All so long gone now, and soon to be relegated to another century entirely.

What is left to her? She rarely lets herself think this way, but something about this day is making her melancholy. That young family across the street with their new baby is at the beginning of a life that they think will last forever. Time will move so slowly. The creeping predawn hours during which the mother will sit nursing in her rocker, half watching the flickering light of whatever muted television show happens to be playing. *Beyond exhausted,* she will tell her friends. Her husband's hulking form, sleeping under the heavy blanket. The fascination and boredom of early parenthood. The hours and hours sitting on little chairs outside of classrooms during school phase-ins. She will wish time away. Check her watch. Wonder why it all seems to be taking so long. Then suddenly— it will feel as if it has happened overnight—there will be no need for bedtime stories, lullabies. No hand-holding. She will lose sight of what's happening. It will speed up, like the pages of a calendar in one of those old-fashioned movies, flipping, flipping, one day, week, month into the next until, if she's not careful, she will no longer recognize her child, her husband, her life.

Her daughter will live in Los Angeles and work in an office where an assistant answers her phone. Her twin granddaughters will hardly know her.

Her son will get up one morning and board a flight to Buenos Aires.

"Mimi?"

Ben is calling her from upstairs. She had stopped in front of a photograph of the four of them, taken when the kids were in middle school and they had gone on a family vacation to an island. Sint Maarten, Barbados—she's not sure which one. For a number of years, when Ben's practice was thriving and the kids were still young, they flew south each March, to one resort or another where she and Ben would sip tropical drinks on their lounge chairs while Sarah and Theo played Kadima in the sand, growing browner with each passing day. Here, they are gathered together on a dock, the sun setting behind them.

Who snapped the photo? A guest at the resort, perhaps. Or a member of the staff. It would have been Mimi—chronicler of small memories—who asked: *Please, would you mind?* Handing off the camera. *It's autofocus. All you need to do is press the button, right there.* Ben has his arm around her. He's wearing a white tennis shirt—so this must have been before his sciatica started acting up, permanently sidelining his game—and his smile is open, unguarded. Sarah is going into her senior year, and Theo has three years left. She remembers the pride she took in her kids, who hadn't grown sullen and uncommunicative like most of their classmates.

Look at them! Happy, sunny children. She had a secret,

fierce, vain (she knows now) belief that this was due, at least in part, to the way she had raised them. She chaired the school auction, spearheaded a local food drive, started a neighborhood beautification committee, sewed costumes for the middle school production of *The Taming of the Shrew*— always with a rueful, self-deprecating stance that she both meant and didn't. *Oh, please. It's nothing.*

"Mimi?"

"Coming!"

She climbs upstairs.

Ben is sitting on the edge of the bed in their room, a towel wrapped around his waist. He's still such a handsome man, her husband. He's grown more distinguished-looking with each passing year. His mane of hair has grayed, his face settled into its contours and shadows. But now he appears startlingly frail. He's staring into a corner of the room. His hands, she notices, are clasped so tightly that his knuckles are white.

"Darling, what's the matter?"

He opens his mouth, but no sound comes out.

"Ben! You're frightening me."

She sits down next to him. The bedspread is damp from the wet towel. She puts a hand on his knee. He's fine. He has to be fine.

"It was a close call," he finally says.

*But it turned out all right*, she wants to say but doesn't. She understands perfectly well. One incident is an invisible trip wire that in turn sets off another and another. Time collapses. There is no straight line. Memory, history—things that happened fifteen years ago, or fifty—are as alive now as if they had just happened, or are about to happen. *Close call.*

There's no room in Ben's life for a close call.

"Maybe you shouldn't have—"

She hesitates. He's still looking away from her, as if he can't quite bear it.

She presses on.

"I mean, what if something had—"

He turns on her. "Don't say that! What the hell was I supposed to do? The woman was in precipitous labor!"

She should have kept her thoughts to herself. It's just that she feels protective of him. The question is left unasked and will remain unanswered. What would have happened if something had gone wrong?

"Sorry," she says quietly. "Benjamin, we're here now. That baby is safe." She strokes his knee. The skin rough beneath her hand.

He gives a small, almost imperceptible nod. She can practically see inside of him, the way the pieces are falling back into place, the sharp edges tucked away. Stories—a thousand *what ifs*—receding like the tide.

"Come. Let's go downstairs. I'm making us a nice dinner."

She has set the dining room table with the good china and silver. Two place settings across the expanse of scarred oak that has seated as many as sixteen at once. Thanksgiving, Passover, so many New Year's Eves. Wax drippings, scratches from years of pencil marks during homework. A burn mark from back when people smoked. A table that they bought when they first moved to Division Street. A family table.

Now, she readies the salad while Ben sits in the den, nursing a Scotch by the fire. He's playing his favorite Beethoven quartet—the C minor—on the stereo. The pulse of the house returns to its usual resting rate. She's tried to prepare a celebratory meal. Always, she wants to make things special. What else is there to do? Baby spinach, bacon, and blue cheese for the salad. A chicken recipe from *The Silver Palate Cookbook*. A bottle of California cabernet recommended by the man in the wine store.

She'd briefly considered and then dismissed the idea of inviting guests for dinner tonight. Who would they have? Almost everyone has left. A few random people from their past still live in Avalon, but they're couples she and Ben only socialized with back when the kids were little because it was the neighborly thing to do. Or because the kids were in the same soccer league, or religious school class. Not because they had anything in common other than having procreated at the same time and moved to this community. Most of their friends moved away from Avalon after their youngest went to college. As in a further rite of passage she hadn't prepared for or known was coming, FOR SALE signs started appearing on front lawns. One afternoon, on her way home from the market, she saw a broker in a tweed skirt and sensible heels marching a young couple up the front walk of the Platts'. The Russos followed and, in quick succession, the Hellers. New families moved in—a new generation. Pregnant mothers, athletic-looking fathers in baseball caps, toddlers in strollers. Squint and it could have been any of them, twenty, thirty years earlier. The houses on Division Street, the whole of their children's memories, turned over one by one.

Those who left decamped to the city, where they caught the new production of Wagner's *Ring* cycle, dined at the top-rated Vietnamese restaurant, attended lectures at the New York Public Library. *You'll love it*, they'd try to convince her and Ben. *We're out every single night. It's like a second honeymoon.*

She flips the bacon in the frying pan. Turns on the vent so that the whole house won't stink. It was hard to know what to say to her well-meaning friends. They were only trying to help. It isn't misery that loves company—no, no. Happiness loves company, and misery—misery just wants to be left alone. Their small group of friends had begun to fray, divided between the lucky and the unlucky. The lucky ones—untouched, unscathed so far by the myriad possible cruelties of life—were attending opera and eating noodles in fish sauce.

Mimi rolls her neck. There's no sense going there. She doesn't feel sorry for herself. She won't allow it! She loves her husband. Loves his shoulders, his hands, his jaw. His gray-green eyes. His measured, infinitely kind nature. She's never heard him say a mean word about a soul—and it isn't because he lacks discernment. No. Quite the opposite: Benjamin Wilf misses nothing.

She pours some Marcona almonds into a small bowl and takes it into the den. Refreshes Ben's Scotch. He's reclining in his leather chair, his head tilted back, eyes closed. Transported, as always, by the quartet. Without opening his eyes, he reaches out a hand and pulls her onto his lap. She rests her head in the crook of his neck. His pulse against her cheek. The fire sputters and hisses. *This,* Mimi thinks. *This right here.* The two of them, their quiet home. Their shared history. Everything they have built together, for better and for worse.

"Hungry?" she asks. He nods.

But they don't move. They stay like this, two bodies so at home with each other that it is as if each of them had grown and shifted to accommodate the other's shape over the years, like two grafted trees. Ben runs a hand through her hair. At first, they don't hear the phone ring. The quartet is playing at a high volume, and the only phone downstairs is in the kitchen, two rooms away.

Mimi raises her head off his shoulder. "Wait, is that—"

"Probably a sales call."

"On New Year's Eve?" She climbs off his lap. "I'd better get it."

She walks quickly into the kitchen and reaches for the phone just as the answering machine picks up.

*You've reached the Wilfs. Please leave a message.* Ben's deep, matter-of-fact voice. She waits, listens for the beep.

Breathing. At first she thinks she hears only the staticky sound of the tape unspooling—of no message being left at all—but then she realizes that someone is on the other end. More breathing. The sound of hesitation. Of being unsure whether to—

She grabs the phone and picks it up. "Hello?" she says. "Hello?"

New Year's Eve. She hadn't allowed herself to think—to even consider the possibility.

"Hello?"

There is no response on the other end, but she can feel a presence, rather than an absence. And she knows. For the first time in five years, she's certain.

"Theo?" She says his name out loud. "Theo, is that you?"

A clatter in her ear. A phone being dropped. *Please don't hang up. Say something. Anything.* Ben has followed her into the kitchen and is now standing next to her, so close she can feel the warmth of him. In the beginning, when Theo first went away, every morning Mimi awoke feeling hopeful. *Maybe today,* she would think as she lay in bed, willing herself to get up. *Maybe today.* But when the days turned into weeks, then months, then—inconceivably—years, her hope sharpened and turned against her, a twisting knife.

"Hi."

A long pause during which she can't seem to breathe.

"Mom? Hi."

She turns to Ben.

*Theo,* she mouths.

"Where—I mean—oh God, I don't even know what to—"

"I'm back in the States. I'm in LA. At Sarah's house."

Her children are together. Sarah and Theo, together. With her free hand, she reaches for Ben.

*Where is he?* Ben whispers.

She shakes her head fiercely. *Wait. Just wait.*

"Mom? Mom, are you there?"

Just her son's voice saying the word. *Mom, mom, mom.* She wasn't sure she would ever hear it again, and now that she finally does, it sounds foreign. A bulletin from a faraway land. Another language altogether. How could he have disappeared like that? No matter how he felt, didn't he have some responsibility to his family? To the people who love him? For all these years she has girded herself against him—thinking the worst. What if she never saw him again? What if—God forbid—something happened to her, or to Ben, while he was gone? What if he never came back?

The room seems to tilt off its axis. The world slowly spinning. She hands the phone wordlessly to Ben. The hoarseness in Ben's voice, the tears—only the second time in thirty years she's seen him cry—streaming down his stubbled cheeks. The things he's saying are hard for her to grasp—*come home, we love you, don't worry*—like scattered beads from a necklace that has snapped. Bright gems rolling every which way. She is on her hands and knees on the floor, gathering them up.

"I'm here," she says. "I'm here."

# Waldo

H E'S CROSSING MOUNTAINS. Valleys, softer than moss. All words he doesn't yet know—it will be three years of no words before his parents send him to the cold office building where a lady will show him flash cards. *Bug. Dog. Girl. Bed.* Trying to get him to use his words.

*Use your words, Waldo!* He will hear this many times and understand just what is being asked of him. But the words won't come. They will be locked in a place within him. His mother will worry. Her creased forehead, her puzzled eyes will imprint themselves on him, something he will carry all his life. Whenever he disappoints a woman he loves, it will be this look on his mother's face that he sees without knowing it. He will be a grown man someday—an esteemed professor of astrophysics—who is unable to use his words. *Talk to me, Waldo!* his wife will say a thousand times. *Talk to me!*

But for now—for now he is pressed against his mother's belly. He has not yet failed at anything. He has disappointed no one. The world is pinkish red through his unopened eyes.

Her smell. Coconut, lavender, musk. His father, a shadow looming. He feels something both soft and rough against his lips.

*Here's your baby boy, Alice.* The voice of a stranger, a man. Someone he will encounter one moonlit night years from now. *Precious.* His mother. *I don't know what we would have done without you.* His father. It is nothing but music to him, a chorus, the chirping of crickets, the whoosh of blood. He doesn't yet have to hide from his father. To fold into himself again and again like an origami puzzle until he's small enough to be overlooked.

He is warm in the soft valley. *Thu-thump. Thu-thump. Thu-thump.* His mother's heartbeat is all he has ever known. The two of them are alone in this busy room—the squawk of a two-way radio, men in boots, the ringing telephone—as if the towel beneath them were a raft and they had been set to sea. Floating. He is outside, but the memory of being inside is alive in him. *Thu-thump.* A door closes. The man who called his mother Alice has left the house. His father is kissing his mother's damp forehead. *I love you.*

This is the beginning. The warmth and sweat and watery milk from the soft, rough place. The shock of air. Skin against skin. The ride with his mother in the back of the car with the flashing red lights. The bright place where he is taken from his mother and put in a bassinet, examined by people in white coats who don't love him, who touch him with a professional indifference. *Close call.* He hears them conferring. *Benjamin Wilf.* A name that someday will sound to him like an echo. *Do you remember him? He's the one who—*And then the voices lower, become a rumble.

At the foot of his bassinet, a handwritten sign: SHENK-MAN. This is he. Waldo Shenkman, the latest in a long line of

Shenkmans, heir to all of it—the rage, the fear, the kindheartedness, the confusion, the loneliness, the instinct for survival that stretches back from the hospital in Avalon to a house in New Jersey to a shtetl in a country that no longer exists. This too, he will carry. He will move through his life, as we all do, without knowing what has preceded him or what lies ahead. A playground, children pointing, laughing. *Dumb, dreamer, nose picker.* A screen illuminating the whole night sky. *Andromeda, Antlia, Apus.* A gray-haired neighbor in a down jacket who makes him feel safe for reasons he won't understand. His father, screaming, his face contorted in fury—that same father who today looks through the plexiglass window of the nursery, falling in love.

Already he is a boy alone in his room, a teenager bent over a computer, a young man in a graduation gown scanning the crowd for his parents. He will always look for his parents wherever he goes, even long after he knows he will not find them. Here he is, a professor in front of a classroom, a devoted husband, a father who longs to connect with his children, a small, delicate man who draws people to him even as he pushes them away. The end of his life is here too, as he is swaddled and returned to his mother. *Waldo Shenkman,* his mother whispers. She unwraps him and places him at her breast, and once again he hears the *thu-thump, thu-thump,* though it is growing ever fainter.

# August 27, 1985

---

# All the Wilfs

B EN PLAYS THE scene over and over again. He rewinds, looks for the precise spot to freeze the frame. He tries to identify the moment he could have done anything other than what he did. The moment he could have looked from the open driver's door of the Buick at the poor girl, blood gushing from her head wound, and made a split-second decision: *Don't touch her.* Some of his doctor friends would have done precisely that; acted out of a kind of reflexive self-protection, concerned first and foremost with insurance and malpractice. But was there anything he missed? Could he have noted the angle of the girl's neck? Known not to move her?

It's no comfort to him that it wouldn't have mattered. He's already spoken with the hospital and she'd suffered not only a cervical fracture but the worst sort of spinal fracture, $C_1$. She was as good as gone the second the car hit the tree. Ben winces. His entire body convulses as if he were trying to break free of a trap. Mimi moves toward him, props herself on one elbow. A thin light from the hall spills beneath their closed bedroom door. He can feel her terror. He's failed them all. He's lost patients before; it happens to every doctor. But this? She wasn't his patient. He never should have intervened. So why did he? He knows, of course. Theo on all fours. Not far from the open driver's door. It made no sense, unless—but it couldn't be. It couldn't be, but it was. All of this had flashed through his mind as he raced to the car. He was acting not as a doctor but as a father. It was his own children he was trying to protect. His fifteen-year-old, behind the wheel. His seventeen-year-old, who had certainly been drinking but falsely confessed to driving.

Before he went to bed, he confirmed his suspicions by rooting through the trash in the garbage bin. Sure enough, he heard the telltale clink of beer bottles. He pawed his way through week-old leftovers and empty milk cartons to see how many. There were three. No, four. In such a tiny girl. The myriad of ways the night could have unfurled—now he sees the face of Misty Zimmerman's mother, socked by grief, mouth twisted into something lopsided and grotesque—are very nearly more than he can bear. His children. His idiotic, careless, carefree children who, at least until this night, hadn't yet lived long enough to understand that there are fates from which their parents can't save them. He feels an aching sense of doom.

"Mimi, we should talk," he says. He sits up, bowing his head into his open palms.

"We don't have to talk, Ben," says his beautiful wife. She climbs behind him and presses herself against his curved back. Her cheek, he can feel, is damp with tears. "Let's not talk."

The mist has lifted, leaving no trace. The sky is now bright with a constellation that one day many years from now a small boy in Red Sox pajamas will be able to identify as the summer triangle: Altair, Deneb, and Vega, the brightest stars in the constellations of Aquila, Cygnus, and Lyra. Misty herself so solid and alive in one moment, so completely broken the next. Down the hall, past the framed prints from the Van Gogh Museum, Theo knocks on Sarah's door. He waits for her voice, an answer, an invitation. *Come on in!* But he is met with silence. He doesn't dare test the knob. *It was me,* she had said. *I was driving.* Never before has he felt so loved. His sister is willing to take the fall for him. Forevermore, love will confuse Theo Wilf. His future selves, like so many wobbly tops set spinning at this very moment. He deserves nothing. He has killed a girl. That knowledge pierces his deepest interior. He wants to wake his parents, to climb into bed between them the way he used to as a little boy. His father would treat the burn on his belly. Cover it with ointment. He wants to tell them everything, safe in the knowledge that they will find a way to fix things—to fix him—no matter what.

Instead, he heads downstairs and opens the refrigerator. His hands are shaking a little as he places cold cuts between two thick pieces of leftover challah smeared with Mimi's homemade mayonnaise. He drinks milk straight from the container. He swipes at the wetness on his face as he stands at the kitchen counter. He doesn't bother with a plate. He doesn't take the sandwich up to his room. There's no time; he's in a rush. His stomach hurts. But bite after ravenous bite, he will try to fill the gnawing void before it devours him.


Sarah is lying on her back, on her bed, staring at the ceiling. She's stone-cold sober now. She hears Theo's knock and rolls

135

away from the door, all the way to the edge of her bed, in the fetal position. *It was me. I was driving.* She hadn't known what she was going to say until she had already said it. Misty, bleeding on the ground. Theo, retching. Their father in his light blue pajamas, lifting Misty's head, trying to stop the river of blood. Their mother's scream. *It was me.* Well, it *was* her. She can see the arc of the car keys as she tossed them to her little brother. Even in that moment she wondered what the hell she was doing. She wanted to help Theo, inject a little courage, a little daring into the kid. But also? She'd already had three and a half beers. She'd vowed to herself when she got her license that she would never, not ever, drive drunk. *You drive, Theo.* Her little brother had looked at her then, confused, excited. She told herself it wasn't the beers—but of course, that's exactly what it was. The real reason. She was protecting herself, and now a girl is dead.

She hears the creak of the stairs as Theo heads down to the kitchen. She wants to follow him, to tell him that it wasn't his fault—it was her fault. She's the older sister, and she knew better. Misty Zimmerman is dead because of her. Instead, she stands and looks out her window at Division Street below. The Buick has been towed. Bits of shattered glass shimmer on the grass. Yellow tape and chalk mark the pavement. By morning, there will be the first bouquets left at the base of the tree, as if offerings at an altar. Over the next months and years, these will continue and become a neighborhood tradition, long after the name Misty Zimmerman has faded from collective memory. Someone will wind an elaborate set of twinkling lights around the oak's trunk and string them into the tree's lower branches by Christmas. Others will plant wildflowers and grasses in the spaces between the tree's massive roots. As the years go on, people will no longer be aware that a girl died here. They will know only that there is a bit of magic and unexpected beauty, here in this unlikely spot.

Mimi lies still. She concentrates on the rise and fall of her breath. If she moves, Ben will know she's awake. If they open their mouths, they will say things that they will always remember, and never be able to take back. Their silence is a third presence in the room. She can't stop thinking about Misty Zimmerman's mother. Mrs. Zimmerman—her first name is Ruth—is divorced and lives three blocks over, near the station, in a row of houses that have been converted to apartments. The ex-husband has moved out of state. Mimi knows this only because the woman works part-time at Avalon High as an assistant librarian. They've had no more than a nodding acquaintance at the morning coffee cart. A shiny dark bob—a mommy haircut—and bright red lips, even early in the morning. And now Ruth Zimmerman's only child is dead. Dead—Mimi digs her nails into her palm—because of *her* children.

She knows Theo is in the kitchen wolfing down a sandwich. As surely as if she were standing inches from him, she sees the streaks of tears on his cheeks. She hears Sarah rustling in her room, next door. There have been advantages and disadvantages, over the years, to the cozy quarters of their home's second floor. She and Ben haven't had quite as much privacy as they'd wish—they've burst out laughing at the creak of their bedsprings—but all things considered, she likes keeping her children close. Now, she sends out a stream of silent words—a sort of prayer—to each of them. If she focuses intently, she is convinced, her thoughts will create a field of protection around her son and daughter. *Not your fault.*

*Could have happened to anyone.* But she knows this isn't true. She searches for something true and useful. Is it enough that she loves them with a ferocity that pushes past all sense of right and wrong? Tomorrow Ben will have to give a statement to the police. *Who was driving the car, Dr. Wilf?* Mimi's nails dig harder.

Ruth Zimmerman didn't look at any of them as Misty was moved to a stretcher, then taken in a slow-moving ambulance to the hospital. Tonight she sits by her daughter's bedside in the ICU, listening to the whir and beep of the machines that are the only thing keeping Misty breathing. There is no hope for that child, and probably not much for her mother either, because who can survive such a loss and keep going? But maybe, just maybe—a thought so selfish she will barely acknowledge it—this terrible night will be the bullet that grazes them and then moves on.

She hears Theo making his way upstairs. The sound of Sarah's footsteps as she walks from her window back to bed. Mimi moves, finally, spooning herself into Ben. He lets out a shuddering sigh. They are all here now, in their safe and solid house, on their pretty street, in their lovely town. An ancient prayer comes to her. Not a Jewish one—she has no idea why she knows it. She must have heard it once as a child, and now holds on to each word like bits of flotsam in a choppy sea that might keep her from being swept under. She repeats it again and again, an obsessive silent lullaby to her family until the first light of dawn. *All shall be well, and all shall be well, and all manner of things shall be well.*

# December 22, 2010

# Theo

THE SNOW IS coming down hard and fast by the time he's on the Saw Mill River Parkway. It's the worst kind of weather to be on a bike, and he's not dressed for it in his leather jacket, chef pants, and sneakers. At least he had the presence of mind to change out of his Crocs. His high beams only make things worse. The world is white on white. He has some experience with snow blindness. In Patagonia, while making a summer trek in El Chaltén he had been caught in an unexpected blizzard. It was pure luck that he managed not to wander off the trail. All signposts—the Piedras Blancas glacier, Cerro Torre in the distance—vanished as if perhaps they'd never existed at all. It was just him, Theo Wilf, spun around, seeing nothing, hearing only the whistling of the wind.

Eyes glued to the guardrail on the winding two-lane parkway. He passes no cars. No one is driving anywhere on a night like this. Where is his mother? The old voice in his head, the one that shuts up only when he's in the kitchen, starts whispering as he counts off the exits—two more until the turnoff for Avalon. Ahead in the distance, he makes out a plow, feels the grit of salt on the blacktop. *Piece of shit,* the voice goes. *Disgusting turd. Motherfucking loser.* Guilt and silence have hardened over the years into something intractable. Leaving was his one attempt to save himself, but he would have had to stay gone forever for that to have worked. The pull of home—his parents, his sister—no. He had to come back. It turns out there are some things you can't outrun.

He nearly misses the exit. He passes the mall, all lit up even in the middle of the night: the bright windows of Pottery Barn and Neiman Marcus, and then that odd, cheery children's store selling play structures that hadn't existed when Theo was a kid and they still climbed actual trees and built actual tree houses.

He tries to catch his breath as he navigates the dark streets of Avalon. The snow has sharpened into ice, pelting him from every direction. Now he's on Poplar, now Division. The porch lights are on at his parents' house. His father's house. As of tomorrow, someone else's house. Through the bay window he sees a figure, and then his sister at the front door. She's holding a big cotton tarp, the kind movers use. He pulls the bike back onto its kickstands—no need for locks here in Mayberry. Avalon: the town crime forgot.

Sarah rushes down the porch steps. She's even less prepared for the weather than he is. Are those heels she's wearing? She throws the tarp over his shoulders. Stares at him, then puts her arm around him—she feels surprisingly sturdy—and pulls him inside. What did he just see in her eyes? It has once again been years since they've been together. The last time was before he opened Twelve Tables and gave over completely to his demons. But she, too—he steals a glance at her as he shakes himself off in the foyer—looks the worse for wear. Tiny, queenly Sarah has dark circles beneath her eyes, her forehead artificially smooth; but she has aged most dramatically around her mouth, the tense set of her jaw. The easy smile of his big sister is gone.

"Fuck, Theo." She collapses on the sofa. A few pops of bubble wrap. A near-empty bottle of Courvoisier on the floor. "Fuck, fuck, fuck."

Her voice is thick.

"Should we wake up Dad?" His first words.

"There's no point. There's nothing we can do until daylight. They have a search party out looking for her."

"How could this have happened, Sarah? Do you know what that place costs? How could they have let Mom ... what? Just wander off?"

"I know."

"Did they say anything else? Anything that—"

"Just the bingo thing."

Sarah picks up the bottle of Courvoisier and eyes it. Puts it down again.

"I have a very bad feeling," she says.

"Me too."

"She's out there somewhere"—Sarah flings one arm toward the window—"in the cold."

"Maybe someone picked her up."

"I'm not sure which is scarier."

Theo keeps standing, shifting from one leg to the other. He's soaking wet, shivering. He sees Ben's winter jacket, an ancient L.L.Bean parka, hanging on the coatrack. He shrugs off his leather jacket, peels off the tee shirt that clings to his skin. He has no self-consciousness in front of Sarah, not of the rolls of fat that spill over the waist of his chef pants, his big belly marked by the shiny crescent scar. He's not thinking about anything other than his mother. They have to find her. They have to find her now and bring her home, or back to the memory unit. Order must be restored in the world before their father wakes up.

He wipes himself off with the tarp, slides Ben's parka across his gooseflesh nakedness.

"Let's go, Sarah."


The two of them in Ben's old Volvo, Theo in the driver's seat. Sarah's in no shape. The key's in the ignition. The rash of car break-ins that will spread across the suburbs, including Avalon, is still in the future, poor souls hooked on Oxy looking for wallets, cash in glove compartments. Tonight, in sweet Avalon, the more recently renovated houses may be protected by alarm and surveillance systems, but what's left of the old guard (their father may be the last of the old guard) never saw the need. Unlocked front doors, keys dangling from ignitions, all proof of the good choices they made, the respectable lives they've lived.

The snow finally seems to be tapering off as they pull out of the driveway and make tracks down the pristine, empty streets. This is the first time the two of them have been in a car together with Theo driving in twenty-five years. They scan every corner, every shadow. Sarah's eyes are wild. Theo is steady, both hands on the wheel. His field of vision has widened like that of an animal in danger, seeing the periphery. Where is his mother?

"If you were Mom, where would you go?" Sarah wonders aloud.

"But she's not Mom," Theo says. "Not anymore."

Sarah sighs. Her breath smells of brandy.

"This is impossible," she says. "She could be anywhere."

It's close to dawn by the time they've completed three loops around Avalon, winding their way down every street. Peel back this night, and their childhood is everywhere. The snow glistens blue in the light of the moon. The sky is now bright with stars. *A bull. A snake. A crab. A child holding a harp.*

"Let's make one more loop."

"Wait, what's over there?"

"That's a reindeer with its lights turned off."

"We've got to get into her head. Into what she might have been thinking."

"But that's the problem, Sarah."

They fall silent as they pull back into the driveway. All the cells, the vertebrae, the blood and bone, the long fingers and fine, arched feet, the startling light eyes, the mane of wavy hair that are still Mimi Wilf—she is a living spark in this world even if she can't remember her own name. Sarah slumps down in her seat, gnaws at a fingernail. Theo reaches over and pats her shoulder. It shouldn't feel so awkward.

"We've got no right—I mean, we need to wake—" Theo stutters, just in time to see a light flicker on in the kitchen, and their father in his flannel bathrobe, rising early to face his moving day.

# Shenkman

WHEN HE SLEEPS, especially after miles upon miles on the RowPro, he is a child once more. It is only in deepest slumber that he meets his young self, that frightened, awkward boy he has worked so hard, all his adult life, to leave behind. He appears—young Shenkman, age indeterminate, sometimes six, sometimes eight, maybe ten—as a cross between an apparition and a cartoon, all huge-eyed and pointy-chinned, a big head atop a skinny body. Grown-up Shenkman teleports into his boyhood self and gazes outward from those eyes, even as his snoring is driving Alice crazy; she has taken an Ambien and sleeps with a pillow over her head. Now it's 1975 and he's in the godforsaken New Jersey suburb where he spent his formative years. The place stinks, literally. There are nice parts of the Garden State, but where Shenkman and his family live is not the nice part.

His father is an executive at the Budweiser plant in Newark. He has a big important job and works hard to support his family, according to him, especially when it comes to

Shenkman asking him for anything: lately Shenkman has been angling for a new Rawlings catcher's mitt stamped with Johnny Bench's signature. And also, a batting net cage so he can invite his across-the-street neighbor over to play. He wants to grow up to be a catcher. He isn't fast or nimble, but he's pretty good at reading the seams of the ball as it's coming at him.

Shenkman rolls over on his stomach. He's flying somewhere in the netherworld. He doesn't want to wake up, so he keeps himself there a while longer. His childhood may be boring, even unhappy, but he can imagine all different kinds of futures for himself, fanned out like a deck of cards. Nothing is impossible: major league catcher is at the top of the list, but also astronaut, surgeon, captain of industry. He doesn't have the words to say it, but he knows he doesn't want his father's life. A dull job, a tense marriage, three undistinguished little Shenkmans, an eventual early end due to a combination of hypertension, inertia, and a weak heart that will give out at fifty. Boy Shenkman—now a teenager—sees his father lying in his casket, hands arranged in a pious clasp.

With this, the dream needle screeches to a stop, and Shenkman bolts awake. The digital clock reads 4:43. The worst time. He won't be able to fall back asleep. It's too late to take one of Alice's Ambiens, and too early to climb out of bed and start the day. He is not a major league catcher, or an astronaut, or a surgeon, or a captain of industry. It's as if he has a set point, the highest he'll ever be able to go in life, like those high striker games at amusement parks where you hit the lever with a mallet, trying to get the bell to ring. *Step right up! Test your strength! Who are the men out of the boys?* Only, the game is rigged. It's people like Lindgren and his ilk who always and effortlessly pull ahead. He, Shenkman, will never hit the lever with enough force. Just as his father didn't, before him. He's a middle man. A man in the middle. A middle-aged man with an unhappy wife and an exceptional (he knows this) son who may be *too* exceptional. If that's a thing.

Shenkman climbs out of bed. Sometimes, when he awakes this early, a session on the RowPro is just the thing to jump-start his day. Added benefit: Lindgren won't be rowing. Lindgren is surely asleep in his Upper East Side town house with his Lindgren-esque wife curled up next to him, all tawny limbs and wheat-colored hair. They could be brother and sister. Lindgren's alarm will go off at seven thirty. He and his wife will fuck in the shower before sitting down to breakfast with their little ones. They'll spend the day sledding in Central Park. Their snowsuits and boots are all lined up in a mudroom straight out of an issue of *Domino*. These are not children who would slip out of their house in the middle of the night. These are not children who pick their noses. They would happily allow different food groups to touch on their plates. These children do not have strange obsessions; they have not memorized the names of all the constellations. Shenkman has never felt so lonely.

Before the gym, he heads down the hall to Waldo's room. Maybe he was too hard on him. The hangover from his rage is always worse than the rage itself. He can do better. Be better. He has every right to be aggrieved, and he did the right thing, taking the iPad away from Waldo. But he shouldn't have exploded like that. On the way home from the office later, he'll pick up one of those anger management books.

He cracks open Waldo's door, slowly so that it doesn't creak. He just wants to commune with his son, and he seems to know how to do that only when the kid is asleep. It takes a minute for his eyes to adjust. Waldo's room is pitch-black, but still Shenkman knows every nook and cranny. He scans the corners, piled with the stuffed animals of Waldo's earlier childhood, each with a name and entire history. He sees the framed poster of Jacoby Ellsbury. Incredible, that his boy is a Red Sox fan. Even in this, Waldo is unlike him.

Shenkman does this a lot: watches his son as he sleeps. It's a habit he got into when Waldo was an infant. Shenkman couldn't believe that his boy was actually here, slipped, literally, through the noose of his own umbilical cord, right there on the kitchen floor. Alice seemed less traumatized by Waldo's birth than Shenkman was—maybe because she went through it, rather than helplessly witnessing it. What if that doctor had not been living across Division Street? What if he hadn't heard Alice's screams? Shenkman sometimes passes Benjamin Wilf in his car or catches a glimpse of him while taking out the garbage. The wife, he hasn't seen in ages. She used to be out front tending to their flower beds, or occasionally she read on the front porch. Over the years, he's made a point of avoiding them. What is there to say? His gratitude is so wide and deep that it feels, instead, like shame.

He takes a couple of steps toward Waldo's bed. He wants to touch the soft curve of his cheek. *I'm sorry* is on the tip of his tongue. He won't say it, but maybe Waldo will feel it. He looks down then, Shenkman, at the perfectly made bed where his son should be sleeping. The coverlet is smooth as a lake at dawn. Two teddy bears sit side by side in front of four plump pillows. For a second he wonders if he's having one of those nightmares so real that you wake panting, disoriented, the world tilted and strange. He shakes himself. Or perhaps he is shaking. His legs are rubbery as he races downstairs. Maybe Waldo is in the kitchen. Maybe Waldo is in the den. Maybe Waldo—Shenkman runs to the gym. The light is on, and now he sees: the iPad is gone.

# *Benjamin*

T HE MOVERS WILL arrive at seven. It's still dark out, and he could probably use more sleep, but with Sarah upstairs—the strangeness of his daughter once again under his roof—he wants, no, *needs* a little time for himself. He hasn't packed the coffee maker yet, and there's still a carton of milk in the fridge for him to heat up in a dented little pot.

What is a house when emptied of its people, stripped of furnishings and art, family photos, vases on countertops, linens in cupboards, a stocked pantry? Pans, strainers, a wok. Place mats, flatware, wineglasses. Tupperware, Ball jars, tins of herbs labeled in Mimi's hand. Shelves upon shelves of books. Mimi gravitated toward literary fiction, mostly written by women: Alice Munro, Margaret Atwood, Laurie Colwin, who had died of an aortic aneurysm, far too young. He still keeps up on medical journals but also reads history and biography: Richard Ben Cramer, Walter Isaacson, and he's just heard that Ron Chernow's new book on Washington is excellent. Now, the shelves are bare. The family from Cleveland hired an interior decorator who has already been by with her measuring tape. Will they rip out the bookcases in favor of a wide-screen television? Redo the kitchen? Break down the wall between the living room and the den? That was something Mimi had always wanted to do, make a big family room. They should have sprung for it. How long will molecular traces of the Wilfs remain inside 18 Division Street?

As he puts on the coffee and heats the milk, he scans the house once more. He closes his eyes and hears the voices of the people he loves most. *Good morning, darling. What time is pickup? What's for dinner? Smells good. How long can one boy spend in the shower? Give me the play-by-play. Ben, there's a dead mouse in the laundry room.* The sizzle of shallots and bacon in a frying pan. (Theo.) Girlish laughter seeping beneath a bedroom door. (Sarah.) He can even hear the particular quality of the silence he and Mimi shared in the years after the kids were out of the house: companionable, loving, spacious, their precious double solitude. He knew that it couldn't go on forever. Still, he had always imagined they'd have more time.

He should have been alert to the signs from the start, but the truth is that he didn't want to see them. First, she lost words. Mid-sentence, she would stop, puzzled, and actually say it: *I can't find the word for what I mean. It's just gone, Ben.* But he chalked that up to forgetfulness, a normal part of aging. Sometimes she misplaced her purse. Again, normal. She'd ask him the same question several times. Even this, he managed to experience as mild annoyance—was she not listening?—and not a cause for concern. It wasn't until she called him from her daily walk: *I don't know how to get home.* What did she mean, she didn't know how to get home?

"Where are you?" He heard his own voice become less husbandly, more doctorly. "Look around you, Mimi. What do you see?"

"I don't know—a yellow house. A white fence."

"What else?"

"The peonies are in bloom."

"Are there street signs, honey? Look for a street sign."

He went to a cordoned-off place inside him where he was all strategy and analysis. Every surgeon has the ability to act decisively now, feel the effects later. *Mimi is sick.* The words entered him. *It's likely that Mimi has Alzheimer's,* delivered in the affectless voice of a newscaster.

"There's one. Maple Street. And the other one is Railroad."

Jesus Christ, she was six blocks from home on a corner she knew so well she could have found it blindfolded. And she was lost.

"Don't move," he told her. "Stay right where you are."

He ran the six blocks and arrived, panting. Mimi, his bride, stood tall at the corner of Maple and Railroad, her hair aswirl, hands tucked into the pockets of her jeans. She gazed down Railroad Street in the direction of town as if contemplating whether to stop at the fishmonger to pick up that evening's dinner. Any neighbor driving by would simply have waved to Mimi Wilf—wife, mother, secretary of the wetlands committee, board member of the after-school arts program, longtime beloved citizen of Avalon—without a clue that anything was the matter.

"Ben! What on earth?"

"Mimi, I—"

And then he stopped. No worry creased Mimi's brow. Her

eyes were clear. She didn't know that she had just lost her way. She didn't remember calling him. Wave upon wave of sorrow washed over him, even as his mind raced: maybe there was another explanation. Maybe she'd suffered a transient ischemic attack, a tiny stroke; that would be preferable. Or something else. She had just started taking statins for her elevated cholesterol. Memory loss could be a side effect. But as he looped his arm through Mimi's and began to walk home, the small slips and confusions of the last many months began to arrange themselves into a coherent picture. This wasn't a near miss, a blip, something solvable. He was losing her. She was losing herself. He didn't want to hurt her. He *lived* to not hurt her. How long before she would have a moment of awareness, feel the falling of the blade that would forever separate her life—their lives—into all that came before, and now this?

"My love." She leaned her head into the crook of his neck. Twilight fell as they strolled up Maple Street. He inhaled her warm, amber scent, as familiar to him as his own. "You must have missed me."

He'd held on for three and a half years. He didn't tell Sarah or Theo. Sarah was living on the other side of the country, and she had her hands full, between her job and the twins. He heard something strained in her voice each time he called; she was overwhelmed. He hadn't wanted to alarm Sarah. And Theo—Theo had returned to them. He was working as a chef in a restaurant in Tribeca, saving up to open his own place. A few times, Ben and Mimi drove to the southernmost part of Manhattan to have Theo cook them dinner. He sent dish after dish to their table whenever they came. Chef's prerogative. This was how he showed his love—Mimi had explained this to Ben, carefully avoiding the fault lines, the damage they both knew lived inside their son. They would take what they could get: warm glazed potatoes with caviar, Meyer lemon gelée, yellowfin tuna ribbons, caramelized foie gras served with port-infused figs. Each dish would be presented with a flourish by a waiter eager to tell them that Chef Theo had personally arranged the finishing touches himself.

Now Ben nearly scalds the milk. His whole being vibrates, as if he were an instrument that had become tightly tuned overnight. The sounds, voices, slivers of memory don't cohere but rather become kaleidoscopic. He thinks of the boy, Waldo, his device tilted to mirror the night sky. His fluency with the thing. The way, by pressing one button, like a wee wizard, he was able to take them on a trip through time and space. *Andromeda, Antlia, Apus, Aquarius.* It was comforting, somehow, sitting beside the small boy who was able to navigate their precise location in the vastness. The stars, rather than appearing distant and implacable, seemed to be signal fires in the dark, mysterious fellow travelers lighting a path; one hundred thousand million luminous presences beckoning from worlds away. *See us. We are here. We have always been here. We will always be here.*

As Ben takes his first sip of his last cup of coffee in this house, he thinks of Whitman's lines, then, from "Song of Myself"—his favorite passage from his favorite poet:

*I bequeath myself to the dirt to grow from the grass I
love,
If you want me again look for me under your boot-soles.*

*You will hardly know who I am or what I mean,*
*But I shall be good health to you nevertheless,*
*And filter and fibre your blood.*

He is a practical man, but still in a wordless place within
him, Ben Wilf has come to believe that we live in loops rather
than one straight line; that the air itself is made not only of
molecules but of memory; that these loops form an invisible
pattern; that past, present, and future are a part of this pattern; that our lives intersect for fractions of seconds that are
years, centuries, millennia; that nothing ever vanishes. And
so he is leaving this place he first moved to as a young man
at the start of a great adventure, he is moving a few blocks
away to be with his wife who soon will no longer remember
him, his own children are living out their destinies (here he
feels a pang for them both). But they have *lived*.

He has answered his own question. The Wilfs will always
remain within the walls of 18 Division. Just as the girl who
died that August night long ago will always live inside the
great oak. His parents are the breeze that crosses Classon
Avenue in Brooklyn. The Mimi he has loved for more than
forty years is still alive in the patient who now sits being
spoon-fed oatmeal in the memory unit, staring into a different kind of space. The first European settlers of Avalon are
buried in the town's graveyard, but they are also—along with
every other citizen in the town's history—as present as the
canopy of stars.

156

# Waldo

IN ANOTHER HOUR, the sun will come up. It's the day after the winter solstice—the second-shortest day of the year. His iPad tells him that. Yesterday—which feels like forever ago—his dad wouldn't let him wake up early (okay, really early, like three in the morning) to watch the total lunar eclipse. That's why he went outside last night, sat with the old doctor, and showed him the sky. He wanted somebody to share it with. He doesn't have brothers or sisters. He doesn't really have friends. And his parents get so mad at him every time he talks about Star Walk. His mom pretended to be interested when he first got it, but he knows the difference between when his mom is paying attention and when she's faking it. Her eyes go kind of cloudy, and her hand drifts down to her phone. And his father straight up hates Star Walk because he thinks Waldo should be doing more normal things. He caresses that word whenever he says it: *normal,* as if it were the end goal, the best way to be.

Well, he's in for it now, Waldo is. If his father finds him, he's going to kill him. But then his next thought is worse. What if his dad doesn't find him? When stars die, first they become red giants, then white dwarfs, then black dwarfs. This takes a few billion years. But he's just a boy. And he's cold. So tired and cold. He looks at the weather app on his iPad. Last night's snow has stopped, and it's twenty-eight degrees. The old lady is curled up next to him, softly snoring. Her hands are in the mittens he gave her, clasped against her chest, and his wool cap is pulled down to her eyebrows. Her hair falls over half her face. He checks to see that her feet are still in the socks, stuffed into her slippers. Inside the play structure it's not too dark. Bright lights from the parking lot stayed on all night like a hundred fake moons.

He has about 60 percent battery charge remaining. His teeth chatter, and he can't feel the tips of his fingers. Sixty percent is a lot. He can risk a few minutes of sky time. He boots up the app, touches his screen, and the familiar pulsing circle takes a minute to zero in on his location. Star Walk can find the sky above him anywhere, from his bedroom on Division Street (oh, how he misses his bedroom), through wood and brick and concrete, the sprawling buildings of the mall. Waldo could be in a dungeon right now and still he'd be able to trace the constellations, the world that's always there whether he can see it or not.

Before they fell asleep, he had shown the old lady where they were. It seemed to calm her down. Or maybe it was the background music, which sounds kind of like a harp. The harp made him think of Lyra, the constellation, so he told her everything he knew about it. *To find Lyra first you look for Vega, one of the brightest stars in the night sky. You can really only see it clearly in the summer, but it's one of my favorites. The second-brightest star in the constellation is*

*Beta Lyrae—two stars locked together in orbit. One star is blue, and the other one is white. They're so close that they circle each other every thirteen days.* Before her eyes closed, the old lady beamed a smile at him, tears trickling down her cheeks. *Thank you, Theo,* she whispered. He didn't bother to correct her.

# Sarah

Later, she will come to think of lives as books divided into chapters. Take hers, for instance. Bright, shiny Sarah Wilf occupies the first third of the book, the setup, the ascent of the narrative arc. She is the golden child of Avalon. There have been other golden children before her and there will be golden children after, just as there have always been the duller siblings of these golden ones, who bear the scars of being compared too early in life and found wanting. You don't get over that shit. The chapters starring Sarah Wilf as a girl on the rise will come to a screeching stop on a summer night in the middle of an inauspicious decade. A terrible thing will happen, and there will be no visible consequences. Misty Zimmerman's death will ultimately be ruled an accident, though not before her own father's good reputation is called into question. All the while, she will remain silent. No one thought to breathalyse her. She'll tell herself she did what she could. She protected her little brother. It would have been worse if it had come out that Theo was driving.

Now she's well into the middle of the story. Or, she has arrived at the first plot point of the second act, as Peter would put it. Or perhaps this is the second plot point. Screenplay language, the only language he speaks. Second acts—middles—always contain two major plot points, according to all the dog-eared screenwriting books on the shelves of his study. These plot points are usually spaced neatly apart, for the sake of dramatic pacing. But she is in the middle of her life, which seems to be exploding on both coasts at the same moment. So, is that one plot point, or two?

She has put her phone on airplane mode, though she checks it every few minutes to see if there's any word about her mother. All is quiet on that front—too quiet—and all the noise is coming from a small apartment in Laguna Beach: *Call me back, bitch. You can't just ghost me.* Then, cryptically: *Hell to pay.* Followed by a few hours of silence, and then: *Remember we took pictures.* Four words, and a chill goes through her. How could she have been so foolish? She's left a voicemail for Dr. Baum. But it's the wee hours in Los Angeles, and Dr. Baum is surely asleep. Seventy-eight-year-old Beverly Hills psychoanalysts with good boundaries don't keep their phones by their beds in case a patient is in crisis. They cater to the worried well. Sarah has abdicated her spot in the club of the worried well and has entered a danger zone. The drinking is one thing. Plenty of functioning alcoholics in the club. And the affair? Same, same. It's her *choices,* Dr. Baum would say. She is growing more self-destructive with each passing day.

And now she's being threatened. There's no other way to think of it. There had been the better part of a bottle of Belvedere consumed, mixed with fresh-squeezed orange juice and a basket of croissants from room service; a pathetic attempt to make the whole escapade look like nothing more than a decadent brunch. She had chosen a hotel downtown. No one she knew from the Westside would be at a hotel downtown late morning on a random weekday. No one from the Westside crossed the 405 if they could help it; if they did, it wasn't for brunch. The NoMad had the right louche vibe with its rooftop cocktail bar, a giant carved stone face of the demon Orcus, his wide-open mouth a fire pit, presiding over the pool.

Not that they were lounging by the pool. A DO NOT DIS-TURB sign hung on the door, the safety chain in place. She had told him what she wanted: to be punished. (She again thinks of Dr. Baum. What had she expected? She is getting even more than what she'd asked for.) He'd come prepared. Somehow, she had known he'd have just the right toys. In his bag he carried no change of clothes—after all, it wasn't like they were planning to spend the night—but he did have a full array of cuffs, wrist and ankle restraints, silk ties, blindfolds.

She hadn't even known she wanted this until the want had overtaken her. She told herself it was because sex with Peter had become nonexistent. But of course, that wasn't nearly the whole story. She'd had enough therapy to be able to analyse her own desire: *Punish me,* she had said. *Punish me.* There are very few lines, once crossed, that come to define you forever. If you have children, you are a mother. If you kill someone, you are a murderer. If you aid and abet, you are an accomplice. If you fuck someone other than your husband, you are an adulterer. She is all these things. *Remember we took pictures.*

The room was on a high floor and flooded with light. It featured a modern take on an old-fashioned bathtub, in which she soaked after he left, her mind quiet, wiped clean of its usual static. He had used a black silk cloth to blindfold her, and another to tie her wrists together, and two more on her ankles, first soft, then tight, her legs spread apart. *You like that? You're just a horny little cunt, aren't you.* He shoved her legs farther apart, then his hand slick inside her.

At some point he took off her blindfold. *I want you to watch me fuck you.* He had a tattoo of a wolf's face on his chest, and a spider on his left biceps. She watched the spider as that arm reached over to the nightstand and grabbed his phone. He paused above her. *Smile, bitch.* Then he flipped her over and rammed himself into her, one hand on her ass, the other still holding his phone. She had asked for this. This obliteration, this pain. This reckoning.

She imagines Peter checking his email as his car idles at a stoplight on Sunset. Scrolling through his inbox. What would the subject line be for the missive that will blow up her life? *Your wife. About Sarah.* No. He wouldn't use her name. Never once has he called her by her name. *Bitch. Cunt.* She deserves every bit of the storm that's about to rain down on her. But Peter? Peter has done nothing to deserve this. He's a simple guy, a nice guy who hasn't been able to catch a break. He's tried to be okay with the ever-increasing chasm between them. People never remember his name. At parties, they look past him to get to her. No wonder he rolls away from her in bed. Now he's going to see images—how many, she has no idea, how idiotic of her, how filled with self-loathing to have allowed it to happen—of his wife tied to a bed with a stranger's cock inches from her bare ass.

And what about the studio? She closes her eyes. Could those photographs find their way to her boss? Sure, they could. Stuff like this happens all the time—usually to men.

She sinks into a pool of shame so familiar and so deep she may drown in it.

"Sarah?"

She jumps at the sound of her brother's voice. She looks around at her childhood: the dented basketball hoop her parents never took down, her mother's herb garden, fallow for years. Upstairs, her bedroom—now just boxes and a mattress—is painted pink and orange, with a shiny white headboard and a wall thumbtacked with hundreds of photos, ribbons, and postcards. Ben had called her when he sold the house. Did she want the memorabilia? The warm light of the kitchen window frames her father as he stands by the stove. There should be a word for the moment just before heartbreak, when the very air quivers with all that is about to come.

"We have to go in now. We have to tell Dad." Theo's hands are still on the wheel, the car idling as if perhaps they might take off again and come back to a different story.

The sky has begun to redden. At the sound of the car doors closing, she sees her father move to the window and stare with incomprehension at his two children as they approach.

# *Mimi*

OH, BLISS! HER boy is next to her. Her beautiful, beloved boy. Parents aren't supposed to have favorites, and she would never tell anyone, but Theo is hers. She loves her daughter, of course. But Sarah doesn't need her the same way Theo does. Some children grow like orchids, some like weeds. Theo is an orchid. Sarah is a weed. She would thrive anywhere. She would strain toward the sunlight from a crack in the sidewalk. But Theo needs care and feeding. Theo needs his mother's eyes on him in order to thrive.

But where are Ben and Sarah? Oh, of course! Sarah has hockey practice. Mimi will cook something with Theo today. He loves poring over recipes with her, rolling up his sleeves, putting on an apron. *Mom, let's make boeuf bourguignon. Or here—this jambalaya looks good.* His little hands next to hers as he peels the pearl onions, washes and slices the mushrooms. She worries about her boy in so many ways but not here in the kitchen. Here she knows that he is standing on two solid feet in the world.

"Lady?"

Why is Theo calling her that terrible name? She isn't a lady. She's his *mother*.

"Lady, you're shaking."

She wants to tell him that she's fine—he should never worry about her—but no words will come. Her teeth bang against each other, her jaw as tight as a nutcracker. Her whole life swirls around her, a vortex, spinning, out of reach even as she is inside of it.

"Lady, I'm scared."

Theo is scared! She feels something sharp. Theo is on the grass, on all fours. A flashing red light. Theo is crying in his room. She can hear him through the walls of his room. He is wailing, inconsolable. Is that blood? No, no, no. Wait, now, what's this? Theo is climbing into a taxi. Theo—it's impossible—Theo has vanished. He has gone far away, and he may never return. He sends postcards. *Forgive me,* he writes. *This is the only way.*

But here he is, and he's clutching something to his small chest. Tears leak from the corners of his eyes. He is saying words she doesn't understand. *Andromeda, Antlia, Apus, Aquarius, Aquila. Ara. Aries, Auriga. Bootes. Caelum, Camelopardalis.*

"Don't be frightened, Theo," she says. Or thinks she says.

"The stars are watching over us, lady. They know where we are. They'll find us."

A long time ago, during a time that seems like it could be now, she had an ocular migraine; her vision broke apart into what seemed like hundreds of colorful prisms, like sunlight hitting cut crystal. It would have been beautiful if it hadn't been so terrifying. Now, the world has gone prismatic. Everything and everyone she has ever loved is inside these prisms. Her long-gone parents. Her husband with his kind eyes and generous smile. She has been so lucky. Her babies— oh, her babies. They hug her around the knees. They reach their arms up to be pulled out of the bath. They sing in the backseat. *The wheels on the bus go round and round.* They are safe in their beds.

*Cassiopeia, Centaurus, Cepheus, Cetus, Chamaeleon.*

It sounds like a lullaby, or maybe a prayer. Her eyes drift closed. She can go now. They are safe in their beds.

# May 14, 2020

---

# Waldo

*e/him/his.* HE STARES at the top of the form. The pronoun is optional, and he doesn't have to fill it in, but still it stops him. *They/them.* That's not right. Maybe he's an *it.* His mind is swirling. He's home. Applying for virtual internships because everything is virtual. *Virtual: not physically existing as such but made by software to appear to do so.* Back after two and a half years away. He's been staying in Berkeley during summers and breaks, working in the lab, but the pandemic has changed everything. He hasn't left the house in weeks.

His father is downstairs, scrambling eggs. This has become an increasingly elaborate process that includes jalapeños, grated cheese, and either bacon or sausage, depending on what's in the fridge. Ever since Shenkman was furloughed—just last month—he has grown softer and gentler with each passing day. Waldo doesn't know what to make of this new version of his father. His mother would have helped him to figure it out. At the thought of his mother, something presses hard against his rib cage, from the inside out. This is grief, his last girlfriend told him. Her name is Sophie McNeil, and she's a year behind him at Berkeley. When they were together, she gave him books: Kübler-Ross on the five stages, Sontag on illness as metaphor, Pema Chödrön on things falling apart (his favorite).

He closes his laptop, looks out the window, across Division Street. He knows no one in the neighborhood anymore. He never really did—not after he was eleven and Dr. Wilf moved away. It was just the closed universe of the Shenkmans, and when his mom got sick it might have seemed that their world would shrink, but instead it expanded to include visiting nurses and, eventually, hospice. There were more people in their house than ever before; the bustle and efficiency of waiting for death. That hard thing presses even harder. He knows better than to fight it. Riding the wave of it is the only way. Isn't that what Pema would say? *You are the sky. Everything else—it's just the weather.*

"Waldo?"

His dad's voice from downstairs.

"Do you want some eggs?"

"No, I'm good."

Every day is the same. The same pajamas. The same socks. The same smells. The same tree outside his window, its branches just beginning to redden with budding leaves. Occasionally a few hardy people pass by, walking, jogging. They wear masks. Even if he knew them, he wouldn't be able to tell. Their masks sometimes have words: *VOTE,* or *BE POSITIVE,* or *I'M ACTUALLY SMILING.* It's impossible to recognize people based on their eyes alone. It's the lower part of their faces that reveals them: the set of a mouth, the clench of a jaw. Sometimes, in the distance, he will hear the wail of a siren. If he listens closely, birdsong. His mom always made sure the bird feeder was full. Though it has been empty for years now, generations of birds carry the memory and keep returning. They hop on the metal lip of the feeder and peck at the glass; tiny brown hungry bodies, open beaks.

The nights are the same, too. The same dinner, Waldo seated across the kitchen table from his father as they joylessly masticate some version of chicken and vegetables. And every night, as he has done since he was a boy, he opens his bedroom window and tilts his iPad—the very latest version bought with the money he makes as a research assistant—to the stars. *You are the sky,* he repeats again and again. *You are the sky. You are the sky.*

There is so much he doesn't know how to say, so he makes lists. He doesn't show anyone these lists. Who would he show? Sophie is gone, back to her parents in Minneapolis, and besides, *Listen to me Waldo, I can't, I just can't anymore.* The lists help him to order his insides. Maybe they'll become a record, a map for future explorers.

When I look at the sky, I am looking for my mother's face.
She is only the second dead person I have ever seen up
  close.
Last night was moonless so I could see the Andromeda
  Galaxy.
It's 2.2 million light-years away.
It will probably collide with our galaxy in 4 billion years.
When galaxies collide they pass through each other. Like
  ghosts.
My dad always stares at me when he thinks I don't know.
When will I be able to leave?
Upload Bumble profile.

Astrophysics doctoral program. Where?
Maybe get a kitten.
Check in with Dr. W.

That last item—*check in with Dr. W.*—is on every list he scribbles in his nearly indecipherable hand. He wants to tell Ben Wilf that he thinks of him all the time, but he hasn't called in a while because he avoids anything that makes him feel too much. Ever since he's known the role Dr. Wilf played in his being here, in his very existence, he has felt a secret kinship, something far beyond what he feels for his own father. He tolerates Shenkman. The memory of Shenkman's rage is lodged inside Waldo, not too far from the thing that pushes against his ribs—he can trace his way from one to the other, like the Great Square of Pegasus pointing to the Andromeda Galaxy.

Dr. Wilf—*call me Ben*—wrote to Waldo when he first heard that his mom had fallen ill during his freshman year of high school. A letter arrived, an actual letter sent through the actual mail. Ben Wilf does not have a physician's typical scrawl, and Waldo had the sense he had even chosen the stamp, a photo of the total eclipse of the sun, with great care. His handwriting was angular, elegant, befitting the man. *I want you to know that your mother is a very brave woman,* he wrote. The ink was blue, paper the color of stone. *I witnessed her bravery firsthand when you were born. And I really just want to say I'm sorry, Waldo. What you're going through is really hard, but it will be okay, or so I hope.*

He struck up something of a correspondence with Ben Wilf after that. Once Waldo was at Berkeley, they were in the same time zone, if not the same city. Ben was living in Los Angeles with his daughter. (Waldo has a dim memory of her from a morning a decade earlier, weeping, reeling, holding the lifeless woman he knew only as an old lady, nothing more.) Ben has granddaughters just a couple of years older than Waldo. *We're quarantining together. Staying safe.*


"Hey, Waldo—got a minute?"

His father fills the doorway. A slant of sunlight beams from the east-facing window onto the wood floor near his bed. Waldo can track the time of day based on where the light hits. He sits in this room all day, every day. His class on stellar structure equations will start in half an hour. Eighteen students in little onscreen boxes, some with fake backgrounds like beaches or mountains, others who are still in their pajamas, settled into their childhood beds. Each student's name is at the bottom of their box, along with, if they so wish (and most of them so wish), their pronouns. What was it his mother said to him a long time ago? She used words like *unique* and *special*. She called him a unicorn. She said this with love. This was during the years between when he ran away and when she got sick. She quit her job at the law firm because of him. She never told him that, not ever, but he heard his parents' whispers behind their closed bedroom door as loudly as if they were shouting into a megaphone: *you can't do this, Alice, we can't afford / you don't understand, I have to / what am I supposed to do / figure it out / I'm his mother and if I don't get him the help he needs—*

"Waldo?" Another interrupted reverie. "I asked if you have a minute?"

This is new Shenkman. Beaten-down, tired, gentle Shenkman. Old Shenkman would have taken two giant steps into his room and grabbed him by his shoulders. *Are you fucking deaf?* But that Shenkman has vanished into this person who might possibly be an avatar.

"Class starts in a few minutes," Waldo says.

"This won't take long."

His father sits down heavily on the bed and looks up at him.

"I'm selling the house," Shenkman says. "I mean, I have to sell the house."

Waldo nods. He doesn't have words, as usual. From the time he was eleven until he was fourteen, his mom drove him into the city three times a week for a variety of appointments: speech therapy, occupational therapy, cognitive behavioral therapy, talk therapy. She took him to an institute in a Midtown building to be evaluated over a series of days. Waldo didn't mind all the therapy. He didn't mind being evaluated. It made him feel special. Project Waldo. Operation Waldo. Besides, he was getting to spend time with his mother away from the tinderbox of 23 Division Street, a home in which a word, a gesture, could set the air on fire at any moment.

If anyone had asked him, amid all the questions they did ask him—crazy ones like whether he heard voices in his head (no), or if he had suicidal thoughts (no), or if he ever tried to hurt himself (no)—if anyone had asked him if he thought he needed all that therapy, he would have answered that in the negative as well. His mother was right. He was a unicorn. He didn't fit into a tidy container, like the other boys. His brain was wired differently. He just needed to survive his own childhood and he would be fine—more than fine. Now no one calls him dumb, dreamer, nose picker. Now they call him a boy genius, and point to the pioneering research he's done (as an undergraduate!) that has helped detect the faint gamma ray pulsations in a rapidly rotating neutron star.

"Waldo?" His father is . . . oh no. His father is crying. This does not compute. Two fat tears spill like train tracks down Shenkman's cheeks, then get stopped by the stubble of his beard.

"Dad—don't worry about it, I don't—"

Waldo glances at the shaft of sunlight. Class starts in twelve minutes.

"It's just that there's an opportunity," Shenkman says. "Because of these times. People are leaving the city. They want to live in Avalon. And towns like Avalon. So property values are skyrocketing. I'm buying a small place—a condo in Florida. Sarasota. You'll have your own room, of course. And besides, the whole thing is good for you too—money for graduate school."

Waldo doesn't tell Shenkman that he won't be going to Florida. And he won't be needing money for graduate school. He's already being recruited by the astrophysics doctoral programs at MIT, Harvard, and Stanford.

"Dad, I'm sorry."

What he means is that he needs to stop this conversation. But Shenkman chooses to hear other layers of meaning.

"It's not your fault, Waldo. I don't want you to think this is your fault."

In the slump of his father's shoulders, Waldo sees. The strange gentleness that has come over his father has a name: defeat. He has fought and fought, and now he is done fighting. He wants to retire to Sarasota and find a nice lady on one of those dating apps for people over fifty. There is freedom in surrender. Maybe this is what life does to some people. Sort of like a spider pulsar system. Two stars: a massive neutron star and a much smaller one that doesn't stand a chance. The neutron star is a pulsar, which over light-years will eventually overwhelm its companion until there is nothing left.

179

Waldo feels like crying himself, something he hasn't done since the day his mother died. He wishes he could put his arms around his father, but he doesn't. He can't. Newton's third law: for every action in nature, there is an equal and opposite reaction. A long time ago, his father raged at him and he ran away from home. He spent the night keeping Mrs. Wilf warm, until her body stiffened and grew cold in his tiny arms. The old doctor who brought him into the world became bound to him as if by intricate, invisible thread. His mom became his advocate and his savior. And maybe—here he squeezes his eyes shut—maybe it cost her too much. Maybe it *was* his fault.

His father stands. "We'll have to pack up the house," he says. "The new owners take possession in two weeks."


Waldo Shenkman, narrow, long-lashed, delicate boy genius, boots up his laptop and makes sure it's plugged in for his three-hour class. But before he signs in to his professor's Zoom room, he picks up his handwritten list. He thinks about what it will feel like to pack up this—the only house he has ever known, the place where he was born, the place where his mother died—and quickly thumbs a text without giving it a moment's thought. A moment's thought would stop him, and he doesn't want to be stopped. *Hi Ben it's Waldo. This is a crazy idea and I know we're in the middle of a pandemic but is there any way I can come visit you?* He is, in this very moment, as aligned with the trajectory of his life as he has ever been. He hits send, then whispers: *I am the sky, I am the sky, I am the sky.*

# December 22, 2010

---

# *Benjamin*

H IS BRIDE. HIS wife. His life. She slipped away slowly. Parts of Mimi remained present for so long that it had been possible to have minutes, even hours, of pleasure together. Her smell: fresh, milky, a hint of the oil (the immortelle flower) she spread over her face each morning. She had always hummed—while cooking, gardening, showering, walking—and she still hummed, though now the tunes had changed. It took Ben a while to realize what was different, and when he did it was with a sharp pang: these were now childhood melodies. She was careening backward in time. Mimi nestled her head into his shoulder whenever he visited her. She spread her crocheted blanket across their laps as they sat on a sofa in the vast living room of Avalon Hills, tucked them in as if they were companions on a long ski lift ride, keeping warm, dangling high above the mountains.

His breath catches. He's behind the wheel of the Volvo. No damned way one of his kids is going to drive. Not now. Not when his Mimi is—he swallows hard—*missing*. They didn't wake him up. They let him sleep while his wife was in peril. Who did they think they were? What right? He can't recall ever being so angry.

"It was a judgment call, Dad," Sarah says.

She's next to him. Theo's in the backseat.

"Poor judgment," Ben says tersely.

"We just thought it would be best if you—"

"I'm not a child, Sarah."

This is what happens with grown children and their parents. He's seen it in his practice. They begin to take over. They think they know best. Meanwhile, where the hell has either of them been—for years now? Theo, he forgives more than he does Sarah. Theo's weaker. More fragile in nature. But Sarah's tough. She has resources. She's visited, what . . . twice since they moved Mimi to the memory unit? Yes, she has the twins. But she also has help, and a husband who, let's face it, has time on his hands.

Ben gives his head a shake, clearing it. Rage will do him no good right now, and yet it's all he feels. At his children. At Avalon Hills. It's unconscionable that a resident could go missing. Isn't that what they advertise—what he's spent most of his retirement savings paying for? Safety. Supervision. Security. How could Mimi have slipped out unnoticed? Though he isn't aware of it, he's tracing the same route Theo and Sarah drove just a few hours earlier; the Exxon station, the Stop & Shop, the mini-malls lined with smoke shops, delis, Thai restaurants, nail salons, depressing real estate that hadn't existed when the kids were little. *Mimi. Darling. Send me a sign. I need a sign.* Ridiculous, of course. He has seen the insides of many human bodies, and he doesn't believe in signs, or God. But still Ben tries to merge his consciousness with the greater consciousness, as if perhaps there were clues to be seen, spirits to guide him.

Now there are more cars on the road. The early morning rush has begun. The denizens of Avalon are being dropped at the train station for their commute to the city, or parking in their reserved spots; those who drive into town, or work in one of those corporate parks elsewhere in Westchester, are heading to the parkway. A familiar car passes in the opposite direction, a familiar face at the wheel. The boy Waldo's dad, Ben recognizes. The wife is next to him. *Steady, Alice. Push again, dear.* He registers something he will remember and understand later. They look as haunted as he is, their jaws tense and rigid, eyes wide.

Mimi loved the water. Could she have made her way to the river? He shudders at the thought. It's too far. And terrifying, the thought of her leaning over an embankment. She would have felt a familiarity on the commercial streets of Avalon. My God, she had spent enough time there over the years. They'd chosen the house on Division Street because it was only a short walk from downtown; it had felt less suburban, somehow, not to have to get into a car for every errand. Now, as Ben drives the length of Main Street for the fourth time, he looks at the shuttered shops. The deli is the only business open at this hour, serving up egg-and-cheese sandwiches to commuters. He feels utterly powerless—an unfamiliar feeling. There's usually something he can do. A path forward. A way of figuring things out. But she could be anywhere.

His cell phone vibrates in his pants pocket, startling him. He struggles to fish it out. Sarah reaches for it and he swats her hand away.

"Ben Wilf," he says. His voice comes out in a croak. He clears his throat.

"Dr. Wilf, we've found the tracking device Mrs. Wilf was wearing." This is the liaison Avalon Hills has assigned to communicate with the family. A social worker. As if this were something that can be managed.

Ben steers with one hand, puts his phone on speaker with the other.

"Unfortunately she was somehow able to remove it," says the social worker. "And the signal stopped transmitting, so it won't be of help in locating—"

"Where was it?" Sarah cuts in loudly. "Where was the tracking device?"

The briefest of pauses.

"On the side of the parkway. Not far from the mall."

In stunned silence, Ben makes an illegal U-turn. Sarah is, for once, at a loss for words. She turns her narrow shoulders away from him and stares out the window. Theo raises his knees to his chest and rocks himself the way he did when he was a little boy. Ben drives quickly, deftly. When he used to prep for surgery, he would mentally consult his checklist of safety protocols, which, of course, he knew well, but going down the list helped him to put his mind in order. Mimi on the parkway. Mimi in the snow on the parkway. Near the mall. Mimi tearing off her GPS bracelet on the parkway. He remembers the blade falling, the moment he realized she had Alzheimer's. But his wife has still been here, even if only a fractional part of her. He's still had his Mimi. A line from an Emily Dickinson poem drifts like a lyric through his head: *My life closed twice before its close.* Is this it? The second time?

# *Shenkman*

ALICE IS SEETHING. He can feel the heat coming off
her, as if the bottomless fury she is directing at him
has a temperature. The tip of her nose and the tops of
her ears are red, her eyes swollen. He had shaken her awake—
which took some doing, given the Ambien—and hadn't even
tried to sugarcoat it, or protect her. What was the point? It's
a catastrophe. The biggest one since New Year's Eve dusk
eleven years earlier. Just three words: *Waldo ran away.* That
first catastrophe turned out okay. He dares for a second to
hope that this one will too.

Alice doesn't have to say it: *It's your fault. Your temper.
You're out of control. You scare him. It's no wonder.* She
doesn't have to say the words, because he already knows.
Shenkman knows. He doesn't deserve his magical son. It's as
if the universe made a colossal mistake. He was not meant to
be a shepherd for this boy. He defaults to bargaining mode:
if they find Waldo, if Waldo is in one piece, okay, alive,
unharmed, he will commit to change. Real change. Maybe

there's a rehab for rageful fathers. Or maybe something else is wrong with him. He doesn't drink (that's Alice's department) or do drugs, he doesn't watch internet porn (at least not much) and he's never hired a hooker, he doesn't gamble—but he is sick inside. *Forgive me,* he says to the god he hasn't thought about since his bar mitzvah. *Just this once.* He'd give a limb. He'd cut his life short by a decade. Or two.

"We don't even know what we're looking for," Alice says. He has never heard her sound like this. All softness gone. Every last bit. Her voice is like an elastic cord stretched to its limits. "You're driving in circles. We don't know where the fuck to go."

Shenkman kicks himself for not installing a tracking app on the iPad. He could have easily done that—if he could have foreseen an event such as this, which, of course, he could not. Waldo is not quite eleven. Eleven-year-olds don't need to be tracked, because their parents always know where they are. The farthest Waldo had ever ventured was outside on Division Street, just last night. Now he could be anywhere. Shenkman imagines Waldo getting on a train. Would anyone stop him to ask where his parents are? He knows Waldo took his allowance money with him. How far could he get on ten bucks? Shenkman has never been a believer in the kindness of strangers, and now more than ever, the world feels like a vast, cold place. Dog eat dog.

As they head down Main Street, Alice swivels her head from one side to the other as steady as the sweep of a surveillance camera. They pass a car he knows. An old beige Volvo. You don't see too many of those in aspirational suburbia. The old doctor is behind the wheel, a younger, dark-haired woman next to him. It's just a blur, an instant. Shenkman feels it in a flash, a wish—as if he himself were again a child—that the old doctor might be able to pull another miracle out of his sleeve.

"I want a divorce," Alice says. She's staring straight ahead now, her fists burrowed into her own belly as if she might be able to tuck Waldo back into a safe place. "I'm saying it now. No matter what happens. I don't want to be with you anymore."

Shenkman looks over at Alice. It's her fear talking. It's her completely justified anger at him. She'll come around.

He swings through the parking lot of the Stop & Shop, then drives to the entrance where all the carts are lined up. You never know.

"You've got nothing to say?"

She refuses to look at him.

"Alice, let's not do this. Not now. All our focus—"

His phone's ringtone—the opening beats of Lady Gaga's "Poker Face"—blasts through the car speakers.

"Jesus!" Shenkman explodes. It scares him. He jabs a finger at the steering wheel to accept.

"Hello?"

The hissing sound of a cell phone.

"Fucking sales call—"

He's about to jab his finger again to hang up.

"Shenkman, hey, buddy. It's Jack Lindgren."

He and Alice look at each other, baffled. *Who's that?* she mouths.

"Listen, dude—this is weird, but your son? Waldo? He just wrote me," Lindgren says.

"What the hell?"

"I guess I was the last person who emailed you, so—"

"Where is he?" Alice screams.

Shenkman puts a hand on her thigh. *Just shut up.*

"He asked me to call you. I don't know what this means, but he asked me to tell you that he's at the mall."

Shenkman floors it out of the parking lot.

"His email sounded really freaked out, man. I'm sorry to—"

Alice speaks up.

"Thank you." She begins to weep. "Just thank you, thank you."

He weaves in and out of the early morning traffic. His teeth are clenched so tightly they might break, and he can feel a vein throbbing at his temple. The colors around him intensify: the awning of the dry cleaner a brighter red; the graffiti on the overpass neon blue. Signs are everywhere. Signs and wonders. He doesn't have any idea what any of it means. Just this: His son is alive. His son is at the mall. His wife is crying by his side, and he risks taking her hand. Maybe, just maybe, they will be given another chance.

# *Waldo*

HIS BATTERY IS down to 5 percent. Outside the playhouse he hears nothing but the onrushing wind. Stores in the mall won't open for hours. It's after dawn now. A single shaft of sunlight trickles through a crack between the cedar planks. It's as if someone had lit a candle. For the first time, he can make out a small ladder that must lead to the spiral slide. If he were home, he'd be getting ready for school, double-checking that he had all his homework and textbooks in his backpack. He always forgets something. His mom would have lunch ready for him, the same thing every day, the only thing he'll eat: two slices of ham and two slices of Swiss cheese on organic white bread. No mustard. No mayo. A wax paper bag of carrot sticks. A soft chocolate chip cookie. A note with $x$'s and $o$'s and a smiley face. Sometimes she forgets the carrots or the cookie, but she never forgets the smiley face.

Lists help. Any kind of lists. The lady's lips are now blue. It's been a long time since she's moved, and her breath is no longer making clouds in the cold. Her arm fell across his chest as she slept, and as he lifts it he feels its stiffness and its weight. He's crying, though he hardly even notices. His eyelashes stick to his cheeks. The old lady is dead, he knows this. He knows this even though he's never seen a dead person except in the movies. If this were a movie, maybe someone would rescue her. She'd spring back to life. He would give anything right now for her to open her eyes and call him the wrong name again.

*Lady?* he whispers as if there were other presences in the playhouse. *Lady, who are you? Why did you come in here?*

Maybe if he keeps talking to her, he can reverse time. Maybe dying isn't real. Maybe his words can breathe life into her. Maybe this is a dream. He's still crying, he can't stop. This is his fault. The lady came because of him. She thought he was somebody else. Somebody named Theo.

"My name is Waldo Shenkman." He keeps talking. "I'm almost eleven. I'm in the sixth grade at Avalon Elementary. I live on Division Street."

The lady doesn't stir. If she could, if she were still in the land of the living, she would tell Waldo that she knows just who he is. That she watched him from across the street as he became a toddler, a kindergartner shuttled in and out of his parents' cars, a wee boy who emanated a special quality that made you want to reach him across time and space. That she swelled with a quiet pride that her husband had a role in ushering this perfect soul into the world. *It was a close call.* But the lady is gone.

"Lady, we have to do something." He corrects himself. "I have to do something."

On the home screen his dad has a bunch of apps, mostly work stuff, which means money. Waldo hasn't paid attention to any of them, because the iPad has only one function as far as he's concerned. He swoops a finger across the mailbox. There's only 3 percent battery left now. He hits the first name in his father's inbox.

Hello whoever this is you don't know me but my name is Waldo Shenkman. Would you please call my parents and tell them that I'm in the mall. I'm scared. I'm so scared and so cold. And something has happened. They have to come find me. Please call them. Thank you and I'm sorry.

If this random person receives his email, or writes him back, he won't know. The iPad screen goes black and lifeless. The lady is dead and the iPad is dead. For the rest of his life, these next minutes will leave an imprint on Waldo Shenkman. He leans back—all sixty-three pounds of him—against the wall so new it smells like wood shavings. He doesn't know if his parents are coming. He can't feel his fingers or toes. Maybe he's going to die too. Maybe he's going to become a dead star, like the Crab Nebula. The Crab Nebula still has a crushed heart beating at its core. It pulses and pulses. It's in an ultradense sphere that makes it a hundred billion times stronger than steel. He's seen a time-lapse movie. The crushed beating heart ripples outward in waves, and looks a lot like the sonogram video his mom once showed him. *That's you! That's Waldo.*

He is in the presence of something so much bigger than he is—as big as the whole sky—he can feel it. To even try to understand is to explode something inside his head, so he doesn't try. He sits and stays as still and as quiet as he knows how. The lady may be dead, but the playhouse is filled with her life. He looks down at her papery, translucent skin, and somehow he is no longer scared. Not of the lady. Not of death.

She's at a threshold—hovering, diaphanous, all the selves she has ever been. In the playhouse there is a small child, smaller than Waldo. A teenage girl walks down a city street. A young woman falls in love. A wife becomes a mother. A bright, loving presence. The whole crowd encircles them. It isn't scary. It isn't anything at all. Maybe every person has an uncrushable heart a hundred billion times stronger than steel. He watches the dance of light and shadow on the walls. Someday, this will be helpful to him.

# Sarah

HER FATHER IS driving too fast but, she has to admit, expertly. What had she and Theo been thinking? Treating him like a child. Like someone who needed to be protected, who needed a good night's sleep while their mother had gone missing. *Poor judgment,* he'd said. Perhaps the harshest thing Ben has ever said to her. It felt like a slap—because it was true, truer than he can know. Poor judgment has become her middle name. Her two middle names.

It's still far too early to reach Dr. Baum. And besides, what can he possibly tell her? He's not big on advice. *On the side of the parkway. Remember we took pictures. Not far from the mall. Call back, cunt.* For just a moment she closes her eyes, pictures her girls. They are her only safe place. But wait, she could lose them. Could she lose them? No. She's the mother. And the breadwinner. No matter what she's done. Her mind is sharp, settling into producer mode the same way she knows her father settles into doctor mode. What needs to be fixed? And how to fix it?

Her poor mother. A terrible thought: she honestly doesn't know whether it would be better to find Mimi alive or dead. The only certain thing is that they must find her. Mimi is a husk of her former self. If Sarah's honest with herself—and she makes a practice of honesty if not exactly discipline—she has already grieved her mother. Mimi has been gone for years. The first time Sarah had realized just how far gone was after she'd called home and they'd spoken for fifteen, twenty minutes. Sarah had hung up, happy and relieved. They'd spoken of all the usual things: Mimi asked after Peter, and Sarah's friends, each by name; she suggested a new recipe for zucchini bread. Maybe things weren't as bad as their father had led them to believe. But then her phone rang. It was Mimi, her voice light and musical as always. She was just checking in, she said. It had been so long since they'd spoken.

Sarah had visited only twice since Ben moved Mimi to the memory unit. She knows this is a failure on every level. She sucks, she really does. Both times she saw her mother, she was filled with a mute, infantile fury, as if perhaps Mimi could just snap out of it. As if she were playacting. It was impossible, that this person could look like her mother, sound like her mother, but not be her mother. It's been a long time since Sarah has kidded herself that a fleeting, familiar smile or gesture means a damned thing. These are reflexes, the way newborns smile when they pass gas. Her father and even her brother have held on far too long to the idea that there is an essence of Mimi that remains.

"The parkway." Ben's jaw bunches. There's going to be hell to pay.

"We'll find her, Dad." Theo breaks his silence.

Ben slows to a crawl as they approach the mall. His

knuckles are white against the wheel. A tractor trailer blares its horn as it passes in the left lane.

"Fuck you," Ben mutters. "Sorry. Not you, Theo."

It's possible his children have never heard him curse before.

They look and look, and see nothing, of course. Footprints would long ago have been covered by snow. Mimi had walked along this exact narrow shoulder of the parkway. She had somehow ripped off her tracking device. What had she been wearing? What was on her feet? The last time Sarah saw her, Mimi's long stride had become a shuffle. She shakes off the image of her mother struggling against the howling wind.

Ben turns into the mall's entrance. Nothing has been plowed. Hours from now, the parking lot will be jammed with last-minute Christmas shoppers. But now, it's a pristine field of white, close to a foot high. The Volvo loses traction and fishtails.

"Shit," Ben says under his breath.

They're acres away from the shops.

He guns the motor and the wheels spin.

"Dad—Dad, stop."

Ben is breathing heavily. He guns it once more. The air smells of rubber.

"We're going to have to walk."

They abandon the car, leaving it at an angle, and begin trudging toward the shops. Ben's got his big snow-shoveling boots on, along with all the requisite winter layers, thank God. Theo, too, has managed to scare up something resembling winter gear. Sarah's still in her thin cashmere coat, so perfect for chilly LA evenings. Its hem drags in the snow and she hoists the whole soggy mess to her waist. At least she's wearing knee-high rubber rain boots, which probably once were Mimi's.

The shops are lit up like a mirage in the distance. Why on earth would Mimi have found her way here? She never liked the mall, and largely managed to avoid it; she preferred instead to give her business to the mom-and-pop shops in town. What would have drawn her here? Certainly not the mannequins in Neiman Marcus's windows—she had always sniffed at the absurdity of high fashion—or the dull holiday decorations at Pottery Barn.

The uppermost layer of snow whips around them. The mall is anchored by two department stores—Neiman's on one end, Macy's on the other. In between, most everything is indoors. Hundreds? There must be hundreds of shops. You could buy a puppy. You could get your ears pierced. You could buy an aspirational designer handbag. What the fuck are they doing? They don't even know for sure that Mimi made it here. Maybe she's still on the parkway. Maybe she ducked under the guardrail and is wandering through some random backyard.

It's Theo who sees it first.

"Play Heaven!" The wind carries his voice. "There." He squints and gestures with one mittened hand.

Off to the side of the mall, the store looks out of place, its entrance rough and fanciful, like the portal to a magic tree house. The three of them push forward. The model playhouse is off to the left side of the entrance. Theo's right. It's the only spot in the whole mall that looks like their mother. Home-made, rustic, inviting.

Snow has spilled into the tops of her rubber boots, pooling around her feet. She can hardly feel herself move. They're almost there. If this is hard for her, what can it be like for her dad? He leans into the wind, one foot in front of the other. Something fierce and protective ignites within her. Her dad.

Her beloved dad. He has to have the strength to withstand whatever comes next.

"Dad? You okay?" Sarah shouts.

Ben doesn't respond. His bushy eyebrows are coated with snow. Behind them, the steady whoosh of cars and trucks on the parkway; people going about their daily business.

As they draw closer, there's the closed door displaying the crooked welcome sign, and a shudder runs through her. Sarah knows. She pictures her mother duck inside, seeking shelter. It makes all kinds of sense. If anything can make sense. She gets there first, pushes the door open, then crouches as she fits herself through.

The light outside reflected off the snow is so bright that it takes a moment for her eyes to adjust. It's snug and shadowy, with one angle of sharp sunlight like a laser onto what looks like a pile of rags. At first she thinks: Nothing. No one. She was wrong. They were wrong. Mimi isn't here.

"Hello?" A soft voice. A boy's voice.

Her breath catches in her throat.

"Who are you?" The little voice quavers.

She wheels around, then sees him. A small boy kneeling in the darkest corner.

"Don't be scared," she says out of instinct. She is a mother, after all.

Ben is now trying to squeeze through the door. He turns to the side, shimmies through. Before the door creaks shut behind him, light fills the small playhouse for just a moment, like a strobe flash.

"Waldo?" Ben stares at the boy.

"Dr. Wilf?" The boy begins to weep.

"Waldo, my God, boy. What in the world—"

"Dr. Wilf, the lady—"

*The lady.* Sarah looks again at the heap of rags and sees the long gray waves, scraggly now but unmistakable. *The lady.* And this small boy knows her father. Her mind goes white and staticky, and she trips as she takes a step in her rubber boots to the heap of rags that is her mother. Now she is upon her. Grabbing her. Holding her. Lifting her. And she hears herself saying *Please, please, please,* even though she doesn't think she's speaking aloud.

"Sarah, don't, she may be hurt—" Ben is on his knees next to her. "Mimi, what, I can't—"

Sarah can't bring herself to say it. She opens her mouth and what comes out instead of words—*she's gone, Dad*—is a noise, a keening sound she has never heard or known. She was fine. She was so fine. She had grieved. She was done. She'd considered that it might be better for them to find her mother dead. And here she is. Here they are.

Ben reaches over and touches Mimi's cheek.

*No, no, no,* Ben whispers. *Oh, darling. Not like this.*

"Dr. Wilf? You know the lady?" The boy's eyes fill up half his face.

Theo sways by the open playhouse door, blocking the light. He can't squeeze inside.

"Dad?"

Ben's head is buried in his hands. When he removes them, they are damp with his tears.

"Dad?" Theo, again.

"Stop, Theo," Sarah wails, "can't you—"

"Other people are here."

# Shenkman

**T**HERE'S ONLY ONE store at the mall Waldo knows. That play place that sold them the knotted pine thing that is slowly rotting in their backyard. Thing cost as much as a trip to Cancún. Waldo was never into it. Yet one more way Shenkman has tried and failed to make his son in his own image.

The all-weather tires on the Lexus skid and then find traction, plowing almost professionally through the parking lot, past an abandoned car parked at an angle, hazards flashing. Footprints lead away from the car in the snow.

"Faster," Alice says, with that new tightness in her voice. "Who knows how long he's been here. If he's even here. You're so sure of yourself."

Shenkman is indeed certain of only this one thing. Alice acts like she has a secret passageway into Waldo's brain, but no matter what, he, Shenkman, is the father. And fathers know things. Even when fathers completely screw up and allow every last bit of their own damaged souls to infect their children, still there is a connection. Like the deep layer of dissolvable sutures his knee doctor used when he repaired that tear in his meniscus, there are threads beneath the surface binding him to his boy, and his boy to him.

A shape comes into focus in the whiteness, a hulking large person standing at the entrance to a model play structure. Shenkman slams the brakes, not the best move, which causes the SUV to skate in a half circle before stopping.

"Asshole," Alice mutters.

He jumps from the car, running as much as it's possible to run in a foot of snow. The sun is rising in the early morning sky, and he can see that the large person is a man. This man is wearing a parka with a hoodie underneath, sopping wet, stretched over his head. He's clapping his mittened hands together and appears to be in a dreadful state, his mouth a maw of grief. What has he done? What has he done to Waldo? A catalog of horrible images plays out in Shenkman's mind. Every child on the nightly news. Every child for whom there's an Amber Alert. Every child on a milk carton. Those poor, luckless families facing the worst.

Shenkman—there is no other word for it—Shenkman roars. All the blood in his body rushes to his head as he grabs the man by his shoulders and shakes him. He is a wolf now, Shenkman, and even though this man easily outweighs him by eighty pounds, he is prey in his teeth, no match for the force of his rage.

"Where is he?"

"Who?" the man pants.

"You fucking monster, where's my son?"

Shenkman shoves him hard, and the man yells as he hits the ground.

"Dad?" A tiny voice from a tiny boy. Waldo sticks his head

out of the playhouse door, and the rest of his body follows. "Dad, Mom?"

Alice nearly collapses. Her knees start to buckle, and she grabs on to Shenkman, righting herself. Their boy. Alive. In one piece. Emerging from the dark interior of the playhouse, clutching the iPad to his chest. Alice lurches toward Waldo, grasping at him as if he might disappear again.

She turns to the man on the ground, who is now struggling to his feet. His chin is scraped and bleeding.

"You kidnapped him." It comes out in a hiss.

"Mom! Mom, stop! I don't even know him!" Waldo's voice shakes.

The man stands tall and removes his hoodie. He looks levelly at Shenkman and Alice, his face torn and gentle. He's still breathing hard.

"My parents are in there." He gestures to the playhouse door, which has swung shut once again. "My mother—" His voice breaks.

"It's the old lady," Waldo rushes to say. "The old lady got lost and she—"

Shenkman stares at Theo. Nothing makes sense. A lost old lady? This strange man's parents? He fixates on the crooked welcome sign. Nothing has ever looked less welcoming.

"And then Dr. Wilf—"

Shenkman and Alice look at each other over Waldo's head. *Go across the street and ask my wife for my medical bag.* Shenkman looks again at the man he just attacked and sees, beneath the heavy bloat, the combined fine features of a couple who on one long-ago afternoon filled their lives with ineffable grace. *Okay, Alice. Push on the count of three.*

"I'll show you," Waldo says.

"Waldo, no!" From Alice.

"It's okay," Shenkman says almost against his will. He's being carried along by something he doesn't understand, but he knows this is an opportunity to do the right thing. Whatever that means.

He follows his son—has he ever followed Waldo?—as he leans his narrow shoulder into the playhouse door and pushes it open. Then Shenkman crouches down and squeezes himself inside. He hears the sound of weeping before he apprehends what he's seeing. There, in the corner, sitting on the floor, is Benjamin Wilf. He's holding—my God, he's holding Mrs. Wilf (Shenkman never knew her first name) against him. A woman around Shenkman's age is next to them. Small, dark hair, heart-shaped face. She looks up at him.

"Who the hell are you?" she says.

"This is my dad," says Waldo.

Ben Wilf raises his head.

"We've met," he says quietly.

He turns to Shenkman. "Apparently your boy was here." He says. "With my wife."

"I ran away," Waldo says.

"So did my wife."

"She was a nice lady, Dr. Wilf," says Waldo. "She kept calling me by the wrong name."

"What did she call you?"

Waldo hesitates. "Theo," he finally says.

Ben Wilf nods as if this makes sense.

"She was confused."

The small, dark-haired woman is holding her iPhone, which glows in the dim light of the playhouse.

"Dad? I think we should call—who do you call? Not 911, right? Since she's—"

204

"We do call 911," Ben says. "They have to pronounce her dead."

"But you're a doctor—"

"I'm her husband, Sarah." Ben Wilf swallows hard. The daughter strikes Shenkman as a tough cookie, despite her tears. She's someone you would want with you in an emergency. She'd lead the way out of the burning building, the avalanche. She has the watchful eyes of a survivor.

She's speaking into her phone now. *I'm calling to report a death.* She delivers the facts. Name. Relationship. Location. Shenkman thinks for the first time of what it must have been like for Waldo to watch Mrs. Wilf as she passed. How long were they together in this shack? The woman is wearing a knitted hat and tube socks. Shenkman realizes with a start that these are familiar.

"I tried to help her, Dr. Wilf," Waldo says. His voice, so high and piercing. So young.

"I'm sure you did, Waldo."

"I talked to her about the stars. Just like we did, you and me."

The stars, the goddamned fucking stars. Shenkman feels the boil, the thing he's never been able to control. And what does Waldo mean, *just like we did*? How has Wilf spent time with his son? But something stops him from spilling over into rage—that same something he doesn't understand. Maybe it's the presence of the dead. Maybe it's the residue of the terror he felt, the certainty that he had lost the thing most precious to him. Even though he missed the memo on the care and handling of that most precious thing.

"Canis Major," Wilf says gently. "A very cool constellation. I remember, Waldo. You told me that Sirius is the brightest star in the night sky."

In the light now seeping into the playhouse, it's possible to see something Shenkman tends not to see: Waldo blushing with pride.

"What else did you tell Mimi about? I'd love to know."

Waldo's words come in a rush.

"I showed her Taurus. And Alpha Persei. I showed her exactly where we were in the universe. I think it made her happy. She smiled."

Wilf offers a slow nod.

"She would have liked that, Waldo. You did good."

They all fall silent. The hushed interior of the playhouse has become, at least for these few moments, a sacred place. A place where Shenkman has put down the burden of his personality and is at one with these people, even the deceased. He remembers her light, arresting eyes, her unusual wide mouth. She'd had an openness to her when she answered the ring of the doorbell nearly eleven years ago, a sense that whatever was on the other side was going to delight her.

A siren pierces the quiet, drawing closer. Why bother with a siren? People and their protocols.

"They're here, Dad."

Ben Wilf nods, but makes no move.

"We should go outside. Give them room."

"You all go," Wilf says. He is weary, Shenkman sees. As if he might just curl up next to his wife and be taken, too.

They file out, first Sarah, then Waldo, and finally Shenkman. Alice is standing there with her arm around the large man, whose name, Shenkman now knows, is Theo. In the distance, the third vehicle to enter the mall's parking lot on this morning makes its way across the sun-warmed snow. An EMT truck, red lights flashing.

"Hey listen," Shenkman says, approaching Theo, who

shrinks back almost imperceptibly. "I'm really sorry." He isn't used to apologizing without a caveat, a defense. But he doesn't even try. The man has just lost his mother. No, Shenkman couldn't have known. But still, he might have taken a beat. Maybe asked a question before reacting and becoming violent.

"I'm sorry I tackled you." He pauses. Alice is glaring at him. "And I'm so sorry about your mom."

Alice lets go of Theo, who walks over to his sister. They huddle together as the EMT truck pulls up to the playhouse and two guys in black coats and boots jump out. A radio squawks.

"She's in there." Sarah's voice is carried by the wind. "Our dad is with her."

# *Alice*

S HE SITS IN the back of the Lexus with Waldo, the way
she used to when he was an infant in a backward-facing
car seat and that's what a good mother did. Shenkman
is chauffeur. She notes the back of his square head, the straight
line of his shoulders, built up from several lifetimes on that
machine of his. Alice knows that this is the time to purge herself of every hate-filled thought. *I want a divorce.* She can't
divorce Shenkman. Maybe if there were no Waldo. Definitely,
if there were no Waldo. But her boy is right here next to
her, thank God. She breathes him in: wet wool, unbrushed
teeth, the still-sweet sweat of childhood. They are a family.
Stewards of this boy who is holding her hand, his fingers
trembling. Shenkman is driving cautiously, unusually so, as if
to prove to her that he can control his road rage, at least. No
*fuck you, douchebag*, no flipping of the bird, or tailgating
some asshole in a Porsche who cuts in front of him.

"Do you think it's true, Dad?" Waldo asks. The iPad is
tucked under his arm. He's never going to let it out of his

sight again, if he can help it. If *she* can help it. Alice understands that for Waldo, the device is a lifeline. "Do you think it's true that I helped the lady—Mrs. Wilf?"

Alice watches the back of Shenkman's head. *Say the right thing. For once.*

Shenkman takes a moment instead of his usual barking back. "I do, actually." He clears his throat multiple times, an old nervous habit. Even though Alice can't see his face, she can feel him searching for the words. Shenkman used to do this when they were first together—when he was trying to express his love for her and didn't know how. Her heart aches for him, just a tiny bit.

"I think this falls under the category of things we can't understand," he says. "But let me try. I have a story to tell you, Waldo. You know Dr. Wilf?"

"Don't be mad at me, Dad. Last night I was showing him—"

Shenkman shakes his head.

"I'm not mad. But I want you to know that you've met Dr. Wilf before. A long time ago."

His eyes meet Alice's in the rearview mirror. *Yes, this. Go ahead.* She's always wondered if they should tell Waldo about the day he was born. Shenkman and she rarely discuss it anymore, but it's a current that runs between them: at school plays, when they grab each other's hand as Waldo recites his lines; at the winter solstice concert, his little face glowing in the third row; at the educational psychologist appointment, when they were first told that Waldo's IQ was genius level. It all so easily could have been otherwise. She knows that she and Shenkman both carry in their lonely hearts the shadow story—the one in which Benjamin Wilf was not across the street unloading groceries from his car, the one in

210

which the ambulance came too late. The one in which Waldo Shenkman did not live to become this strange and serious, miraculous boy.

"Dr. Wilf is the reason you're here," Shenkman says. "Dr. Wilf saved your life."

As Shenkman tells Waldo just the bare minimum of detail, trying not to scare him—*you came early, we couldn't get to the hospital in time, Dr. Wilf delivered you right there on the kitchen floor*—Alice notes that Waldo doesn't seem in the least surprised. He's nodding his head, as if this were not news to him. Maybe he's in shock? Maybe this is too much?

Alice rushes in to fill the gap. "We don't need to talk about it now if you don't want to," she says. "We can just—"

"Yeah," Waldo says. He's looking straight ahead, though not at anything in particular. "Everything is connected. Everything. The lady. The doctor. Me. You. It's like we're part of a galactic supercluster."

Alice looks to see whether Shenkman's shoulders are inching up. *Let it go.* She beams the thought at him. But she can already see that he's going to let it go.

"Tell me more," Shenkman says, his voice more gentle than she's heard it in years. "Tell me about the galactic supercluster."

"A supercluster is a large group of smaller galaxy clusters. Our supercluster is called Laniakea." Waldo speaks rapidly, as if Shenkman might shut him down. "Superclusters are . . . well, they're the largest known structures in the whole universe. Not all galaxies are part of superclusters. Some of them are way off by themselves, alone in the void of space."

He sounds almost as if he were reciting something from a textbook by memory. Like he's trying to say something bigger, deeper: private thoughts for which he doesn't have language. *Everything is connected.*

They're in downtown Avalon now, stopped at a light. The sun is high and bright; last night's snow is melting. People are out walking in their big puffy coats and boots, and Alice feels a piercing tenderness for all of them. There's the lady who owns the dry cleaner, unlocking the door to her business. And there's their insurance guy, coming out of the health food store with a smoothie. Benjamin Wilf kneeled beside her once, long ago. *Give it all you've got, Alice.* Waldo kept Mimi Wilf warm and made her feel safe at the end of her life. Maybe all of them are simply a chorus of souls, light touching light.

They pass house after house. Alice is transfixed. She looks at each front walk, each door and window. An old brick house surrounded by boxwoods wrapped in burlap. A yellow Victorian with newspapers piled on the front porch. Empty flower beds. A broken fence. Has she ever paid attention before? No—she's always been too busy, she and Shenkman, to notice that they are part of a neighborhood made up of all sorts of people who are living their lives in this particular place, at this particular time. Who knows about the impact of any action, any decision or omission, however seemingly random or small?

Why, for instance, had they never invited the Wilfs to dinner? Why, in fact, had they avoided the other couple, as if they had been privy to something too intimate? It would have been so easy. She could have slid a note under their door, or picked up the phone. Alice imagines now what it might have been like to gather around the kitchen table, faces warmed by candlelight, wine flowing. Their shared experience might have become the basis for a friendship, closeness, rather than a source of embarrassment. She hadn't even known that Benjamin Wilf had been living by himself in that house for these past years—that his wife had Alzheimer's. He must have been so lonely. And here they were, the selfish, fearful, oh-so-private Shenkmans, on the hamster wheel of their lives. Work, produce, strive, grasp, sleep, repeat.

No more. She's going to do everything differently, from here on in. Quit her job—this comes upon her with absolute certainty, though never once before had she ever considered it. Maybe get Shenkman into therapy. Or couples therapy for the two of them. Definitely therapy for Waldo. She almost laughs. Therapy for all! She's going to reach out to Dr. Wilf, learn to be a good friend and neighbor. Here she has been so afraid, so busy trying to shore up and protect their lives that she has forgotten how to live.

Beginning with today. Today she's going to spend the afternoon making a lasagna. No, two lasagnas. She'll drop one off at Benjamin Wilf's front door. She will take a walk with Waldo at dusk and watch the setting sun turn the world pink. As the stars populate the evening sky, she will let him tell her all about it.

"Mom?" Waldo's hand has stopped trembling and is finally warming up in hers. "It wasn't scary. I mean, it was scary being in the dark and cold and everything, but when the lady, Mrs. Wilf, died, it was like everything had no beginning and no end. Like we were light-years away and here, all at the same time."

As they round the corner onto Division Street, Alice is consumed by her own sense of urgency. She needs to get it right, immediately. There is no time to waste. Without thinking, she puts a hand on her lower belly, on the exact spot where, in just a few years, a single cell will fail to correctly divide. She will still be a young woman when her son's words return to her. She will recite them to herself as she slips away. *Everything is connected. No beginning and no end.* But now, she sees two huge moving trucks parked in front of 18 Division Street. Three men are standing on the Wilfs' porch, smoking cigarettes.

"Oh no," Alice breathes.

"What?" From Waldo.

They sit in the car for a moment, the three Shenkmans, all looking across the street at the empty house. The magic tree presides over it all. She—Alice thinks of the majestic oak as a she—had been here long before they arrived, and here she will remain, once they're gone. Her roots spread far beneath the pavement, invisible, a whole system they'll never see. Hundreds of tiny lights twinkle, even in the sunshine.

# August 27, 1985

# *Benjamin*

ONCE MIMI IS asleep, there is no waking her. He has envied her this over the years. Her peace. Or perhaps envy isn't quite the right word. He would never wish to rob Mimi of her essential nature, her baseline contentment. Of course he wouldn't. He just wishes a little of it would rub off on him. Even tonight she is on her side, facing him. He studies her face: the clean line of her jaw; the fluttering of her eyelids as she dreams. Her mouth is slightly parted, and if he dares get closer, he knows he will feel the warmth of her breath. The very physical fact of her—the sheen of perspiration on her collarbone, her dark-nippled breasts, the small mole behind her left ear that she may not even know exists—this is what returns him to himself every day.

He climbs out of bed, feels for his slippers, then pulls the quilt over Mimi's shoulders. He needs to move his body through space. He needs air. He avoids the creaky stair in case either of the kids is awake. *His kids.* Even the thought of them now feels different to him, devoid of simplicity and innocence. They are culpable. They are *criminal.* Lying in their beds.

He grabs the green fleece jacket that hangs by the back door. The late summer night has grown chilly. Or maybe it's him. He feels ice-cold inside as he steps out and walks down the driveway. The shattered glass on the sidewalk and on the newly paved black asphalt of Division Street sends a chill through him. Though it's not a crime scene (he shudders), there are white chalk marks and bits of reflective tape the forensics team has used, o's and u's and short dashes, arrows, indecipherable as hieroglyphs along the road and on the oak tree itself. The police had to do this, he knows. For their records. For insurance purposes. Though he can't stop terror from creeping in. The roulette wheel spins and spins. Here is a body in a pool of blood on the ground, but it is the hefty body of Theo. Here is Sarah, cowering on the porch, submitting to a breathalyser held by a cop. His daughter, hands cuffed behind her back, escorted into a squad car. Mimi's wail, that most primal maternal sound, as the car pulls away silently, red lights flashing.

He walks down Division and turns on Poplar. His neighbors' houses are all dark, except for the faint glow of a night-light on the second floor of the Platts', and a downstairs lamp left on for the Berkelhammers' half-blind old collie. He thinks of the girl whose death—he's sure they'll remove her from life support tomorrow or perhaps the next day if the parents insist on waiting for a miracle that will never come—whose death will forever be a stain on the souls of his children.

He passes the Chertoffs' and sees the blue flickering light of a television in the master bedroom. Seymour must have insomnia. He has the urge to throw a pebble at their window, ask Seymour to come out for a walk with him. He can usually keep his own counsel, takes pride in that, in fact. But his kids are responsible for a girl's death. And he is ricocheting between his own horror and selfish gratitude that they didn't die in that car, that it wasn't them. That they have escaped ruin. There will be no consequences.

He carries on, rounding the corner onto Maple. His heart is beating irregularly, an arrhythmia. Hardly surprising. He disgusts himself. Never before has he acted out of such a primitive protectiveness. All that mattered to him—literally all that mattered as he sprinted to the crashed Buick—was saving his children. Is this who he is—who they all are? No different from any creature in the natural world whose sole job is survival?

He will metabolize this new knowledge. He'll learn to live with it. He may be a middle-aged husband and father living in suburban Avalon, but he is also a scrappy kid from Classon Avenue who made it into Stuyvesant and far beyond, who stood on the shoulders of his immigrant parents and aimed himself like an arrow, straight and true, at a life of purpose and meaning. A good, useful life. That's all he has ever wanted for himself. And all he has ever wanted for his family. But Sarah and Theo? They have far less road behind them. No mental habits, no muscles for this. No discipline. They are soft, his children. Soft and—at least until this very night—without guile. How will they carry this burden?

*We don't have to talk, Ben,* Mimi had said to him. *Let's not talk.* He understands that by this, Mimi did not mean let's talk tomorrow, or later, or down the road. Mimi believes the best recourse will be never to speak of this again. Next week, they will attend Misty Zimmerman's funeral. Theo will wear a suit, his dark hair slicked back, his face a round moon.

Mimi will buy Sarah a navy-blue knee-length dress. They will sit in the sixth row of the synagogue, backs erect and proud. They will send a card from the whole family, bring a platter of homemade cookies to the shiva.

The words that might have been spoken will instead be swallowed. Unexpressed, they will wind their way through and around each of them like vines choking a stand of untended trees. Years from now, once his children are off to college, he will quietly make an anonymous donation to Avalon High in Misty Zimmerman's name: an annual scholarship for a student gifted in a foreign language. He'll never tell a soul. But now, Ben stands in front of his own home, beneath the oak's canopy of branches. The trunk is shredded where the car hit, as if its guts were spilling out. The bright night sky illuminates the peaked roof; the window boxes on either side of the front door, the shiny brass knocker in the shape of an eagle.

Fifteen years they have lived in this place. His children are every age they've ever been within its walls. There's Sarah doing her chemistry homework at the kitchen table. *Dad? Can you help me with molecular compound structures?* Her hair tucked behind her ear. Her determined scowl that made him want to kiss the top of her head. And there's Theo. Fixed forever in Ben's mind at age four, his arms always reaching up for his parents. *I wanna go wheee!* His voice was adorably hoarse for a little kid. He would insert himself between Ben and Mimi and command them to swing him back and forth until their arms ached.

The roulette wheel spins again. One night many years from now, beneath this very oak tree, a small boy will set his whole world whirling on the screen of a device that has not yet been dreamt up. For the briefest of moments, Ben will feel he can hold it all—past, present, future—in his hands. But now he has no such portal. No window through which to see the lives that will unfold for the three people he loves most. He bends down and picks up a sliver of glass from the ground. It could have been them, him and Mimi, sitting vigil at the hospital, as the parents of that poor girl are doing. It could have been—but it isn't. Not on this night.

# November 2, 2014

---

# Theo

IT HAD TAKEN a while to find the right spot. The first few leases fell through, as rentals and property values in Brooklyn continued to climb, and he had very specific requirements for the space: it needed to be light-filled and cheerful, ideally with a garden for outdoor seating. The rapidly gentrifying neighborhood is now populated by women (mostly white) in bright, shapeless smocks and Swedish clogs, pushing state-of-the-art baby carriages down uneven sidewalks lined with former tenements in various stages of renovation. The husbands (if there are husbands) wear faded band tee shirts older than they are, and hoodies that look like they might have been scored in a thrift store.

Owning two restaurants has far more than doubled the work. Twelve Tables is open four nights a week—Thursday through Sunday—and Mimi's is a breakfast joint. Or at least Theo likes to think of it as a breakfast joint. He tries to keep the vibe at Mimi's simple and rustic; just honest food and drink, a place his mother would have been proud to have named after her. But when news spread that Theo Wilf was opening a second spot in Bed-Stuy, lines formed around the block. The press was followed by offers from venture capitalists. He apparently has a brand. A potentially valuable brand.

When he first opened Twelve Tables, he made a practice of taking photos of the empty restaurant, the busy kitchen, the "before" of each evening. He thought of this as offering people a glimpse of a place they'd likely never actually see, since there were so few tables and the restaurant was fully booked through Christmas of the following year. The @12Tables Instagram account has close to seventy thousand followers now, and there are at least two unofficial Theo Wilf fan pages. As soon as he tries to shut one down, another springs up. Which means that he is recognized on the street more often than he wishes (which is never).

He is the unlikeliest slightly famous person. Why would anyone care about him? He wants only to feed people, to transport them through their senses. He doesn't want to talk to them, or join their table at the end of the meal. Satisfaction, for him, comes in the form of empty plates returned to the kitchen without a drop or morsel left. And he doesn't want anything to do with the VC folks who keep calling. He doesn't want to "scale" or "amplify" or be on a "high-growth pathway." The younger ones invoke David Chang; the older ones mention Danny Meyer. They don't understand his lack of interest. How can he not want this? They think he's playing a game.

He's takes his usual route, Atlantic to Nostrum to Gates. It's only a couple of miles—about thirty minutes at a brisk pace—from Twelve Tables to Mimi's, and he tries to walk whenever he can, though sometimes he takes an Uber in the interest of time. His father has pleaded with him to take better care of himself. It's a perfect day, the sky cloudless, the hardy urban trees at the peak of their autumnal glory. He FaceTimes Ben on his route to show him that he's trying, he really is. Here's his dad's face filling his iPhone screen. He's on a windy beach, wearing sunglasses. Theo can barely hear him.

"Theo! Look who's here!"

Ben tilts his screen inexpertly. Is there a cutoff point for learning new technology? Ben has lost zero marbles in the nearly four years since Mimi died. But when it comes to devices and screens, he throws up his hands. Theo gets it. His father just doesn't care. There's limited time now. His eightieth birthday is on the horizon. As far as Theo can tell, Ben spends his days reading poetry. He returns again and again to Whitman but has become interested, too, in contemporary poetry. He spends hours each week at a small bookstore called Diesel, not far from Sarah's house. He'll send Theo an email with a typed-out poem by Marie Howe or W. S. Merwin. Sometimes he leaves long messages that begin: *Theo, darling, listen to this.* Theo saves these messages. They're a map of his father's inner world. He knows he will want them someday.

Theo sidesteps a bike messenger who really shouldn't be on the sidewalk. Three men pass him wearing big fur hats— Satmar Hasidim who have wandered far from Williamsburg. Two girls are ahead of him. Or are they girls? It's hard to tell. They're narrow up and down, hair shorn and bleached white. Their hands are tucked into each other's back jeans pockets. The beauty of this borough—the sheer human scale and breadth of it.

His nieces grab their grandfather's phone.

"Uncle Theo!"

They're seventeen now, Sydney and Olivia. They'll be heading to college next year. He can't believe there was ever a time when he couldn't tell them apart. Sydney takes after Peter, lanky and golden; Olivia is a mini-Sarah, just as Sarah is a mini-Mimi. Theo knows it shouldn't matter, that it's all just a mishmash of genes, but whenever he sees her he feels comforted, as if there were still tangible evidence of his mother in the world.

He wishes his mother had lived to see her granddaughters grow up. That rocky time in Sarah and Peter's marriage and, more than anything, Sarah's recovery, seems to have deepened them both. They participated in family week at the rehab, went to Al-Anon. Why is it that some kids can weather the storms of their childhood whereas others—himself, Sarah—spend their lives running from the damage? Never mind. He knows the answer to this. He and Sarah *made* the damage.

Oh, how he loves being an uncle. He's never going to get married. Never going to have children. He knows this. Every once in a while there's been a woman. He can't do the dating apps, which is pretty much what every single person does. He's tried, but he's not clever like you need to be, and he's allergic to describing himself like a product on a shelf. So that leaves chance. Chance brought Prachi into his life a couple of years ago, and for a brief while there, he wondered if maybe this was it. They met through Twelve Tables, he guesses you could say. Everything in his life happens through Twelve Tables, so that's no surprise. Frieda and Joe Glasser, patrons of his from day one, introduced them. Theo would never have agreed to being set up, but the Glassers had a light touch and managed to make it seem as if it were no big deal that they were bringing one of Joe's graduate students to dinner with them. It definitely wasn't a setup. No, no, no. Later, he learned that they had told the same to Prachi.

He noticed her through the burgundy curtain that night. Her shiny cap of cropped black hair, her long neck, her open-throated laugh. It was summer, and she wore a sleeveless, cream-colored top. Her arms were lean, muscular. He was visited by a surprising image: those arms wrapped around him. It had been a year and a half since Mimi had died, and the last time Theo had hugged anyone was when he said goodbye to his dad and Sarah at JFK. He clung to Sarah for a moment, feeling the narrow wings jutting from her back. His father, his sister. His mother in the ground. This was what had become of them.

"Uncle Theo?" Olivia's voice sounds like it's coming from the inside of a seashell. "When are you going to come see us?"

"Soon," he says. Soon is what he always says. But it's hard to get away. Twelve Tables is all him. No one else, not for a single night, has ever taken the helm. Mimi's could do without him for a few days. He's hired a team of chefs and sous chefs and the place is a well-oiled machine, even by his standards. But is that the real reason? He feels tethered and safe when he stays within the three points of his life: Mimi's, Twelve Tables, and his loft.

"How about you come see me?"

He hears the call of a gull on the other side of the country. On the sidewalk, a pigeon pecks at a discarded pizza crust. He has a thought so fully formed that he must have dreamt it. It has the quality of déjà vu.

"Actually, why don't you guys come work at Mimi's? Maybe over winter break? Or for the whole summer! We'll call it an internship."

Theo sees that Ben hasn't strayed far from his granddaughters. Can he hear the invitation? As Theo turns right onto Malcolm X Boulevard, he sees the usual crowd spilling out from Mimi's. He takes a deep breath, then envisions a volume knob inside his mind and turns it down. He's learned how to do this. Reduce the noise. It's a cacophonous symphony that never entirely stills itself: the sickening crunch of metal; Sarah's scream; the hiss coming from the Buick's crumpled front end; the samba beat in the kitchen of La Cabrera, the crackling fire; the sound of his mother's voice on the phone breaking as she asks if it's him. *Theo? Theo?* His sister's wail coming from inside the playhouse; the siren in the snow; Prachi asking what he's thinking, what that look in his eye means, why he won't talk to her, where he's gone.

"Awesome! Yes!" Both his nieces are giving him the thumbs-up. Have they ever bussed tables before? Or worked in a kitchen? Or worked at all? It doesn't matter. He'll get them up and running. He'll redo the back of his loft, build a wall so they have privacy, turn it into a real guest room. They are seventeen going on eighteen. They have already been complicated by life. Their parents' near divorce. Their grandmother's death. Their mother's addiction. But these are the gentler hills. Mimi used to be fond of the phrase *with any luck*. He thinks of it now. With any luck, his nieces will continue to grow strong and hardy, like the trees that cast their canopies over Malcolm X Boulevard. With any luck, he will be around for a long time to watch over them.

# Benjamin

IT HAD SEEMED logical, after they buried Mimi in the Wilf family plot in Brooklyn, after the truncated shiva—three days instead of seven—held in the empty shell of their home surrounded by boxes, that he'd go with Sarah. The movers had been called off, the family relocating from Cleveland blessedly flexible and kind about when they needed to commence their massive renovation. There was, of course, no question of his moving to Avalon Hills. Not any longer. The whole idea had been to be reunited with Mimi. Besides, he held the assisted-living facility responsible for Mimi's disappearance. He could have sued them. Friends recommended litigators who were partners at fancy-sounding Manhattan law firms. He might have won. But so what? He knows how destructive and all-consuming these cases can be—as if being awarded damages could pave over the raw, ongoing work of grief. He has enough money to live on. His kids are all set. Nothing will turn back the clock and return Mimi to him. If there's one thing Ben has known since he held his wife's lifeless body in his arms, it's that he refuses to spend whatever time he has left consumed by a desire for recompense. There will be no recompense.

What has surprised him is how he has taken to life in Los Angeles. Each morning he rises early as he always has and takes a long walk around the canyon. He's the oldest person in the neighborhood. The runners are out in full force, the middle-aged speed-walkers, the cyclists in their neon jerseys and colorful helmets. The hard-core among the runners gather at the top of a long and steep set of stairs. Some do uphill sprints with what appear to be their personal trainers. It's a culture devoted to a kind of gluttony of health, or what they now call wellness.

Sarah, Peter, and the girls live in a Mediterranean-style house with terra-cotta floors and stucco walls, heavy dark furniture offset by their impressive black-and-white photography collection. Ben knows little about photography, but he's boned up: Horst, Man Ray, Elliott Erwitt, Sally Mann. A particularly beautiful Irving Penn, an image Ben has seen before, or feels he has: the fleshy curve of a woman's hip, punctuated by a single dark mole. It reminds him of Mimi.

He had missed Mimi in the years before her death as he lost her bit by bit, as if parts of her were being erased; only smudges, traces remained. But she was *there*. He had still been able to feel comforted by her presence. He was a husband. There is a name for what he is now. *Widower.* He had never fully appreciated, in all the years he took patients' medical histories, how it must feel to check that box.

During the days, Sarah's house is empty. The housekeeper comes and goes, the gardeners and the pool guy. Money. It's the one thing he doesn't have to worry about when it comes to either of his children. Sarah has done remarkably well for herself. Her latest project, a limited series on Showtime adapted from a controversial French memoir, has just received three Golden Globe nominations. In her office—the downstairs of the guesthouse—her awards are hidden in a corner of a bookcase, including the most famous statuette of all. Now that she's middle-aged and sober, she has settled into her work with a quiet determination, rather than her old frenetic energy.

Ben doesn't know exactly what went on between Sarah and Peter, why their marriage seemed so tense and strained for a while there. The truth is, he doesn't want to know. It isn't his place. If he hadn't been living on the second floor of the guesthouse, he never would have heard the shouts, the slamming doors. He has theories, of course. Peter is no longer a dues-paying member of the Writers Guild. He stopped writing scripts a couple of years ago and enrolled in graduate school. This spring, he'll have his master's in social work and start a family therapy practice. It couldn't have been easy for them, with Sarah's tremendous success in the same industry that has been indifferent to her husband. It might not have mattered as much if their roles had been reversed. Blatantly sexist, to be sure, but that doesn't make it any less true.

But Ben knows it's more than that. Something to do with Sarah's month in rehab shortly after Mimi's death. Something to do with the phone that wouldn't stop ringing that night she arrived from LA. Something to do with that dreadful summer night so very long ago, and the choices that each of them—he and Mimi, Theo and Sarah—made that buried the truth of what happened deeper with each passing year. Ben wonders if Peter even knows about it. He suspects not. They had never spoken of the accident and its aftermath, the four of them. There were times words danced on the tip of Ben's tongue. Two years after the accident, on a family road trip from Avalon to South Carolina, he almost came out with it. The car felt like a safe bubble, a confessional booth on wheels. What would have happened if he had simply offered: *Let's talk about it*? There would have been no question as to what he meant.

Instead he slid in a cassette of an audiobook they'd agreed on. It was easier to listen to a narrator reading *The Bonfire of the Vanities* than to take the risk. But what had the risk been, really? He's thought about it a lot. It's a thorny place to which his mind drifts when left to its own devices. The most sense he can make of it is that they'd shared a terror that if they spoke of what happened that night, their words would form a complete narrative more terrible than the shattered part each of them carried alone. But silence may have been a mistake. No. Silence had definitely been a mistake. Ben heard somewhere—on a PBS documentary?—that Carl Jung had once described secrets as psychic poison. That's what it felt like: poison, leaking into all of their lives, Sarah's and Theo's most of all. Christ, they had still been kids.

Theo, too, will be fine, at least when it comes to money. The restaurants are packed, thriving. Sarah has shown him some of the press. Of course, Theo never would. In photos, he looks a little sheepish, uncomfortable; he wears his success like an ill-fitting suit. Success won't keep him warm at night. Success won't take away the ache Ben knows is inside his son. In fact, it might even be making it worse, because that pained, self-deprecating look on his face fairly screams that he doesn't believe he deserves it. Ben wonders what Theo does with himself when he returns home to his loft after locking up each night. He never speaks of having a special lady friend, though that doesn't mean there's no one in the picture. It must be lonely.

On the other hand, it seems Theo is taking better care of himself in recent years. He's still on the hefty side, but he's no longer obese. He tells Ben he exercises most days, by which he means a brisk urban walk. Ben can't help compiling a chart in his head, the way he would have for a patient, assessing risk. Forty-four-year-old male, five feet ten, 190 pounds. Genetically, Theo's in pretty good shape: no family history of heart disease or cancer. There's Mimi's Alzheimer's—Ben's sure that already haunts both Sarah and Theo—but nothing to be done about that unless they want to take one of those DNA tests that would identify the markers. If they asked his advice, not that they would, he would advise against it. What's the point in knowing, when there's no treatment?

He often thinks of Avalon, though it had no longer been his town long before he left. His many years living there are like a layer of sediment that has since been covered over by newer layers. Rachel Carson—he has been reading *Silent Spring*—wrote that sediments are sort of an epic poem of the earth. The history of every town is its own minor epic, then. The only tug he still feels toward Avalon is not to his former home but rather to the house across the street.

All is not well in the Shenkman household. The mother, Alice, is ill. When he first heard, he sent Waldo a handwritten note. Waldo called right away. *Dr. Wilf? Please, Waldo. Call me Ben.* Hard to believe the boy is now fourteen. He had sent only the occasional text before that note. Waldo and he have a surprising friendship, if you can call it that. He doesn't quite know what to make of it. He once heard it said it's possible to have bonds with people, even complete strangers, that are soul-to-soul. The idea has stayed with him. What does it mean that he helped deliver the boy? What does it mean that Waldo was with Mimi when she passed? Is it coincidence, pure and simple? Is there even such a thing? Ben thinks, sometimes, about the time he spent sitting with Waldo, nestled among the gnarly roots of the oak. Later that night, Mimi would slip through the doors of Avalon Hills. And because of that night, because of *him—Hey, kid! What are you doing? What is that thing? Is that some kind of game?—* Waldo packed up his belongings and ran away from home. All is somehow connected, traceable if only he knew how to look.

It was startling to hear Waldo's voice now that it had begun to change, cracking and skipping like a vinyl record. That new voice wobbled. He was crying, Ben realized. It didn't take much, just a gentle question, to get the boy to talk. Ben had no way of knowing how rare this was, Waldo's onrushing words; that with every other adult in his life, he was silent bordering on mute. *My mom is getting sicker, Dr. . . . Ben. She's really sick.* Ben pieced it together from the torrent. Sounded like ovarian, maybe uterine cancer. Not the good kind, as people liked to say, as if there were a good kind. She'd had surgery. Now she was undergoing chemotherapy. Waldo spelled out the different kinds of drugs as if they were Latin names for constellations. He had typed and saved them on his phone. He had a list. He wanted Ben to tell him what it all meant.

Now he calls or texts every day. No matter what Ben's doing, he drops everything to respond. It's clear no one else is talking to Waldo. His mother is too busy trying to survive, and the father? Ben doesn't pretend to understand the father. Ben has been fueled by many emotional states in his life, but he has never experienced a chronic state of rage. He saw it the morning Mimi died. He heard it when Shenkman screamed at Theo outside the playhouse. Of course, that was understandable—the man was mad with fear about Waldo. But even when the family came to pay a shiva call, Ben noticed it. Shenkman's very physiognomy seems to dictate his destiny: the thick arms and shoulders, the short neck, the brow frozen into a permanent scowl. He kept looking around the empty house as if the secret to some elusive happiness might be hiding behind the stacks of boxes. What could he possibly be saying to Waldo? Angry people don't tend to grow less angry when life throws them a curveball like this one. The poor woman. The poor kid.

After a walk north of the pier with his granddaughters—something he does as often as they'll allow—he's sitting at a picnic table in the courtyard of the Brentwood Country Mart. This is his favorite spot because of the perfect one-two punch of a great independent bookstore and a great café. He's become a regular here, even though he doesn't exactly fit in. He enjoys watching the little ones running between Reddi Chick and the toy store. Their moms or dads often look familiar, something that puzzled him until he realized he knows them from television.

Today he browsed the poetry section of Diesel until a slim volume caught his eye, *The Night Parade* by Edward Hirsch. Perhaps it's the book jacket: a dark, blurry photograph of a woman in an overcoat walking on the platform of a train station, the line of lights above her head like an arrow made of stars that reach up to a cloudy night sky. It's hard to tell if she's moving toward the camera or away from it. He thumbs through the book—the author photo shows the sharp features and soulful eyes of a man he might have played stickball with back on Classon Avenue. What happened to the boys of his youth as they scattered like marbles bouncing away from Brooklyn and into their lives? Every once in a while a name passes through Ben's mind. Old men now, all of them. Some must be dead.

Sounds, smells, words return to him. The dull thwack of a broom handle connecting with a Spaldeen. The bang of a truck going over a manhole cover. The feel of a paper bag filled with hot chestnuts in his hands. The gush of an open hydrant in summertime. His childhood friends were sons of immigrants who had arrived in Brooklyn from Germany, Italy, Ireland, or Poland, like his own parents. The kitchens in their small apartments smelled of cabbage or sausage or simmering tomato sauce. *Benny!* His mother's voice calling for him from the stoop. *Dinner!* All the mothers called for all their children, but it was her voice that reached his ears. That still reaches his ears if he listens hard enough.

He takes a sip of his cappuccino. It seems almost a desecration to ruin the barista's perfectly articulated leaf in the foam. His phone vibrates on the table. He imagines Waldo alone in his room, searching the sky for answers written in the stars.

"Hello, my dear boy," he says. "Tell me how you are."

# Sarah

A T FIRST IT was like this: a soft, invisible quilt that enveloped her and made her feel safe, warm, comfortable in her own skin. A few drinks diluted her sense of not belonging. It was just that easy. She became voluble, floaty, brave, and funny. She became that girl—the one she otherwise did not quite know how to be. It might have been a phase she'd eventually outgrow. She might have learned new, healthier ways to cope. She has friends who did plenty of risky things when they were young and laugh about their exploits now, while doing everything in their power to ensure that their own teenage children don't do the same. They have all sorts of reasons that it was okay for them but not for their kids. Drugs are stronger now. Their digital imprint will follow them when they apply to college or for jobs. But the real reason is that they know, on some level they know, that their survival has been simply a matter of good fortune. The cocaine could have been laced with fentanyl. The Mollys they took on the dance floor could have contained meth. The stranger in the bar could have been a sociopath.

The talk among the moms in Sydney and Olivia's high school often veers into this territory. Sarah tends to avoid the moms in general—she feels out of place among them—but once in a while there's a curriculum night, a science fair. There's always some drama: a DUI, a party that got shut down by the police, a girl who had her stomach pumped. When she gets pulled into one of these sotto voce conversations, Sarah watches their faces. While it wasn't exactly public that she went to rehab, it wasn't exactly private either. She'll notice one of them look quickly at her, then away. It has been a struggle, not to feel ashamed. She lost control. She nearly destroyed everything: her girls, her husband, her job, herself.

It has been three years since she's had a drink. She goes to meetings every day, mostly big, crowded ones where she can sit near the back of the room and just listen. Where she won't be noticed or singled out. Where she won't be known. Early in her recovery she had been invited to private meetings around town. In a city, an industry that is so much about pecking order that actors are given actual letter grades denoting their box office worth, private recovery meetings were no surprise. Famous and famously sober people often prefer to gather in their own backyards. She attended one or two but felt paralysed by self-consciousness. She knew too many of these people: the actor who had walked off the set of one of her shows in the late 1990s; a couple, writing partners, who had once pitched her a comedy about reproductive medicine; a fashion designer who dressed one of Sarah's stars in a bizarre see-through gown when she was nominated for an Independent Spirit Award.

The private meetings were small enough that everybody had to talk. That was the deal. You couldn't just lurk. But whenever she opened her mouth and said *Hi, I'm Sarah and I'm an alcoholic,* her pulse raced. She doesn't know how to talk about herself. She is very, very good at telling other people's stories. She is known, as a producer, to be an unusually good reader of scripts when it comes to character and motivation. She has an excellent sense of structure. But her cheeks redden and she stumbles when she tries to share in meetings. It's as if the whole of her life rushes in, and she doesn't know where to begin.

Today she's at her regular late afternoon meeting that acts as the bridge between her workday and her homelife. She grabs a paper cup of burnt coffee, settles into a metal folding chair, then scrolls through her Twitter feed so that no one will talk to her. She has a sponsor she calls dutifully on Sunday evenings, an older woman who treats her with a maternal warmth that makes her eyes sting. Her sponsor has gently suggested that she reach out more, become more a part of the community. And she knows she should, but years have gone by and she continues to be a bystander. She tells herself that she's not drinking, and isn't that all that matters?

Except the thing is that it all just keeps getting harder and harder. She's begun to wonder whether clarity is overrated. She feels better physically; the pink light of dawn without the wooziness of a daily hangover has been a revelation, and she even feels tiny glimmers of gratitude when she sits outside early in the morning and thinks of her family, how lucky they are to be together. It's an unexpected gift that her dad is living with them. The girls have a relationship with him that wouldn't have been possible if not for the turn of events that brought him west. That Peter stayed with her after her hideous betrayal is nothing short of a miracle. She knows all this—she knows it in her head, but she doesn't feel it. Not the way she thinks other people do.

A man in the front of the room has been telling his story. Sarah realizes she hasn't heard a word. He's Black, looks to be in his fifties. It's hard to tell with former drinkers. He could easily look a decade older than he actually is. He's bald and thin, wearing a collared shirt, blazer, and jeans. The room is crowded—they're at capacity with two hundred people—and he speaks into a handheld mic.

"It happened because I was drunk," he says. "And I have to live with that every day of my life."

Around the room, people are wiping away tears. She leans forward in her seat. What happened? What does he have to live with every day of his life?

His next words hit her with the force of a physical blow. "Twenty years"—his voice shakes, but he maintains a certain inner dignity, as if whatever he says won't topple him—"since Joey drowned. My boy. On my watch."

Sarah wishes for the first time that she were sitting closer. Something inside her is suddenly very awake. And how can this beautiful man sit in front of hundreds of people telling this awful truth? She's heard a lot of people's drunkalogues, but never this. Not this. His son was three years old. They were on vacation with another family. He went into the cabin to fetch a drink. He tells his story in excruciating, necessary detail. It's something beyond confession. It's testimony. Telling the story won't bring Joey back. Telling the story won't take away his pain. But telling the story in these rooms filled with broken souls is what saves his life again and again.

"You're only as sick as your secrets," he says. This is one of the program's maxims. She's heard it a thousand times. It's

242

never meant anything to her—just a phrase that skids across her mind without leaving a trace: *Searching and fearless moral inventory. Made a list of all persons we had harmed and became willing to make amends to them all.* She has somehow managed to believe that none of this applies to her. But now, she is deeply and incontrovertibly aware that *all* of it applies to her. If it's true that she's only as sick as her secrets, that means she must be very sick indeed. She has never spoken of that long-ago summer night. Not even to Dr. Baum, in the privacy of his HIPAA-protected office.


For her whole adult life, several times a year, she has looked up each of the parents of Misty Zimmerman. They're old now. About a year after the accident, Misty's father remarried, his new wife a woman with a couple of kids. They live somewhere with palm trees. On Facebook, Sarah has watched over the years as the kids have gone on to have their own kids, grandkids, golden retriever puppies have become stately old dogs, bouncy houses have given way to summer camps and high school graduations, clambakes. She studies his face for signs of the grief he must privately carry.

Misty's mother's life is less traceable. She's not on Facebook, but public records show that she's living in Georgia—if indeed she is the correct Ruth Zimmerman—and her address is that of a senior living facility. One time, there was a photo from a real estate company website. She sold houses at some point. She was wearing a red blazer and a forced professional smile. Sarah searched for signs of Misty in the woman's hooded eyes, in the deep creases running down from the corners of her mouth. But Misty's mother, however she might have otherwise aged, is marked by the loss of her only child.

It wouldn't be reading too much into a single photograph to say that this is a woman who has nothing left.

The room comes in and out of focus as if pressed from either side like a bellows. Her ears ring. She can hardly breathe. The man at the front of the room is pointing at her. She looks up and sees her own hand in the air. A shiver runs through her. For years to come, she will marvel at this moment, her shock that her hand seemed to shoot up of its own accord. When she tells her story, as she will learn to do—to her brother, her father, her husband, her daughters, her shrink—this will be where she begins. *Yes, you. The woman in the black sweater near the back. Please.* Someone passes her a mic. She feels like she's going to pass out, but if she does, it's okay. The worst has already happened. She is at the bottom of the ocean floor. There's only one thing to do. With all her reserves, she hurls herself toward the light she cannot see.

"Hi, I'm Sarah," she says. Her voice emerges from a small, hard place within her, a shelled, encapsulated thing that has just broken open. "I'm an alcoholic." She chokes the words out. "Once, a long time ago, a girl died and it was my fault."

# *Waldo*

H IS MOTHER ISN'T telling him, but still he knows. Do his parents really think there's anything about them that he hasn't witnessed? He has watched their every move. He knows that when his dad presses two fingers to his right temple, he's trying to stay calm; when his mom pours a third glass of white wine, it means she's sad. He can tell when they have an appointment in the city with the people who ask him questions and fill in his answers on a chart. When they return home, his parents' eyes are bright and kind, and his dad is gentler with him, at least for a day or two. Waldo has heard their whispers all his life. For a long time they were about him. (Sometimes they still are. He is their favorite subject.) Then they fought about money. But now his parents are whispering in a new language: *uterine mass, hysterectomy, lymph node biopsy, chemo.*

In the top drawer of his desk, he keeps Dr. Wilf's letter neatly folded in its envelope with the stamp of the solar eclipse. Word has traveled from Avalon to Los Angeles.

People know his mom is sick. Neighbors, probably. But nobody has said a word to him, not until Dr. Wilf. It would never have occurred to Dr. Wilf that Waldo's parents might choose not to tell him. The tip of his nose and the tops of his ears redden when he thinks about that. He's fourteen years old! Why are they keeping a secret from him? It should be, like, illegal or something.

*Your mother is a very brave woman.* He thinks of his mother giving birth to him on the kitchen floor. He doesn't like to think about this, but sometimes he does anyway. His dad likes to pretend at strength, but it is his mom who is actually strong. *It will be okay, or so I hope.* Ever since the time he spent with Mrs. Wilf, it's like he sees things. He doesn't mention this to the doctors in the city. They're looking for crazy—and this might qualify.

Also, he doesn't really know how to talk about it. Once Mrs. Wilf was dead, she was no longer in her body. Her body was just a thing, like the discarded carapace of an insect. But she wasn't gone. She had escaped. Within the walls of the playhouse, there was a field of energy he could almost reach out and touch. No, more than that. It was as if the two of them—he and Mrs. Wilf—were enveloped by that field of energy. It wasn't exactly like time stopped; more that time had seemed to expand so that they were a part of everything that had ever happened or ever would happen. She would never really be gone.

This new knowledge (and it felt like knowledge) has stayed with him like a superpower. If when we die, we don't just vanish, then there's nothing to be afraid of, right? He sees . . . he doesn't know what to call them . . . not *spirits*, exactly, not *beings*, but a barely visible web, like those intricate spider-webs that glisten when the sun hits them. Those glistening strands form patterns just like constellations. But now he's being put to the test. He wants more time with his mom. A lot more time. He doesn't want her to be a glistening strand, part of the invisible pattern. No. He wants her to be at his high school graduation. He wants her to take him to college. He wants the conversations that they have together in the car every day to go on without end.

He can't stop himself. He Googles some of the words he's written down, words he heard his parents say when they thought he was safely inside his room. *Endometrial cancer. Type 2.* He types all of it into the search engine and is drawn instantly to a list of five-year survival rates. First he sees 70 percent. That's not so bad. In school, that would still be a passing grade. But no, that's for something else, not what his mom has. His stomach lurches. She has a 30 percent chance of survival.

Waldo closes his laptop and stares out the window. The leaves have mostly turned and carpet the ground. The house across the street has been re-sided and painted bright white. A new wood-shingle roof has replaced the old one. The family has a seven-year-old boy and a five-year-old girl, and a couple of times he's worked for them as a mother's helper, even though he's not great with little kids and doesn't really know how to talk to them.

Strange, that the only time he had ever been inside that house was when they paid a visit after Mrs. Wilf died. Then, it was shadowy, dusty, the walls lined with boxes, furniture covered with sheets. The caterers had brought in folding tables and chairs for visitors. Now, the wood floors are the color of sand, and where he remembers walls there is wide-open space. A huge blue-and-white sofa floats like a boat in the middle of the family room. He tried to get the boy and girl to watch *Cosmos: A Spacetime Odyssey* on the giant flat-screen, but they weren't into Carl Sagan. That was the last time he was asked to be a mother's helper.

*Thirty percent.* He's put Dr. Wilf into his favorites on his phone. Each time he calls, he's afraid that Dr. Wilf won't answer. That he'll get sick of him, like everybody else has. He puts on his headphones, huge ones that cover his ears, because they help him feel whole. Dr. Wilf answers on the second ring. Waldo knows he's supposed to call him Ben, and he does. *Hello, my dear boy. Tell me how you are.* And the torrent begins—*my mom is so sick, she's bald now and she's wearing a wig like I'm not supposed to notice, some days now she can't get out of bed, no one is talking to me, they keep pretending*—as if Ben holds the key to the locked box within Waldo Shenkman where words tend to die before they're formed and become nothing more than particles of space dust.

Waldo squeezes his eyes tight and listens to the sound of Dr. Wilf's voice. It isn't so much what he says as how he says it: with certainty and . . . could it be? With love. He hears love from this old man he hardly even knows, with whom he has spent only a handful of hours. Dr. Wilf reminds him of how he feels when he traces the night sky—*Andromeda, Antlia, Apus, Aquarius, Aquila, Ara, Aries, Auriga*—diagramming the constellations the way a musician might practice the same piece of music he knows in the very bones of his fingers over and over again. There is always something new and undiscovered out there—even when he can't see it. Especially when he can't see it.

It's dusk by the time he says goodbye to Dr. Wilf. He needs to get away from his room, out of the house. There's only one place he wants to be. He doesn't need to tell his parents he's leaving. He's not ten going on eleven anymore. He's a teenager. He takes his iPad and slips out the front door, closing it gently behind him. He crosses Division Street. It's just past Halloween, chilly out, and the lower branches of the magic tree have been strung with amber lights and bits of orange and black tinsel. The last of the summer wildflowers are fallow now, nothing more than a tangle of weeds.

Waldo circles the tree, dragging his fingers along the rough bark. It would take five of him, maybe more, linking hands to go all the way around the trunk. He stops at one spot that feels different from the rest, smoother, darker, and rests his palm there. There is a term for this—*wound wood*—that he does not know but feels like a current running through him nonetheless. The bark has grown stronger, a scar over a healed wound. He sits down on the hard, cold earth between two roots that seem to emerge like arms from the ground.

*What kind of bad thoughts?*

*Oh, you know.*

*No, I don't know. Tell me.*

*Like, about dying and stuff.*

He leans his head back. The iPad is in his lap, but he doesn't touch it. Not now. There is life inside the tree. Something. Someone. A girl. Her energy field is all around him. Gossamer threads weave them together. She is around his age, but she is also every age: a newborn baby, a grown woman, a crone. The threads shimmer and dance. He once saw a photograph comparing the pattern of rings inside a tree with the pattern of a human fingerprint. The two images looked almost exactly the same. It was difficult to tell where one ended and the other began. Who is the girl in the magic tree? She lost her life here, he realizes. Something to do with the wound, the scar. Has she been here all along, presiding over the neighborhood? Has she watched him grow up across the street?

The sky is nearly dark. Above him, the first stars. A light goes on in the upstairs guest room, where his mother now spends most of her time. *Thirty percent.* He watches as a shadow moves across the window and knows she's going to die. Not today, not tomorrow, but soon. She won't be at his high school graduation. She won't drop him off at college. She won't be there to tell him how special he is, to wait, just wait, that great things are in store. He wraps his arms around himself. Once his mom is gone, how will he know where to find her? He wishes he could ask the girl. She is casting threads in every direction like electromagnetic waves, infrared photons, radiant beams of light visible only in the darkness. The waves grow longer and longer. And suddenly, Waldo realizes: she's extending her reach beyond Division Street, past Avalon, across highways, overpasses, cities, farmland. There are a few people who will feel her touch—a chill up a spine, a hand in the air, a poem recalled—even if they won't exactly know it.

July 2, 2020

# Shenkman

HIS CONDO IN downtown Sarasota is a short walk
from Whole Foods. That was a selling point. Shenkman doesn't want to get into his car if he doesn't
have to. He calculates how many minutes he spent commut-
ing from Avalon to the city. Forty-five minutes (with no
traffic) each way. Ninety minutes a day at a minimum. Times
five days a week equals 450 minutes a week. Call it fifty
weeks a year (he never took more than two weeks' vacation)
brings the grand total to 22,500 minutes a year. For two decades. He would like those minutes back. He would like to
turn back time all the way to the beginning of . . . well, that
is the problem. Where to begin?

He met Alice during his last year of business school. It was
kind of a setup, but one of those setups that isn't supposed to
seem like one. Mutual friends invited each of them to the
same dinner party. It was all couples except for Shenkman
and Alice, and they were seated next to each other. Nudge,
nudge. Wink, wink. They'd also been given the pertinent details

in advance. He knew she was a third-year law student at NYU; she'd grown up in Forest Hills; her dad was a dentist. She'd had one serious boyfriend but had been single for a while. What had she known about him? He looked pretty good on paper. He had rowed crew at University of New Hampshire, was finishing up business school at NYU Stern, already had accepted a position at Lehman. This was how it seemed to work. Résumés, backgrounds, family histories lining up nicely as if common ground were the best way to choose a person to mate with for life.

Shenkman wonders if that kind of thing even happens anymore: people getting fixed up by their friends. Well, it definitely doesn't happen in this shithole of a year. Anyway, what if he hadn't gone to the dinner? Hadn't met the pretty law student? Life is just a series of accidents, one piled on top of the next like one of those huge highway crashes you sometimes read about, one jackknifed tractor trailer in the fog, and all of a sudden there's a twenty-seven-car pileup. If he hadn't married Alice, he wouldn't now be a widower walking in his mask along Main Street in Sarasota. He would have had a whole other life. A whole other story. A different wife. A different suburb. A different kid or two or three.

Most of all, there would be no Waldo. Something inside of him, some old familiar impulse, strains toward anger, remorse, regret, and comes up empty. He cannot regret the pileup of his life. Waldo is the best thing he's ever done. Even though he can't take much credit—except for his name. He did name his son. That's not nothing. When Benjamin Wilf slipped the noose of the umbilical cord away from the tiny, vulnerable stem of that infant neck, when he laid him on Alice's belly—*little guy just needed an assist*—something about that six-pound red-faced slippery bundle was already fully formed. Shenkman just needed to not fuck it up.

But of course, he went and fucked it up. He royally fucked up one of the only things in life that you can't find a way to fix later. He had sucked as a dad. Would he have sucked as a dad for any kid? Or was it something in the chemistry between Waldo and him that was doomed from the start? He had tried to turn Waldo into the kind of son he wanted, rather than meet him where he was. As a husband, he'd done a marginally better job, though, no doubt about it, Alice deserved more.

One thing he did get right: when she was diagnosed, when she got sick, he was all in. He was, in the parlance of the day, a caregiver. He gave care. He was at every appointment with the oncologist, taking notes. He pulled the few strings he had to get second and third opinions. After Alice's radical hysterectomy, she moved into the guest room, and he kept one of Waldo's old baby monitors by his bedside in case she called out for him in the night. Their master bathroom turned into a stockpile of medical supplies: antiemetics, painkillers, medical weed, and eventually morphine. He bought one of those pill organizers that he had always thought of as being for old people, to keep it all straight.

This is where his mind goes when he thinks of Alice now. Not the vibrant woman he married; not the strong earth mother who pushed Waldo out right there on the kitchen floor, cursing him all the way; not the attorney with the agile mind who was tapped for partner as a fifth-year associate. God, he had been so proud of her. Had he really let her know it? He's read a few books about grief. But no one talks about how long it takes for the person you loved to return to you as who they were before they became sick, before they wasted away. When he sees Alice, she is bald, her skin sallow and nearly falling off her bones. Her nails, her lips, cracked. Her arms like sticks; hands, in those final days, like claws.

Outside Whole Foods there are vats of hand sanitizer. A few shops aim a thermometer at your forehead before they let you inside, but this is Florida, not a Westchester suburb. The sunshine has convinced them all that this whole pandemic thing is overblown. In some parts of the state it's a point of pride to parade around maskless. Here in Sarasota, live music plays every night at outdoor bars where people dance under tiki torches. In Whole Foods, arrows and decals on the floor are meant to direct the flow of traffic and create social distancing, but no one is paying attention. They're either too old or can't be bothered. Shenkman watches it all like an anthropologist. He's always played by the rules, and so he wears a mask, rubs his hands raw with Purell. But he personally isn't too worried. He has a theory that there's a set number of shitty things that can happen in one lifetime, and he's already reached his limit.

The couple who bought his house in Avalon has by now installed two deep freezers in the basement and built shelves to stock enough canned goods, grains, paper goods, and bottled water to last a year. It's like Y2K all over again. They told him they planned to pod—*pod* has become a verb—with at least one other family on Division Street and set up a regular COVID-testing schedule with a local concierge physician. Concierge physician! The couple has a lot to live for: two little kids; enough resources to outbid other buyers in an inflated market; the belief that if they are smart and vigilant enough, they will be able to protect themselves from harm.

He throws Vidalia onions and a head of cauliflower into his basket. Grabs a carton of the oat milk that always seems to be in short supply. There's no comfortable place for him inside his own head. Waldo is so pissed at him, and he has every right to be. Even though pissed is a register outside Waldo's range of expression, Shenkman knows. The damage Shenkman has inflicted on him has become a shell that keeps Waldo in, and Shenkman out. He wonders when he will see his son again, now that the house that bound them together is gone from their lives.

His ties have loosened and fluttered away, one by one. His parents are gone. Alice wished to be cremated even though Jews aren't supposed to be cremated. He and Waldo spent a troubling afternoon together a couple of weeks after Alice passed, carrying out her instructions to scatter her ashes in the Hudson River. It was probably, no, certainly illegal. But still, the two of them drove past the train station and down to the river, the sturdy cardboard box containing her ashes on the back seat. It was a weekday afternoon in early spring, and the promenade along the Hudson was relatively quiet. Just the occasional cyclist, and a few determined walkers getting their steps in.

Shenkman carried the box down to a quiet grassy spot at the water's edge. He didn't know how to do this. He only had buried people before now. He felt an irrational wave of anger at the contents of the box that had once been his wife. So selfish of her! Might she have considered what it would be like for him? Here alone with his . . . But then he looked over at Waldo, who had taken the cardboard top off the box, undone the twist tie holding together the plastic bag inside. He was running his fingers across the remains. The cremains. God, he hated that word. He fought the urge to slap Waldo's hand away. He saw that Waldo looked even more lost in thought than usual. He was calm. Dreamy, even.

Shenkman cleared his throat. It felt like something was stuck.

"Well, then. Well, then, we should—"

"Mom is everywhere," Waldo said, then. "She isn't in this bag. She won't be in the river, or at least not only in the river."

Shenkman sort of liked it when Waldo talked like this. It soothed him, even though he didn't understand why.

"When some stars die, their material goes back into the universe," Waldo said in the special voice he reserved for encyclopedic knowledge. "It takes millions of years for a star to die. Millions. It collapses to form a very dense white dwarf. It's super heavy. Even just a teaspoon of material from a white dwarf would weigh hundreds of tons. Then it takes billions of years for a white dwarf to cool off and become invisible."

All the while he spoke, Waldo tossed his mother's ashes into the river. "But other stars, really huge stars, end their lives suddenly. When they run out of fuel, they swell and become red supergiants. Then they blow themselves up in a supernova explosion so huge that it outshines all the other stars in the galaxy. Eventually, all that's left is stardust."

Waldo paused, then looked into his cupped hands. "I'm oversimplifying," he said, "but you get it. The stardust eventually makes other stars. And planets."

He turned to Shenkman and stared at him with those eyes. Alice's eyes. A few months later he'd be graduating from Avalon High. He'd be off to Berkeley. He wouldn't return home, not once, until the pandemic would force the university to shut down and he'd have nowhere else to go. Shenkman searched Waldo's face for any sign of love for him and saw none. And perhaps that was okay. Perhaps that was as it should be—as it had to be. It was a kind of relief, to no longer feel that he had to fix things.

Shenkman exits Whole Foods, dutifully squirts sanitizer into his open palms. The afternoon stretches ahead of him, scorching, endless. The two onions and cauliflower he bought rattle around in his plastic bag. He heads down Main Street in the direction of the marina. The park is teeming with people, even in the midday heat. Little kids play in the splash park while their older siblings ride their scooters around the perimeter. An older couple, their backs to Shenkman, sit side by side on a swing, looking out over the bay. The picnic tables at O'Leary's Tiki Bar are full of families eating fried seafood and having drinks with little umbrellas in them.

He finds a spot on a bench under a tree and takes a load off. Maybe this is it, then. His wife is stardust, according to his son, who is on the other side of the country, as far away from him as possible. His home of twenty years is now a sub-urban bunker. He spent two decades in Avalon without ever putting down roots. Who had the time or, quite frankly, the inclination? And so here he is, rootless Shenkman, in random Sarasota. He's pretty healthy, unlike his dad, who dropped dead at around his age. He may have a lot of road ahead of him. The RowPro—he made sure his new condo's gym is properly equipped—will keep his heart pumping, his cells regenerating. Maybe he'll even head back out on the open water. There's a rowing club called Sarasota Scullers just past Siesta Key. He shades his eyes and watches a gull as it swoops down to skim its prey off the surface of the glistening bay. It could be worse.

# Theo and His Nieces

AFTER SHUTTING DOWN Mimi's and Twelve Tables, he lay in bed for forty-eight hours in a frozen state that frightened even him. But on the third morning, he woke up with a clear and renewed sense of purpose. He knew exactly what he had to do. Theo went on his public Facebook page—previously managed by some social media person—and posted the following: *I'm here. By myself. If you want food I'm cooking for you. Please call for details.* He then listed his own mobile number, along with the landline for Mimi's. He did the same on the @12Tables Instagram account. He felt, in equal measures, determined, and a little out of his mind. Each step he took was so radically different from anything he could have previously imagined that it was a shock how inevitable it seemed. How necessary.

Now, as he has done every morning since mid-March, he tapes the day's menu to the inside window of Mimi's, written as legibly as possible in his own hand. Today's menu features Argentinian beef empanadas, pork ragù over creamy polenta, okra gumbo, rotisserie chicken pot pie, greens with braised pancetta and garlic. Comfort food with staying power. He also tries to keep a few staples in stock, the ones people have come to count on: baked paccheri with four cheeses, broccoli rabe, and spicy sausage is a neighborhood favorite. Customers order whole casseroles and freeze the leftovers. He's never cooked with an eye toward leftovers, but now nothing must go to waste.

It's the start of a holiday weekend, but this year there are no holiday weekends. Instead of the explosion of July Fourth fireworks, each evening at exactly seven there is a symphony of banging pots and people leaning out from open windows to cheer in support of essential workers. This is happening not only in the five boroughs of New York City but in cities and small towns across the globe. As people line up, standing six feet apart on Malcolm X Boulevard to pick up their dinner, they are accompanied by the elemental sound of spoons banging against pots. He listens for it as he moves through the kitchen, packing orders. A predictable thing in an unpredictable world. A way to measure the passage of time.

The restaurant itself is dark, chairs turned upside down on tables, the floor swept clean, nothing touched since he sent everyone home months ago. A framed black-and-white photo of Mimi hangs on a white brick wall. His dad snapped it in her garden in Avalon, and Theo had it blown up to poster size. His mom is in overalls, crouching next to a bed of kale— she was early to the kale party—and she's radiant, her hands digging into the earth. This is his favorite way to remember her. Each morning as he unlocks and lifts the metal grate and enters the eerie quiet of the restaurant, he takes a moment with his mother and hopes that she exists in some dimension in which she's able to see him. Mimi never fully recovered from his five-year disappearance. In the handful of years they had together after he returned and before her Alzheimer's set in, there was something fearful in the way she looked at him, as if he were a wild creature who just might bolt again. *I'm here, Mom.* He dons his apron and Birkenstocks. Flexes his fingers. Rolls his shoulders. *I'm here cooking.*

For a while, he kept his staff on the payroll, but with no end in sight, he reached a point when he could no longer afford to do that. Between the kitchen, waitstaff, and back-office crew at Mimi's, he employed twenty-six people. Twelve Tables had only three part-time employees and his sous chef. So thirty people—many of them immigrants with families—are out of work. He feels responsible. He *is* responsible.

His daily menu lists two different prices for each dish. In both cases, he's almost giving it away. One price is for people who still have jobs. And the other is for everyone else. All day he talks with old customers and new ones, a raw quality in their voices he recognizes as gratitude. But Theo doesn't want or need anyone's gratitude. These hours in the kitchen are saving him. Somewhere along the way he had lost sight of how he began, with the simple desire to be in the kitchen with his mother, working side by side, a stained cookbook—Marcella Hazan, Julia Child, Jacques Pépin—open on the counter. He would line up all the ingredients before they began, along with measuring cups and spoons, pans, dutch oven, whatever was called for. He preferred stews with complex flavors that would simmer on the stovetop for hours. Mimi would switch on the radio as they worked, and sometimes if a song came on that she liked, she would sing along and he'd catch a glimpse of what she must have been like as a girl.

If he had to distill what those long-ago afternoons in the kitchen with Mimi were all about, it was simple. It was love.

He's always loved the people who dine with him, but that love had a different quality to it. It was more like supplication. With every elaborate dish, each new invention, he attempted to prove himself worthy. He was on one side of a glass pane, separate, apart from his customers, their satisfaction, their satiety, his penance. He sees that now. He had drifted away from what matters most. And now, here he is. Offering food as sustenance, as balm for the spirit, as connection. The glass pane is gone.

His phone rings in his apron pocket day and night. He hears his own voice as unfamiliar music. *Theo Wilf*, he answers again and again. There is no separation now, no fear of exposure or alienation. No reticence or hiding. All that lifted well before the pandemic, in a series of long phone conversations with Sarah. Her words: *It was me, Theo—I said it was me back then because it was me, I was your older sister, it was my fault, I never should have*—and the sound of their breaths, the quiet thrown across them like a blanket. *Do you think of her?* Sarah asked him. *All the time,* he answered, and in saying it realized just how true it was. *Because it was me,* he told his sister. *Not you, Sarah. Me. I was the one driving like a fucking fool.* They went on like this, Theo in Brooklyn, Sarah in Santa Monica, middle-aged, haunted, silenced for decades by their own terror and shame.

His nieces will be coming soon. They'll pod. Their college graduations took place over Zoom, and all plans are now in a state of suspension. One lesson among many during the pandemic is that plans are mere fantasies. Plans are fungible. We make plans and God laughs. Sydney just finished RISD—she's supposed to go to work for Tom Ford in his LA office in September—and Olivia has become a rather extraordinary baker. She was going to apprentice for Nancy Silverton, but now that's on hold. The good news is, this means they are coming. His nieces. They will live once again in the room he built them in the back of his loft, and the three of them will spend their days feeding Brooklyn and beyond under the watchful eyes of their grandmother Mimi.

A siren screams down a nearby street. Hospitals are overflowing with people who can't breathe. Thousands upon thousands are dying lonely, terrible deaths. He's heard that refrigerator trucks are being used as morgues. A madman is in the White House. The atmosphere is weighted with grief as if grief were a tangible thing, a presence rather than an absence. And yet at the center of his life, his hearth, his kitchen, in the restaurant he has named to honor his mother, Theo Wilf, turning fifty, stirs a dense umami cube into his chicken stock.

This too, he thinks as he samples the broth. He thinks of everyone he will feed tonight. The cops, teachers, beauticians, yoga teachers. The homeless, out-of-work actors, emergency room nurses, busboys, doulas, paralegals, UPS drivers. This too, this too. He will feed them all with everything he's got. He dices the remainder of yesterday's carrots and makes a mental note to reach out to his organic farmer friends upstate for whatever the earth is offering up. He will make use of their crops. He will make use of himself because this is the one thing he can do. His phone rings. Forty minutes north, a long-dead girl is sending out lassos of light. She has been doing this for many years, but conditions have to be just so. He has to be ready. Now, she crosses time and space. She is bones in a graveyard. She is cellular matter. She lives within the inner rings of an ancient tree. Every part of her that did not vanish on that summer night loops around him in an embrace he feels only as unexpected purpose and well-being. *Theo Wilf,* he answers the call. And again. *Theo Wilf.*

# Waldo and Benjamin

H E SETS OUT on the cross-country drive with his car
packed with books, photo albums, and boxes. Anything he might ever want to save from the house he
grew up in is now in his Prius, bought with the insurance
money his mom left to him. He is a turtle carrying his own
shell. He has chosen the southern route. His father: *When I
made this trip during college, we took the northern route.*
Waldo, who up until that minute hadn't mapped out his jour-
ney: *I'll take the southern.*

When he pulls out of the driveway and onto Division
Street, he knows this is the last time he will ever see this
house, this neighborhood, this town. Why would he come
back? There is nothing for him here. Twenty years. His entire
life. Will he ever again live in one place for so long? In fact,
he will. In his late forties he will move with his wife and children into a bungalow in the foothills of Berkeley where he
will plant saplings that will grow mighty and strong, casting
shade over him for many years. Dr. Waldo Shenkman will be

a towering neighborhood figure in a world of scientists and academics. He will find himself in just the right place. And he is wrong that he will never return to Division Street. He will visit once with his college-age daughter. They will stand across the street from the old Shenkman abode. But by then the magic tree will be gone, its roots having invaded a leaky sewer pipe nearly a hundred feet away. Some neighbors will have petitioned to save the great oak at considerable expense, others dismissing it as a nuisance. After cutting it down, arbor services will have been able to estimate from the rings in its enormous, beautiful stump that it had been alive for close to five hundred years.

He knows his route: Pennsylvania Turnpike to I-70 west to Saint Louis. I-44 to Oklahoma City, then I-40 west to Arizona, all the way to California. Then I-15 to Los Angeles. Motels feel unsafe. Doorknobs, countertops, bedding—all kinds of normal things—have recently become ominous. He sleeps in his car at rest stops, rising with the sun. When he fills the Prius with gas, he uses a disposable plastic glove. The passenger seat is littered with hand sanitizer and Lysol wipes, blue surgical paper masks.

In New Mexico he wanders off course and spends the night in a state park forty miles from the nearest source of artificial light. Beneath the darkest sky he's ever seen, he sets up his telescope. Just south of Alnitak, the easternmost star in Orion's belt, he sees the elusive Horsehead Nebula, some fifteen hundred light-years away, a crisp black silhouette illuminated from behind by the pink background of charged emission gas. It's a popular target, kind of an astronomy tourist thing—lots of tattoos of the Horsehead Nebula among stargazers—but still his pulse quickens and he lets out a laugh. It may be a cliché, but it's a very beautiful cliché. Even though he doesn't fully form the thought, because it would feel too lonely, he wishes he had somebody to share it with. His ex-girlfriend Sophie. His mom. Ben.

In just one more very long day, he will arrive in Los Angeles. He's made sure not to have contact with a single other person on his drive. He's taking every precaution. *I'd love a visit, Waldo. We just have to make sure we do it safely. I'm no spring chicken.* He got tested before he left Avalon, and he'll get tested again before he sees Ben. He has hardly any friends, just an ex-girlfriend, and no family now to speak of, so this visit has loomed larger with each passing day. It means *too* much. But maybe that will be okay. Maybe it's all right to allow his whole being to yearn for the company of one actual person, and not only to be searching for black holes in the universe. Maybe it's all right to risk loving someone.

As he makes the last leg of the trip, with every mile he puts between himself and Avalon he feels more whole, more himself. The air grows thinner, drier. In the desert, he can breathe. The cacti on the side of the highway look otherworldly, like flora from another planet. He passes crossing signs for moose, armadillos. He will live here, he thinks. By *here,* he means somewhere on the western edge of the United States. It's possible to grow up in the wrong house, on the wrong street, in the wrong town, in the wrong part of the country. It's possible to go to the wrong school. To have the wrong dad. To be pushed to do the wrong things. But it is also possible to survive all these psychic indignities if you have one, maybe two people who recognize you for who you are. His mom saw him. By seeing him, she saved him. And on one winter night half his life ago, an old doctor slung his arm around him and swayed back and forth as if he and Waldo were both hearing the same barely audible music.

He doesn't pretend to understand any of this. He knows only that he is following a pattern that he cannot always make out. It is elusive, chimerical, subject to dead ends and abrupt disappearances. It's easy to forget to look for it. But when it is visible, as it is now, it lights up his way like a comet shooting through the night sky. He has only to trust it and follow. This will be true all his life. He will recognize a current running through him, a force that connects him to the world he apprehended as an almost-eleven-year-old boy. He won't know who is reaching him through time and space, but he will know he is not alone.

And here they are, the once and future doctors Benjamin Wilf and Waldo Shenkman. It has been ten years since they have seen each other. Ten years since the day that changed them both forever. Ben moves more slowly now. He was an old man even then. But Waldo, of course, is the one most changed. Ben recalls him as a boy, a small boy, still a child, with soft cheeks and floppy hair, long eyelashes. He had been pale, remarkably so, as if he rarely saw the light of day, his face illuminated by the screen's blue glow as he tilted it up toward the stars. That boy is still inside this young man with his patchy beard and glasses, dark circles under those same eyes. Eyes, Ben notes with relief, that still contain the spark he remembers, the spark that says: *Underestimate me at your own peril.*

Broad Beach is nearly empty. Two men in wet suits carry surfboards in the distance. A black dog runs in circles on the rocks. They've borrowed Sarah's car, a convertible, for the day, and driven with the top down up the Pacific Coast Highway to the northernmost tip of Malibu. The beach—Ben remembers it from an anniversary trip he and Mimi took in the 1970s—has changed completely in these fifty years, eroded to the point where now the homes along this stretch of shoreline are buffered by huge concrete boulders that act as retaining walls where once there had been sand. In another fifty years, he imagines, it will all be under water: The mansions, one, two, three stories high, jammed right up against each other. The sports cars parked beneath porte cocheres, the soft terry-cloth chaises lined up on the dunes and alongside swimming pools, the azaleas, hibiscus, the scent of lemon in the air—all of it creating the illusion of safety and stability.

"Sad," he says out loud without meaning to.

"What?" Waldo swivels his head toward him.

"This"—Ben sweeps his arm out as if indicating an ancient, lost civilization—"is all going to disappear before too long."

"It won't disappear," Waldo says. He's been reading James Gleick, and repeats a passage to Ben by heart. "If only time could be seen whole, then you could see the past remaining intact, instead of vanishing in the rearview mirror."

"You believe that?" Ben asks.

"It's not a matter of belief. It's physics," Waldo replies.

They stop, the unlikely pair, and ponder the miles of sandbags stacked along the beach's edge. Waldo glances at him. "And besides, I can feel it."

The wind picks up. Ben shoves his hands in his pockets. He feels at ease with this young man, as if they had known each other for a very long time.

"How are you doing, Waldo? About your mom, I mean."

It has been three years since Alice passed. No time at all, when it comes to such a profound loss. Ben knows this. Grief comes in waves. Like the swells crashing against the rocks, it gathers force and breaks when you least expect it.

271

Waldo shrugs. Ben remembers this shrug from the small boy in the Red Sox pajamas. Reflexive, as if he's not used to anyone paying attention so it's easier to push things away.

"Okay, I guess. I miss her."

The two of them look down at their feet as they walk. The sand is scattered with broken mollusk shells, bits of sea glass. Mimi used to bring home shells from their trips to the Caribbean. Imperfect, broken, she didn't care. She collected them in a ceramic bowl that filled and filled over the years. It was about creating a tactile memory of where they'd been, who they'd been, what they'd done. When he packed up the house, no one wanted those shells. He couldn't bring himself to throw them in the trash so he tucked the whole bowl behind a boxwood out back. Maybe one of the kids from the new family would come upon it someday.

"How about you?" Waldo asks.

"What about me?"

"How are *you* doing?"

Ben is suddenly embarrassed. He can't remember the last time anyone asked him this question. He spent so much of his life being the steady one, the one always in charge. It would cost his own kids too much to ask him how he really is. Or maybe it would cost *him* too much. Because the truth is that he's lonely. In these ten years since Mimi has been gone, he's never wanted to meet someone new. Every once in a while Sarah or Peter would mention a friend's recently widowed mother, or whatever, but the idea felt absurd. He has lived his life with Mimi. He doesn't want another chapter.

"My daughter, Sarah, gave me a gift," Ben surprises himself by telling Waldo. "She had a filmmaker she works with put together a . . . montage, I guess you would say . . . of our family photos and videos over the years."

Waldo watches as the black dog dives into the surf and comes running back with a bright red Frisbee. He doesn't want to look at Ben because he's afraid he'll stop talking.

"I've probably watched it a thousand times."

"Does it help?"

Ben's cheeks turn pink.

"Not really." Ben stops. "Pretty pathetic, I guess. But that's the answer to how I'm doing."

Waldo stops in front of a perfect fossilized starfish. He's actually never seen one before. He's seen pictures, but he hasn't spent a lot of time on beaches. He bends down to pick it up. *Echinoderm. Asteroidea.* They live twenty thousand feet below the surface of the ocean.

"I saw her, you know."

The words just come out. Over the years, Waldo kept what he experienced that morning in the playhouse to himself. He was sure it would get him into trouble. That the doctors would have a field day. *Oh, he sees dead people.*

"I know," Ben says. He looks confused. This is hardly new information.

"No," Waldo presses on. "I mean, after."

Ben blinks hard against the wind. He has been haunted by the thought of such a small boy witnessing Mimi's death. And Mimi, her mind so scrambled, mistaking him for her own son. But what's this? Waldo must have been traumatized. Otherwise why would he—

"It was like she was everyone she had ever been," Waldo says. "I remember seeing a child in a white dress. And a lady with dark hair, so long she could sit on it."

Ben is listening. Sound recedes as if the wind had died down, as if the ocean had stopped its waves from churning.

"She looked happy, Ben. Then she was pregnant, wearing

jeans and a plaid shirt. She was holding a little girl's hand. I couldn't make everything out, it was all kind of flickering, like images from an old movie projector. But I know what I saw."

Tears spill down Ben's cheeks. He doesn't even try to swat them away. He lets go of his skepticism and simply sees what Waldo sees. His Mimi, intact. Not vanishing. Everything that has ever happened is still happening. She does not need to be preserved in a video montage. He did not leave her behind in the Brooklyn cemetery alongside his parents. He closes his eyes and takes a deep breath. The breeze picks up again. The wet black dog runs up to them, joyfully yapping. Ben slings his arm around Waldo. The two men are now the same height. They stand, swaying, looking out toward the horizon.

"I didn't make it up," Waldo says.

"I didn't say you're making it up."

"But you think it."

"I'm not so sure I do."

The sunlight is dancing along the whitecaps. It looks as if the sea were filled with thousands upon thousands of flickering stars. Perhaps each one is what remains of every soul who has ever lived; perhaps time is not a continuum, but rather, past, present, and future are always and forever unspooling. The young man standing beside him is the infant he placed on his mother's belly; the husband and father whose salvation comes in opening his own heart; the elderly astrophysicist who devotes his life to the hunt for habitable exoplanets beyond our solar system. The whole crowd is here, invisible, surrounding them. The air shimmers with everyone he has ever loved. He is near the end of his life, and in another sphere, he is also just beginning. He would like to believe this. And why not? He will find out soon enough.

# June 5, 1970

---

# The Wilf Family

S EE THEM, BEN and Mimi Wilf, as they walk up the steps to their new home: 18 Division Street. They love that they will live at number 18, *Chai*, the Hebrew word, also, for life. Ben briefly considers lifting his bride over the threshold, but she is hugely pregnant, so probably not the best idea. She is radiant, dressed in jeans (unbuttoned around her belly since maternity jeans have yet to be invented) and a flannel shirt. Though they have no way of knowing, everyone tells them that the way she's carrying, they're having a boy. Mimi holds Sarah's hand as the two-year-old attempts to navigate the steep stairs with what will someday be her trademark determination.

Their house (their house!) is shaded by a beautiful old oak tree, the tallest on the block. Ben imagines reading in a lawn chair beneath the tree. Their neighbors all seem to have little kids, growing families. He sees tricycles, pogo sticks, small canvas sneakers piled on front steps. It's a far cry from Classon Avenue, this quiet street where Sarah and her little brother—he secretly hopes it will be a boy—will grow up. He can hardly believe his good fortune. He's married to the love of his life, they have a thrillingly precocious daughter, and in just a few more weeks they will become a family of four.

Their first night in the house, Sarah finally asleep upstairs in her brand-new toddler bed, he and Mimi sit on the porch with a beer for him, chamomile tea for her. The front door is cracked open; a beam of warm light splays across the steps. The sound of crickets fills the air. The baby kicks and Mimi laughs, resting her hands on her belly. They are city people, unaccustomed to the deep velvety sky.

A car moves slowly up Division Street, headlights sweeping over them. If you were to see them, Ben and Mimi Wilf, as they begin their lives in Avalon, you would wish them Godspeed. You would hope that they know how lucky they are, how blessed.

# Acknowledgments

A book is written in solitude, and yet it contains within its pages the fingerprints, dedication, and love of others.

Early readers: Molly Zakoor, Debbie Attanasio, Andy McNicol, and Abigail Pogrebin offered incisive and invaluable editorial suggestions.

A long and well-timed phone call with Jeff Gordinier helped me to fill in an essential piece of the puzzle.

Thanks to my writers' group, also known as The Bunker, for the solidarity and literary friendship. You know who you are.

Anne Horowitz is the kind of copyeditor a writer can only dream of.

Deep gratitude to Jordan Pavlin, Reagan Arthur, Alison Rich, Stephanie Bowen, Isabel Yao Meyers, Abby Endler, and the entire Knopf family. Paul Bogaards, it is my honor and good fortune to continue to have you in my corner. Thanks to Poppy Hampson and Chatto & Windus, who have made a home for my work in the UK.

Margaret Riley King, you changed the game for me at this late date. To my whole WME team: Hilary Zaitz Michael, Laura Bonner, Fiona Baird, Ben Davis, I am blessed by your care and support for this book.

A special shout-out to Jennifer Egan, who suggested to me over a decade ago that chronology of any sort is boring. Thanks for reminding me by example that the high wire is the only place worth being.

Guy Birster and Charles Cilona, countless dinners at your divine restaurant RSVP served as an inspiration and entry point into Theo's world.

And finally, to my family. My husband, Michael Maren, is my first and most trusted reader and makes me feel safe enough to take flying leaps. My son, Jacob Maren, listened long and hard to me read from the nascent pages of *Signal Fires* during a time when the future looked bleak. It would not be an overstatement to state that this book would not exist without him.

All my love and thanks.